D0020590

Deadly
Housewives

'JUN 2 0 2006

Don't miss the next book by your favorite author.
Sign up now for AuthorTracker by visiting
www.AuthorTracker.com.

Deadly

Housewives

Edited by Christine Matthews

SAN DIEGO PUBLIC LIBRARY
LA JOLLA BRANCH

3 1336 07230 3283

AVON

An Imprint of HarperCollins*Publishers*

This book is a work of fiction. The characters, incidents, and dialogue are drawn from the author's imagination and are not to be construed as real. Any resemblance to actual events or persons, living or dead, is entirely coincidental.

Copyright Notices

"Dear Christine" and "The House of Deliverance" copyright © 2006 by Christine Matthews.

"The One That Got Away" copyright © 2006 by Julie Smith.

"GDMFSOB" copyright © 2006 by Nevada Barr.

"Lawn and Order" copyright © 2006 by Carole Nelson Douglas.

"Joy Ride" copyright © 2006 by Nancy Pickard.

"The Next-Door Collector" copyright © 2006 by Elizabeth Massie.

"Acid Test" copyright © 2006 by Sara Paretsky.

"Trailer Trashed" copyright © 2006 by Barbara Collins.

"An Invisible Minus Sign" copyright © 2006 by Denise Mina.

"Purzz, Baby" copyright © 2006 by Vicki Hendricks.

"The Next Nice Day" copyright © 2006 by S. J. Rozan.

"He Said . . . She Said" copyright © 2006 by Marcia Muller.

"How to Murder Your Mother-in-Law" copyright © 2006 by Suzann Ledbetter.

"Vanquishing the Infidel" copyright © 2006 by Eileen Dreyer.

DEADLY HOUSEWIVES. Copyright © 2006 by Christine Matthews. All rights reserved. Printed in the United States of America. No part of this book may be used or reproduced in any manner whatsoever without written permission except in the case of brief quotations embodied in critical articles and reviews. For information address HarperCollins Publishers, 10 East 53rd Street, New York, NY 10022.

HarperCollins books may be purchased for educational, business, or sales promotional use. For information please write: Special Markets Department, HarperCollins Publishers, 10 East 53rd Street, New York, NY 10022.

FIRST EDITION

Designed by Sarah Maya Gubkin

Library of Congress Cataloging-in-Publication Data

Deadly housewives / edited by Christine Matthews.—1st ed.
p. cm.
ISBN-13: 978-0-06-085327-3 (pbk.)
ISBN-10: 0-06-085327-1 (pbk.)
1. Housewives—Fiction. 2. Detective and mystery stories, American.
I. Matthews, Christine.
PS648.D4D414 2006
813'.0872083522—dc22
2005055877

06 07 08 09 10 WBC/RRD 10 9 8 7 6 5 4 3 2 1

Contents

Introduction: *Dear Christine*

Being a housewife is the most difficult, thankless job there is. And when a person gets ignored, taken for granted year after year, something happens. She turns deadly. I know this not only from personal experience but from all the letters I get. Like this one:

> *Dear Christine:*
> *My husband's a skunk! I don't know why I even married the bum. He treats me like a slave—makes me cut his toenails and even give him a bath. When he watches his favorite TV show, WWE Monday Night RAW, I have to get on the floor and be his footstool. Last Saturday I snapped when he was getting ready to go bowling and hit him on the head with last year's trophy. It was one of those big suckers and made quite a mess on our bedroom carpet. Can you tell me what to use to get out the bloodstains? I'm having company next weekend and want everything to look nice.*
>
> Wondering in Wilmette

And having been there I always try to help.

Dear Wondering:
Try using a mixture of cool water and dishwashing liquid.
Rub gently then blot. Repeat until the stain is gone. If this
fails, I suggest you move your bed to cover the spot.

Christine

Why, just look at the papers, or CNN or . . . your neighbor. Frustration hides behind gingham curtains. A smile can hide such brutal plots. Like Ann Landers once said: "Nobody knows what anyone's marriage is like except the two of them—and sometimes one of them doesn't know."

And I ask you, is it any wonder we spend our time fending off deadly thoughts? Between carpooling, cleaning, cooking, shopping, scheduling *his* appointments, helping everyone in the house get what *they* want . . . well, a girl has to keep her mind sharp, doesn't she?

In this book I've gathered fourteen delicious stories of revenge, rage, love—you know, the things that feed our passion. Make us feel truly alive! You're going to meet some very interesting characters here, and I hope that after you've made their acquaintance, you'll be inspired to run right out and look for novels by the talented women who created them.

As for me, I've already digested each word between these covers and have my hands full encouraging my sister housewives:

Dear Christine:
Oh Lord, I knew I should have thought this through more be-
fore poisoning Henry's enchiladas. I'm a patient woman, I
really am, but that husband of mine has had sex with all my

friends and two of my sisters. I rolled up his body in a super-size garbage bag, stuck it in a closet, and then threw a bunch of those pine tree air fresheners all over him.

My question for you has two parts: 1) How do I get Henry out of the house? And 2) When he's gone, how do I get rid of the smell? Please keep in mind that I'm a widow now and won't be able to afford anything expensive.

Anxious in Altoona

Dear Anxious,
Borrow one of your sisters' cars, never use your own. I've found that early morning around 4 A.M. is the best time to haul out the "trash." And baking soda is wonderful to freshen up a room. It's cheap and easy.

Christine

Deadly housewives come in such a variety. One of my favorites, Sylvia Plath, wrote in one of her poems:

> *. . . meanwhile there's a stink of fat and baby crap. I'm*
> *doped and thick from my last sleeping pill.*
> *The smog of cooking, the smog of hell.*

Mark Twain was smart enough to know "The reason novelists nearly always fail in depicting women when they make them act is that they let them do what they have observed some woman has done at some time or another. And that is where they make a mistake; for a woman will never do again what has been done before."

Yo, Christine:
My husband and I have been married for two months, but he doesn't seem to realize he's a husband now and still hangs out

*with his crew. One in particular, Rich, stays all night playing
video games until I go to bed. Sometimes I've even found him
eating breakfast when I get ready for work. I took Rich out last
Tuesday, pushed him off our deck before my husband got
home. It was so easy it made me laugh. But so far nothing's
changed. Everyone's still here in my house. Bummer. What
should I do? I really love my husband and want to give our
marriage a chance. I'm thinking that maybe if I get rid of his
best friend, Aaron, things might get better?*

Sad in Seattle

*Dear Sad,
Have you thought about a trial separation? Moving out of
town? Hurry.*

Christine

See what I mean? We've got stories from housewives in all
stages of jealousy, greed, and anger, just trying to work things
out in their own special ways. I'm sure you can all relate to
more than one of these brave women who take things into
their own moisturized hands and finally "clean house."

There's really nothing left for you to do but find a quiet
corner, pour yourself a cup of coffee, and enjoy. But if you're
still a little "anxious," remember the words of Wilma Scott
Heide who tells us:

"I do not refer to myself as a 'housewife' for the reason
that I did not marry a house." And keep repeating to yourself, "I will get even. I will get even. I will . . ."

Hugs & kisses,

Christine Matthews

The One That Got Away

Julie Smith

Forest got all misty when he saw that Roy had a six-pack of beer in the truck. Like it wasn't enough he'd had to come down and bail Forest out, using up almost all the money they had left over from that pirate job they'd pulled on those dumb-ass smugglers near Savannah. Forest felt real bad about that, specially since Roy had just wanted to leave with the money they got from unloading the boat.

But Forest had talked him into sticking around and going after the jerk-offs next time they had a load coming in. Not that it hadn't turned out okay, except for Roy getting grazed by a bullet, which messed up his hairdo for a while. But due to the circumstances, they couldn't get but a little of the pot, which they'd had to unload slowly over the next few months.

Then they'd ended up gambling away most of the profits, hoping to put off actually having to work again. Truth was, there was precious little left when Forest got nailed for D&D in Biloxi.

He popped a brew and tried to apologize. "Roy, I know I hadn't oughta done that."

"Well. Least you missed the guy. But you did have to do it, bro'—I'd'a done the same, swear to God."

Forest was curious. He could vaguely remember taking a swing at some yahoo in Treasure Bay. "I did? How come?"

"You don't remember, do you? He insulted your date, man."

"I had a date?"

Roy laughed. "You were talkin' to some chick, anyhow. Hey, listen, no biggie. We'll figure out something."

So they drove to the beach to polish off the beer and start figuring. "We could pull some kind of gigolo thing," Forest said. "You know, like wait for some fat chick to hit the jackpot and then move in on her. Do her and roll her, make everybody happy—she gets a little romance, we pay the rent."

"You mean *I* could do that. Oh no. No way, José. Uh-uh. My body's a temple of God, man." Roy looked like the Kennedy kid who'd gone down in his own plane, only with a mullet.

"So you say," Forest grumbled. This was a discussion they'd had before. The way Forest saw it, Roy had this great asset and all he wanted to do was hide his light under a bushel. "You need a manager, man. Hey, what's that? My hip tickles."

Roy snorted. "Your cell phone's probably vibrating. When's the last time you got a call?"

Forest looked at his phone. " 'Private caller,' it says."

"Probably a telemarketer."

"Maybe it's opportunity."

"That's supposed to knock, right? Not vibrate."

But Forest was already punching the talk button. "Forest, it's me. Heidi."

Forest couldn't speak. Dumbfounded didn't describe. It *couldn't* be her. "Bet you thought you'd never hear from me again." And then she laughed that silvery laugh, like pure, fresh water crackling its way back to sea over a bed of sun-soaked stones. And he knew it *was* her.

"Well? Aren't you going to say hello?" Her voice was slightly accented.

"So," he said. "Did you marry that guy or what?" He tried to keep the fury out of his voice. She was the one that got away. And without so much as taking off her little lace panties.

But she'd screwed him anyhow. Him and Roy both.

"Of course I married him. We live in New Orleans now."

"Well, what the hell you callin' me for?"

"It's not working out too well, Forest. Say, you still hanging out with that nice friend of yours?" The American slang sounded strange with her fancy-ass accent. She claimed to be Dutch, but a chick like that, who knew? He wasn't even sure he'd ever known her real name. But he did know the name of the man she'd married; it was the guy he and Roy had set up for a big fall, with her help. Or so they'd thought.

But they were the ones who took the fall.

"So," he said. "You're Heidi Handshaw now."

"If you like. But with any luck, not for long. I need to get out of this, Forest. Help me and there might be something in it for you."

"Yeah? Like what?"

"Like half a million bucks."

Forest fell back against the truck seat and exhaled. That was about $475,000 more than he'd ever seen in his life.

"Split between you and your friend, I mean. That is, if you're still working together."

Roy was about to pee in his pants. "Who the hell is it? What's up, bro'?" Forest motioned to him to keep it down.

"No hard feelings, Miss Heidi, but we didn't exactly part friends. Why the hell should we trust you now?"

Roy went, "It's *Heidi*? The Dutch Treat? Oh, shit, hang up. Now." Forest punched him.

Heidi was saying, "I want to make it up to you, sweetness. I've always felt terrible about that—me living in luxury all this time, and you and that nice friend of yours getting cut out. I'm so sorry it couldn't have worked out."

"Yeah, right." Forest hung up.

The phone rang again. He didn't answer it, just slugged down half a can of beer and then told Roy the story, ending up with, "Chick's the Ebola virus, man. I'll probably have to disinfect the goddamn phone."

But to his surprise, his buddy was interested. "Hang on, man, hang on. Don't you remember, we were gonna get revenge? We planned it, remember? We were gonna blackmail her and make her pay with Handshaw's money. Get back our own."

Forest had thought Roy'd been too drunk to remember.

At any rate, neither of them had ever brought it up again, Forest because . . . well, because he was about three-quarters in love with her at the time. But he damn sure wasn't now. The chick was Darth Vader in a bathing suit, which was what she'd been wearing when he met her. He could see her now, tanned legs peeking out from the sarong she'd tied around her, shoulders gleaming with sunscreen . . .

Roy wouldn't shut up. "This is our chance, man. This time we cut *her* out. See, we got the advantage—we see her coming this time. I mean, she thinks we're just a coupla dumb redneck peckerwood bozos."

Forest laughed. "Didn't you ever go to school, man? You know the word *redundant*?"

Evidently, Roy did, because he started laughing, too, and pretty soon they couldn't stop, they were so full of beer and desperation. "Go on," Roy said finally. "Call her back."

But she hadn't left a number, only an address, or part of one, and an order: "Come to Belle Reve in New Orleans—on the West Bank—at two P.M. day after tomorrow. Ask the guard for Mrs. Handshaw."

"Well?" Roy said. "What else have we got to do? If we start now, we can be in the French Quarter in a coupla hours—catch a little action, scope out the place tomorrow."

"I've got to go to court tomorrow."

"Okay, we'll leave afterward. I was kind of wondering how we were gonna pay your legal fees."

Forest sighed. He'd known they were going to do it. He was even kind of excited about it.

Turned out Belle Reve was a gated community, the kind of place that made Seaside, the shiny resort where they'd met the current Mrs. Handshaw, look like a shantytown.

They gave the guard the password, not knowing what to expect, but to their surprise, he said, "Oh yes. Mr. McElroy. Mrs. Handsaw's expecting you." And he gave them directions to a minimansion that probably had five marble-paved bathrooms and a screening room.

Heidi met them at the door before they even had a chance to ring the bell. Forest was just about to plant a big one on her, when she said, "Mind putting the truck in the garage? We don't want to draw too much attention." Somehow, she always managed to move out of the way just when Forest was planning to get physical. Which was something her appearance certainly invited. She looked more like a porcelain figure than a woman—aristocratic profile, pale, pale skin, and great big light blue eyes in a round face that looked so innocent you wanted to buy her an ice cream cone.

But the thing was, chicks like her always went for Roy, not him—hell, all chicks went for Roy. Which should have made Forest suspicious in the first place. How the hell had she picked him over his buddy? Naturally, first time around, he'd thought it was his superior brain and down-to-earth charm, but now . . . well, face it, a piece of him still thought that.

When she finally let them in, she gave each one a kiss on the cheek. She was wearing a flower print sundress with one of those halter top things made for showing off a great pair of garbanzos. Which she had, and it did.

"Nice place you got here," Roy said, stepping in and casing it. Nice bar, nice piano, expensive modern furniture—nothing fusty or Maw-Maw—and a wall of glass facing a pool shaped like a comma.

Heidi's face shadowed. "Not a happy place, Roy. Not a

happy place at all. Let's go out by the pool. You guys like mojitos?"

"Mosquitoes?" Roy said, and Forest punched him.

Heidi spilled that water-over-rocks laugh all over both of them and handed Roy a mint-sprigged cocktail. "Here. Try one."

After that, there was no going back. Neither Forest nor Roy had any idea where mojitos had been all their lives, but after the first one, they couldn't wait to drink up all the rest there were in the whole world. And in Forest's case, he was almost ready to make an honest split with the former Ebola virus, who was once more elevated in his mind to the Queen of . . . yeah. He lifted his glass: "To the Queen of Crime."

At that, Roy and Heidi almost peed themselves laughing, but she managed to gasp out, "So you'll do it?"

"Are you kidding? How could it fail?"

"It couldn't."

Here was the setup. A man two streets over, guy named Bert Caulfield, who shared a cleaning lady with Heidi, was someone she knew from neighborhood cocktail parties, where he'd told her he ran not one, but three pain clinics out in Jefferson Parish. As it happened, she suffered from headaches, so he said to drop on in, he was sure he could fix her up.

She went the next day, but almost left because there were so many people in the waiting room. However, she noticed they were all coming out about two minutes after getting called for their appointments. So she gave it twenty minutes, whereupon she was seen by a doctor with a foreign accent who asked her what was wrong and, when she said head-aches, didn't say another word. Just sat down and wrote her

8　Julie Smith
out prescriptions for not one, but three drugs, which could be filled at an in-house pharmacy—for cash only.

She looked at her watch—the whole procedure hadn't taken but two and a half minutes, including the doctor's final words ("Be sure and come back if you have any more pain") and paying the bill, which was a hundred dollars.

"How good at math are you guys? That's almost a dollar every few seconds, not counting what they'd have made if I'd actually filled the prescriptions. So I just knew Mr. Caulfield was a man after my own heart. I looked up all the drugs on the Internet, and sure enough—they were all narcotics and all highly addictive. Get it? You don't make just one visit—you've got to keep coming back for your happy pills."

By now, they'd had quite a few mojitos and Roy evidently wasn't firing on all cylinders. "You mean the guy's a drug pusher or something?"

Heidi's teeth showed, and water warbled over rocks. "You got it," she said. "It's what they call a pill mill. I figure Caulfield raked in about a thousand dollars in the twenty minutes I was in there."

Roy was still working it out. "So, was it a fake doctor or something?"

"No, I think he was real—he had a diploma on the wall. But his English wasn't so good, and maybe he has a little trouble building up a practice. Also"—she paused—"I'm sure he's very well paid."

Well, they had a big ol' laugh over that one—*of course* the guy was well paid—Mr. Caulfield was basically running a money factory. The question in Forest's mind was how to get hold of a whole big chunk of the goods.

"You mentioned, like—half a million dollars¿" he said.

"Actually," Heidi said, and licked her lips, "that would be a conservative estimate. Did I mention my cleaning lady also works for Mr. Caulfield¿ One day I lifted her keys and duplicated them."

"Uh-huh. And checked out Mr. Caulfield's house."

"I figured there *had* to be something good in there. But, gentlemen, I could never in a million years have guessed."

Roy was about to jump out of his chair. "What¿ What the hell was it¿"

"Well, think about it. If you're taking in that much money—and so very illegally—you are going to want to hide quite a bit of it from—"

"Yeah! The IRS!"

"You got it, Roy. But Mr. Caulfield apparently has quite a bit to learn about the fine art of money laundering, because guess what he's got in his oversize McMansion¿"

"Cash, by any chance¿"

"Garbage bags of cash. Great big black lawn-size plastic bags three feet tall when full—and, my sweets, they are positively overflowing."

Forest was trying not to salivate, and Roy was, too, but it was getting the best of him, anyhow—Forest could see a little bit of drool in the corner of his mouth. "Check this out," Heidi said, producing a plump green bundle, which she handed to Forest. He leafed through it.

"All hundreds."

Heidi nodded. "A hundred of them. Ten thousand dollars. I—what is it you say¿—I liberated them."

Roy leaned back, foot crossed over ankle, regaining his composure, or pretending to. "Well, if you can get into his house, why not liberate the whole mess for your pretty little self? We ain't never noticed you bein' generous before."

She said everybody knew her there, and she'd been able to claim she was taking in Mr. Caulfield's mail while he was away, just that once, but how could she get away with removing two great big garbage bags? Well, she *might,* but the risk wasn't worth it.

"And you think we could get away with it?" Forest said.

"You're gardeners, right? That's what I told the guard. Gardeners are always hauling large plastic bags."

"You also told the guard my name."

A delicate pink briefly stained Heidi's porcelain skin. "Ah, yes, the guard. Well, one little bundle for him." She snatched the money back from Forest. "In fact, this one. We'll never notice it's missing."

"Yeah?" Roy crunched ice. "What's our cut?"

"Half, of course. I owe you guys. I know that." Her eyes looked like little pieces of the sky.

"That's for sure, sweetheart," Roy said. "The part about you owing us."

"Boys, it's a beautiful, beautiful thing. Mr. Caulfield can't even report a burglary, do you realize that? *Because he's not supposed to have that money.* For all I know, he won't even notice it missing for a while. You'll never find a better setup than this one."

"What about alarms?"

"Well, that's the good part. He leaves his off for the cleaning lady—afraid if she knows the code, she'll rob him on her day off, I guess. How screwed up is that? Anyhow, I know all this because she happens to be *my* cleaning lady, did I mention that? But he's too cheap to pay for a whole day—shares Thursdays with Mrs. D'Amato down the street. Mimi's at her house in the morning and Caulfield's in the afternoon, but the alarm's off all day. That's how I got in that other time—went while she was at Mrs. D'Amato's. Anyhow, tomorrow's Thursday—you could just do an instant replay."

Forest was doubtful. "Sounds pretty stupid to me—leavin' your alarm off like that."

Heidi made a little noise like *pfui*. "Forest, this is Belle Reve—a highly upscale gated community, in case you didn't notice. You'd have to have a tank to get in here if you didn't belong. Truth is, Caulfield's probably the only one in the whole place who even bothers with an alarm—and I think we know why, don't we?"

Forest and Roy thought about it. Finally, Roy said, "Sounds reasonable, I guess."

"Why don't you two take a swim? Think about it awhile? You can skinny-dip, you know—look at the fence." Sure enough, she had just about complete privacy back there. Forest was wishing Roy was about five hundred miles away. Something about this chick . . .

"Think I will," Roy said, and he peeled off his shorts, causing Forest to wince at the mental comparison he was making. Roy didn't even have a cell phone, women called him so much. All he had to do to get laid was go to the beach, a bar, the mailbox, the drugstore, and chicks followed him around like a litter of puppy dogs. He could take his pick, but he wasn't even a little bit particular. To him, pussy was pretty much pussy. In all the time Forest had known him, he'd never planked the same chick twice except for Heidi's predecessor, the first Mrs. Handshaw, but that was for the cause. "You coming, Forest?" Roy said.

Last thing Forest was about to do was give Heidi a chance to compare his pink peckerwood jelly belly with Roy's perfect tanned six-pack. Roy pumped iron every day, in or out of the joint. Forest liked to exercise his right elbow, that was about it.

"Nah. Might have me another mojito."

Heidi squeezed his knee and shot him a little close-mouthed Mona Lisa thing as she got up to get it. She gave him another squeeze when she got back. "Forest," she said, "you may not believe this, but I've been thinking about you a lot. Listen, I really thought I was in love with Ben Handshaw when we met. You kind of shook me up a little. I mean I was already committed, you understand? But you . . . I don't know—you *moved* me."

Uh-huh, Forest was thinking. "So what went wrong here?" he said.

Heidi looked away. "Oh . . . you know. Drinking. Gambling." She pulled up her dress to show a bruise on her thigh. "Even that. He never hits me where anyone can see."

"Well, why not just divorce him and take his money?"

"Did I mention the gambling? There *isn't* that much money, honey. Besides . . . we're not exactly married. Nobody knows it here, but . . . well . . . you know."

"I hear you." He heard her loud and clear. Rich guy has affair with Heidi, catches wife with Roy, uses that to dump her, but then thinks, why take on another cheating bitch? Forest could relate. Except there was a piece of him that . . . he couldn't explain it. There was just something about this chick. She was drop-dead gorgeous, there was that. But there was something about her that seemed like it might break—she seemed so fragile and ladylike, he wanted to hold her and protect her and . . . he stopped himself. *Whoa, don't go there, boy.* He knew this chick. She really was the devil in a blue dress—or she would be if she went in for blue. Wasn't nothing in the world she wouldn't do to get what she wanted.

"I was just wondering . . . later, when this is all over . . . ¿ I mean, is there a chance¿"

"Baby, you want to know something¿ You've always been the one that got away. There's not a chance, there's a *certainty*."

They kissed on it, like Forest knew they'd have to. But he hardly felt a thing—or at least hardly anything more than Roy was probably accustomed to feeling.

Later, over a couple of brewskis, Roy got into a little negativity. "I don't know, man. I can't get over the feeling she's setting us up for something."

"I don't think so—she hit on me again."

"You¿ She hit on *you*¿"

"Well, yeah. When she could have had you. Thinks I'm sensitive and gentle, I think."

Roy spewed beer.

"Yeah, I know. My own mama wouldn't make that kind of dumb mistake. So what was she after¿ I'll tell you what she was after. She's trying to rope me in again. Like she did the last time. So we won't screw her out of the take. But think about it—that means there's gonna *be* a take—there really is somethin' in that house, man."

Roy considered. "Could be." He nodded, his long hair

bobbing on his shoulders. "Know what? I don't like the deal she offered us. Why should she get half and we only get a fourth each? Let's ask her to go thirdsies, see what that does."

Well, when she called that night, she wouldn't go for it, which pretty much decided Forest, who'd in truth been wavering a teeny little bit on the issue of leaving her high and dry. The matter was now closed.

They loaded up a couple black plastic bags with newspapers and went into the house at noon the next day. It was a fancy-ass Tudor-style house with marble floors and chandeliers that were probably each worth more than Roy's pickup, but even Forest could see how tacky it was, and Graceland was his idea of elegance. It was the white piano that tipped him off, in addition to the general whiteness of everything else, which was mostly leather with great big ugly brass studs on it. "Man," he said, "if I had this dude's money, I'd get me some actual antiques."

"Not me, bro'," Roy said. "Know what I'd like? I want me one of them pulpits people make into bars."

"Well, if Heidi's not lying, I'd say it's only a matter of time."

Bless her cheatin' little heart, she wasn't, it turned out. The bags of hard, cold cash were exactly as advertised, in a storage cabinet in the den, a high-up one you had to get a ladder for, not the sort of place a cleaning lady would look, but a thorough burglar would. And the current Mrs. Handshaw seemed pretty thorough.

They even pawed through them to make sure the money went all the way to the bottom and wasn't just salted on top. "Hey," Roy said. "This thing's for real."

"Yeah." Forest could barely whisper. It was almost like being in church. For a moment they were both so quiet you could have heard a mouse squeak. But all household rodents held their peace. The sound they clearly heard was human.

Roy was on it first. "Hey, man, what's that?"

Forest noticed his buddy'd just lost his tan. "Shit! Somebody's here. I knew this goddamn thing was too good to be true. Let's get out of here."

"Wait a minute." Roy held up a beefy hand. "It sounds like cryin'. Like a chick, bawlin' her eyes out."

"Not our problem, Roy. We're lookin' at ten to twenty here." (Actually, he had no idea what the penalty was for burgling in Louisiana, but who cared? Whatever it was, he couldn't afford it.)

Like a fool, Roy was already padding down the white-carpeted hall, holding up a hand for Forest to keep quiet.

Like another one, Forest padded after him, but he knocked into some kind of weird sculpture that hung on the wall. The crying stopped. "Bert, is that you? Please come and untie me, baby. I can't even feel my hands anymore."

Forest and Roy froze. "*Please,* Bert! Oh God, I'm gonna die here! I want my mama!" And then she started crying again.

"Sounds like a kid," Roy whispered.

About then the chick started praying, one of those Catholic things they pray in Louisiana. "Hail Mary, full of grace, Our Lord is with thee. Blessed art thou among women . . . oh, Blessed Mother, *help* me! I swear I'll never do anything bad again; I'll devote myself to Jesus—oh, God, I don't deserve to die trussed up like a pig. Oh, God, oh, God, oh, God!"

"Jesus, shit! This guy could be a serial killer." Roy looked like death. He wasn't the type you'd think would go in for rescuing damsels, but Forest had once seen him take on three guys who were pestering a woman in a bar. No way was he leaving now; Forest knew him. And no way Forest was, either. The way he looked at it, you had to make a living some way and robbing the rich happened to be his, but he could *not* walk away from this. His mother, rest her soul, would hunt him down and haunt him the rest of his life.

Roy pushed open the door closest to the sounds, and there, tied to a big old four-poster bed—hands and feet both—was a naked girl, looked about fifteen, and the prettiest little thing Forest had ever seen. Least her face was—he was too embarrassed to check out the rest. It was a face red from crying and it now turned dead white. "Omigod," she whispered. "*Please*. Please don't kill me." And then she squeezed her little eyes shut and braced herself, shaking from neck to toes, like she was freezing. Most pitiful thing Forest had ever seen.

Roy ripped his shirt off and covered her torso, cradling her head and crooning to her. "You're okay, honey. We're the good guys; you're gonna be fine."

She opened her eyes as Forest went to work on the knots in the black silk bands that held her feet. "You're the cops?"

"Not exactly. More like, uh . . . Superman and Batman. You just take it easy now, we're gonna get you outta here. You got any clothes?"

She started crying again. "He cut them up! Cut up all my clothes right in front of me."

Forest had her legs free now, but she winced. "Hurts."

He started to massage them. "Still hurt? The feeling coming back? Tell you what, Roy, you go finish up in there and I'll take care of this little girl. Find her some clothes and all."

Roy was looking slightly greenish. "Yeah. I was just thinkin' that."

"Take your shirt, though." Man was so shook up he'd forgotten his own shirt.

Forest untied the girl's hands, told her to rub them for circulation and rummaged in a chest of drawers until he found sweats and a T-shirt for her. Shyly, he handed them over, averting his eyes, but he was so nervous he figured he'd better keep talking.

"I'm Forest, by the way. We—uh—came over to do some gardening and came in the house for a drink of water. My buddy's just loadin' up the trash now. Can I—uh—get you anything else?"

"My purse," the girl said. "Maybe he didn't throw away my purse."

Forest looked around, saw a raggedy backpack on the floor near the chest. Picking it up, he said, "This it?"

She grabbed it like it was full of gold bars and rummaged till she found a little coin purse. "Oh, thank God! He didn't rob me."

Honey, you just escaped a serial killer or something, he thought. *That's all you can think about?* And then he remembered she was just a kid. And probably didn't have two dimes to rub together. "Did he hurt you?" he said.

"You friends with him?" Once again, she was holding the backpack like maybe it could somehow save her life. She looked like a scared little bird.

"No. No, you've got nothing to worry about. We'll take you to the—uh, cops or something."

"No! No, I can't—"

He was hoping she'd say that. "Okay, take it easy. We'll take you home, then."

"No!" Louder this time.

Forest was starting to get it. "You a runaway or something? What's your name?"

"Oh, sorry—it's Allison." She shook hands with him, her palm sticky with sweat. Her face twisted into something that was almost a smile. She hadn't said whether Caulfield had hurt her.

Forest said, "You sure you're all right?"

"Yes. Yeah, sure. Just scared, that's all. If you hadn't come along—"

"Yeah," Forest said. He usually hated people who said there was a reason for everything, but he hated to think what might have happened if he and Roy hadn't happened to be there right then, relieving Mr. Caulfield of his cash. "Let me just check on my buddy." He walked to the door of the room. "Roy? How you comin' out there?"

"All loaded up," Roy said, already padding down the hall. "Let's get this young lady out of here. Honey, I'm Roy."

For him, she managed a real smile. She was still clutching the bag. "Allison. Can we go now?"

"You got it."

"Roy," Forest said. "Miss Allison's a runaway—that right, missy?"

"Listen, lots of people know where I am," she said, her eyes pretty well terrified. Forest realized he'd sounded kind of sinister.

"You're fine, baby. Really. If you don't want a ride, you don't have to go anywhere with us. I just thought—"

Roy said, "What do I have to do to convince you we're the good guys? Hey, I know, I'll call my mama—you can talk to *her*. Forest, gimme your phone."

Allison laughed. "No, listen. It's okay. I've just kind of—"

"Yeah. Been through a lot."

They went out the side door, where their truck was parked in the carport. Forest saw two black plastic bags in the bed of the truck and cocked an eye at Roy, who nodded that he'd made the switch.

Forest tried to motion the girl into the vehicle, but she hung back. Then he got it—she didn't want to sit between them. "Hey, listen, I'll sit in the middle. You can be on the side, where you can jump out if you get nervous. Look, we might be Bert Caulfield's gardeners"—he made sure Roy heard that part—"but we have it on good authority he's not a nice man. All we want to do's get you home."

And out of our hair. He was ashamed of himself for thinking it, but this was no time to babysit.

"Not home," she said. "I can't go home. How about the French Quarter?"

"Okay, sure."

Once they were under way, Roy said, "So, what happened, Allison? How'd you wind up with a guy like Caulfield?"

"Bar," she said, so low Forest could barely hear it. "Fake ID." That pretty much said it all, he thought—runaway picks up rich guy in a bar, he takes her home, and nobody even knows she's missing.

"Didn't your mama tell you not to talk to strangers?" Roy

said. "I mean, unless they find you tied up naked. Hardly any choice in that case."

She laughed again.

Forest's cell phone rang. "Private caller," it said. "Hey, girl," he said, knowing it was Heidi. "We're good, everything's fine—but we just have to make a little run to the French Quarter right now. Sorry. See you in about an hour."

"What are you telling me?" Heidi's voice was furious. "Forest McElroy, if you don't show up, I swear to God, I'll hunt you down and lop off every one of your appendages. Joint by joint."

"Baby, take it easy. We gotta do a good deed, that's all. We'll be there." And he hung up. "Hoo boy, is she mad!" he said to Roy.

Allison giggled. "Girlfriend?"

"Wife," he said. "It don't get much worse than that."

"He's not kiddin'," Roy said. "Forest's wife is so ugly, *stones* turn to stone when they see her comin'."

"Roy, that don't make no sense at all," Forest said grumpily, but Allison giggled again, and Roy kept her entertained all the way to the French Quarter with amusing anecdotes about how mean the wife was, how bad her cooking was, how bad she smelled, anything he could think of. By the time they got there, the girl seemed pretty cheered up.

"Where shall we drop you?" Roy said.

"Oh—anywhere. I'll find my friends."

Yep. A runaway all right.

"Look, you got any money?" Forest pulled out a hundred-dollar bill he'd taken for luck out of the pile he and Roy had just boosted.

"Hey, thanks," she said, and as soon as the truck slowed

down, she was gone. Just opened the door and split the second she could.

Roy looked at his buddy. "No kiss good-bye?"

"That was one scared rabbit," Forest said. "Listen, we gotta report this. What if that dude really is a murderer or somethin'?"

"Well, I've been thinkin' about that. What do we say? 'Hey, we found this chick tied up while committing a burglary and maybe the home owner's a suspicious person?' Listen, the dude's probably no worse than your average pervert—probably just wanted to think about her all day, tied up like that, then come home and let her go. After—you know."

"Hell, she couldn't be but fifteen—that makes him a criminal right there."

"Yeah? How we gonna prove it?"

He had a point there. Forest decided to think on it awhile. The main thing right now was to get out to Airline Highway and find a fleabag motel and unload the money and count it. Then they could get some cheap suitcases to put it in and then . . . well, maybe split up and each go off and be rich.

Forest's phone rang again. He looked at it. "It's her." He tossed it out the window. "Plenty money to get another."

More than they thought. Closer to two than one million. They were high-fiving and jumping all around when Roy said, "The hell with the suitcases. Let's get drunk and do it in the morning."

"No, man. We gotta be responsible. We gotta do it now."

"We can't leave the money here."

"Hey, I thought you wanted to get drunk."

"Oh, yeah. Damn. We shoulda taken some out and got

the suitcases first. Now what do we do? Can't even go get a burger." One could go, of course, and leave the other to guard the loot, but as close friends as Roy and Forest were, neither of them considered that one for a minute—each one of them knowing the other way too well.

"Only one thing *to* do—gotta bag it up again, take enough out for expenses, and take it with us to get what we need."

Forest shrugged and started putting his pile back in its plastic leaf bag, all but one package. "We'll split this up, okay?" he said. "Just pack up."

When they were finished, they picked up their bags and opened the door, whereupon they were greeted by Mrs. Heidi Handshaw, her right hand closed over a little white-handled gun. "Hi, guys. Nice job. Put the stuff in my car, okay?" She pointed to a little white Taurus, not at all the kind of car a rich lady ought to have.

"Say wha . . . ?" Roy said.

"Hey, Heidi, honey," Forest said casually. He prided himself on thinking on his feet. "Get out of our way, now. You're not gon' shoot us."

"Maybe not," she said, "but my buddy over there wouldn't think twice about it."

"Over where?" Roy asked, just as something big crashed into him—the guard from Belle Reve, a big redhead, running at him sideways. And Heidi did shoot, taking off some of Forest's arm hair.

"Drop your bundles, gentlemen," she said, but actually they already had. The guard scooped them into the Taurus, and then scooped up Heidi, who kept the gun trained on Forest and Roy till the damn car was in motion.

"Say wha . . . ?" Roy said again.

"Get in the truck, Roy. Let's chase 'em!"

What do you know? The car wouldn't start. "Big surprise," Forest grumped, and Roy got out to look under the hood.

Allison! Forest thought. *Tied up all night, all morning—she should have had to pee. Should have been bustin'.* So she hadn't been there that long. The kid was a booby trap of some kind. He thought about the way she'd left so suddenly, the hundred-dollar bill still clutched in her hand . . .

"Wait a minute," he said aloud. "She didn't have her backpack with her."

"What's that?" Roy had returned. "They took our spark plugs, by the way."

Forest was rooting around on the floor. Sure enough, while Roy was spewing out all that dumb-ass chatter about Forest's so-called wife, the kid had managed to drop it on the floor and stuff it under the seat with her feet. Forest pulled it out. "Whaddaya bet this thing has a GPS in it?"

"Holy shit," Roy said, catching on right away. "How we gonna tell? Wouldn't know one if I saw it."

But there was some kind of thing in it had to be one.

"Goddammit," Roy said, "I knew we couldn't trust that foreign broad. How come you were so confident?"

"Let's go get a beer."

And so, as usual, they discussed the matter over their favorite adult beverage.

"She outthought us," Forest said.

"Elementary, Dr. W. For the second time."

"See, what she did, she pretended to want my studly pink body, but she knew I wouldn't buy it. I *thought* I was supposed to think she was tryin' to keep me from double-crossin' her, but actually, she figured out we were already planning to, so she wanted us to think she was trying to get us not to, because that way we'd think everything was okay."

"Not sure I follow that, bro'."

"She wanted us off guard. Subconsciously thinkin' she was tryin' to lure us to the meetin' place. So we wouldn't suspect nothin' about the naked girl in the house."

"Who ya think *she* was?"

Forest shrugged. "Runaway, probably. Just like she said. Heidi probably paid her a few hundred bucks up front, and then we gave her another hundred. *She* wasn't gon' ask no questions."

"Well, look. This ain't no problem, really. We just go to Belle Reve tomorrow and ask for Mrs. Handshaw. Then we shake her down and go on our merry way."

"What if her buddy's in the guardhouse?"

Roy shrugged. "We beat the shit out of him. What the hell's your problem, man?" He pronounced it "hail."

Forest grinned. "No problem at all." He drank up.

Next day, there was a different guard waiting for them, in a different uniform—a young, insecure one who didn't even seem to know who Mrs. Handshaw was. "Well, locate her!" Forest snapped. "She's expecting us."

Shaking his head, the guy went to get his boss, who, Forest was relieved to see, wasn't Heidi's buddy, either. He was a beefy guy, name of Claude, a lot older than the others. Maybe an ex-cop. "You guys got a problem?"

"Lookin' for Heidi Handshaw—Mrs. Ben Handshaw; 405 Pelican Drive."

Claude scratched his head. "Dr. and Mrs. Inglesby live at

that address," he said. "You sure you don't want Mrs. Inglesby?"

"The lady we want's a blonde with blue eyes and a great laugh. About thirty-two, I'd say, but maybe older. Slight accent—could be Dutch. That Mrs. Inglesby?" Forest wasn't sure about a damn thing about Heidi at this point—she could be Icelandic for all he knew.

"Accent, you say? Hang on a minute." He brought back a file and extracted a picture from it. "Is this her?"

"Yeah. How come you got a file on her?"

"You boys mind coming in a minute? I think we got somethin' to talk about."

Roy and Forest exchanged glances. This didn't sound good. But on the other hand at least Claude would be where they could see him—if he tried to call the cops, they'd be right there to stop him. They climbed down out of the truck, and when they were settled in Claude's neat little office, he said, "What made you think this little gal's named Mrs. Handshaw?"

Forest's stomach did a somersault. "How come you got a file on her?" he repeated.

" 'Cause she's my employee—or was till this morning, when she didn't show up for work. She ever shows her skinny butt around here again, I'm gon' kick it halfway to Baton Rouge. I can't run this place with these half-assed temps."

"She's a *guard* here?" Forest asked, but just for form's sake—if she was a guard, everything fell neatly into place.

"I already told you. She *was* a guard."

"Dr. and Mrs. Inglesby on vacation, by any chance?"

"Now how'd you know that? They're in Tuscany for a month."

"Uh-huh. And do the guards have access to keys to the residents' houses?"

Claude was starting to looked panicked. "Not usually. But sometimes they do. They make side deals to feed cats, take in papers, things like that." He shrugged. "It's against the rules, but they do it. You askin' for any particular reason?"

"It might interest you to know my buddy and I've been swimming in the Inglesbys' pool. And your guard served us some really great mojitos over there—probably made with the Inglesbys' rum."

"Oh, shit. I knew I shouldn'ta—"

"She came without references, did she?"

"Yeah, but she had a really good sob story. And that great laugh." He looked like a broken man.

"Okay, she took you in, but she sorta took us in, too— least my buddy Roy here. They had kind of a thing goin', ya know what I mean? And now he's missin' some money. You mind givin' us a name and address?"

Claude said no, he couldn't do that, it was strictly against the rules, but Forest pointed out that things were a little ir- regular here, and anyhow, there was some more to the story Claude might want to know about.

Roy started at that, but Forest shot him a chill-out look.

"Tell you what," Claude said. "I gotta answer a call of nature. I'll think it over on the way."

And he walked out of the office, leaving the file where it was. Forest opened it. "Jesus Christ," he said, handing it over to Roy. It said she was Rosa Klebb, of 121 Fleming Street, New Orleans, Louisiana. "This ain't her!" Roy said.

"Think, Roy. You ever heard that name before? Like in a movie or somethin'?"

Roy thought, and the light dawned. "The babe in the Bond movie. The one with the poisoned blade in her shoe."

"Yeah—Fleming Street, get it? Whaddaya bet there ain't one in New Orleans?"

"Well, I'll be goddamn."

"Yeah."

Claude came back. "Sorry, but I just can't let you boys look in a personnel file. You seem like solid citizens, though. Maybe you could let me in on the rest of the story."

Forest filled him in about the guard who was in it with her, the big redheaded dude. "Oh, Lord, Billy Acree. Been here for three years. I been on vacation for a week. Left Billy in charge."

"I got a feelin' you seen the last of him, too."

"Shit on a stick." He slumped, mouth turned down.

"Well, good luck findin' 'em, Claude. Hope they didn't do too much damage."

"Hey, wait a minute. You boys ain't gon' report this, are you?"

"You kiddin'? We wouldn't do a thing like that to you. Maybe they didn't do a damn thing but borrow the Inglesbys' swimming pool."

They backed the truck out of the guardhouse drive and took off. Forest kept his mouth shut for the next little bit, thinking things through, and finally Roy said, "What do we do now? I gotta know where to point this thing."

"Well, I got an idea. How about if we look at this thing optimistically? We each took out a pack of bills for expenses—that gives us about ten thousand each. Not bad for a couple days' work, right? So maybe we go back home and pay the rent."

"You don't want to track down the bitch and rip her hair out?"

Forest had thought that one out, too. "I don't think so," he said. "You gotta admire the woman's skill. Gotta give her credit—she's the best little con artist I ever seen in my life."

"Hey, Forest—hello? She just did us out of two million bucks."

"Naaah. Just one when you think about it. We were tryin' to do her out of the second mil, remember?"

"That's a technicality."

"Okay, let's do one little thing—let's go over and clue old Bert Caulfield in—let him try to find her. We can just say she and the carrot top offered us the gig and we turned it down. Ain't nothin' he can do about us, anyhow. Can't report the theft—can't kill us in front of his whole staff."

Roy brightened. "Hey, maybe he'll give us a finder's fee if he gets the money back."

"Don't think I'd count on it, my man, Anyhow, there's only one thing I really want at this point."

"Sure, I know, sucker. You still want to get in her pants. Know how they talk about the kind of guy you shake hands with and then have to count your fingers? I don't even want to think about—"

Forest cut him off. "Shows how much you know, bozo. That chick's Satan spawn, I've long since accepted that. But she's an artist, you gotta admit it—an actual artiste."

"So what's the thing you want?"

"I'd just like to know her real name," Forest said dreamily.

GDMFSOB

Nevada Barr

All Walgreen's had was a little kid's notebook, maybe four by five inches, the binding a fat spiral of purple plastic, the cover a Twiggy–Carnaby Street–white boots–flower power mess of lavender and yellow blooms.

Jeannie put it on the café table, opened it, and carefully wrote, "Goddamnmotherfuckingsonofabitch" in her best schoolgirl cursive. The juxtaposition of sentiment and sentimentality pleased her.

Next she wrote, "Divorce Rich," then sat back, looked at the words, and took a long luxurious sip of the cheap but not inexpensive Pinot Grigio a harried waitress in too-tight jeans had brought her.

Rich thought she drank too much. Of course she drank too much. She was married to a goddamnmotherfucking-sonofabitch. She drew a neat line through the word *divorce.*

Divorce was out of the question. Mississippi, usually such a liberal, cutting-edge innovator, was old-school when it came to matrimony; marriage was sacred. Unless both parties agreed, the only grounds for divorce were adultery, impotence, or if felony could be proved.

Not that the GDMFSOB wasn't engaged in one or the other at any given time, but Good Old Rich put Jeannie in mind of the Baptists: you knew they were doing it; you just couldn't ever catch them at it.

And Rich would never grant her a divorce. Not if it meant giving up the "income stream from the family business," as he euphemistically referred to her earnings as a sculptress.

No. Divorce wasn't happening.

That left suicide and murder.

When Rich had been particularly demeaning, Jeanie'd had the occasional fling with Dr. Kevorkian, but, in all honesty, she had to admit that she was a decent individual. She paid her taxes—and his—kept a tidy house, and got her oil changed every three thousand miles. And Rich . . .

Rich was boring.

Not casually boring; he was a bore of nuclear magnitude. More than once she had witnessed him turn entire dinner parties to stone, seen guests' eyes roll back in their heads and their tongues begin to protrude as he replaced all the available oxygen with pomposity. Not being a jobholder himself, he felt uniquely qualified to lecture on the subject. He told her cleaning lady how to clean, her gallery owner how to present art, the man who cast her work how to run a foundry, her agent how to sell sculpture.

Suicide was out. It would be wrong, un-American even, to deny the world her lovely bronzes while simultaneously condemning it to Rich's monologues.

That left murder.

In the ordinary run of things, Jeannie didn't condone murder. She wasn't even a proponent of capital punishment. But her husband wasn't in the ordinary run of things. He was extraordinarily in need of being dead.

"Kill Rich," she printed carefully beneath the crossed-out "divorce."

Another long swallow of wine and contemplation.

Over the eight years of their marriage she had shared all the nasty bits with shrinks, groups, AA, and half a dozen girlfriends. There was so much dirty laundry lining the by-ways of her past they rivaled the back alleys of Mexico City on wash day. Should anything untoward befall Rich, she would be the prime suspect.

There must be no evidence. None.

She scribbled out everything she'd written then tore out the page. Feeling a fool, but being a nonsmoker and thus having no recourse to fire, she surreptitiously soaked the page in the wine and swallowed it.

As easily as that, she decided to kill her husband.

Setting her glass on the uneven surface of the wrought-iron café table, she watched the wine tremble as minuscule earthquakes sent out barely perceptible tsunamis and she thought of the things people die of.

Drowning, burning, choking, crushing, goring by bulls, hanging, falling, dismemberment, being devoured by wild beasts, poisoning, exploding, crashing in cars, boats, planes, and motorcycles, disease, cutting, stabbing, slashing, blunt trauma to the head, dehydration, hypothermia, heatstroke, starvation, vitamin-A poisoning from eating polar bears' livers, snakebite, drawing and quartering, asphyxiation, shooting, beheading, bleeding out, infection, boredom—Lord knew Rich had nearly done her in with that one.

Rumor had it people died of shame and broken hearts. No hope those would work on Rich, though over the years she had given it a go, usually at the top of her lungs with tears and snot pouring attractively down her face. A dedicated philandering deadbeat pornographer, Rich had embraced shame as an alternative lifestyle and his heart was apparently made of India rubber.

"Goddamnmotherfuckingsonofabitch," she wrote on the fresh, yet-to-be-eaten page of her notebook, knocked back the last of her wine, and left the waitress a five-dollar tip.

Two hours later she was again staring at the page. The compulsion to write what she'd done was overwhelming. Vaguely she remembered there was actually a word for the phenomenon, *hyperscribblia* or something. "Don't, don't, don't," she said as she uncapped a razor-point Pilot and put the tip against the smooth paper.

Mildly fascinated and massively alarmed, she watched as the pen flickered down the page, line by line, leaving a trail the dumbest of cops couldn't fail to follow.

"Went to the garage. Shoulder-deep in junk. No room for car. Found motorcycle. Put on gardening gloves. Drove roofing tack three-quarters of an inch into front tire just below fender." On the pen flew, painting the pictures so clear in Jeannie's mind: Rich's praying-mantis form, clad in the endless leathers that arrived almost daily from eBay—chaps, fringed and plain, leather vests, gloves, leather pants, boots, leather jackets, leather shirts, helmets, do-rags, even a leather face guard that made Jeannie want to reread *The Man in the Iron Mask*—or rent *Silence of the Lambs*. Done up like a macho caricature of a macho caricature, the imaginary Rich pushes the bike out with his long spider's legs. Backward rolls the heavy machine, the tack slides unnoticed up beneath the fender.

Words flow across the tiny cramped pages, spinning a tale of how the tack, pounded in at an angle just so, remains static until the curve heading out onto the freeway, where the wheel turns and the bike leans and the head of the tack finally hits the pavement, driven deeper. *Bang!* The tire has blown! Out of control, the motorcycle is down. Rich is sliding. My God! My God! His helmet pops off and bounces across two lanes of freeway traffic. The motorcycle is spinning now; Rich's protective leathers begin to tear, leaving black marks on the pale concrete, hot and lumpy like a black crayon dragging across sandpaper. Leather is rasped away; flesh meets the road. Crayon marks turn from black to red. The driver of an eighteen-wheeler, high on methamphetamines, barrels down the highway, unaware of the man and motorcycle spinning toward his speeding rig. Look out! Look—

"Lover Girl? Have you been in the garage?" Rich's murmuring voice, always pitched a decibel or so lower than the threshold of human hearing, thus forcing the unfortunate listener to say "What?" several times just to make audible something not worth hearing anyway, wisps down the short hall between the garage and the kitchen, where Jeannie sits at the counter.

"The garage¿ No. Why¿" she calls as his rubber-soled slip-ons shuff-shuffle down the hall.

The pages. She shoves them into the Osterizer and pushes *puree*. Jammed. A pint of milk. Bingo. Pasta. "Thankyou-babyjesus."

Rich's bald head on its Ichabod Crane neck pokes around the corner. "My things. In the garage. Did you touch them¿" Rich hates her to move his things.

"No, sweetheart."

"Dinner¿" he asks, eyeing the Osterizer.

Jeannie nods, too scared to talk.

Rich settles on a stool, his pale bulbous eyes fixed on her. Under the blue stare Jeannie pours the mixture into a casserole dish with pasta and sauce from a bottle and sets the oven to three-fifty.

Rich likes it. "Happy tummy," he murmurs as he eats, eyes glued to *Fear Factor* contestants on the television gagging down pig bowels in cockroach sauce.

GDMFSOB, Jeannie chants in her mind as she surreptitiously makes herself a ham-and-cheese sandwich and takes it to bed.

Rich stays up till three, as he often does. Jeannie has learned to sleep. She knows if she tiptoes down the hall like a curious child on Christmas Eve night and peeks in the piled mess he calls his office, Good Old Rich will be hunkered in front of his computer screen, bald head nestled between hunched shoulders like an ostrich egg in a lumpy nest, watching the X-rated cavortings of what he insists is not pornography but Adult Content Material.

Sleep is good.

Plotting is better.

The next day, armed with information from the library's computer—so there will be no history on her own—Jeannie cultures botulism. It is surprisingly easy and naturally deadly. Perfect. Bad salmon. The GDMFSOB loves salmon. She doesn't. Perfect. Until she gets hold of the pen and out it comes: Rich reeling out of the marital bed, dragging himself to the bathroom, Jeannie pretending to sleep as his calls grow ever weaker. She dialing 911, but alas! Too late! Weeping prettily as she tells the kind, attractive, young policeman how she took an Ambien and can't remember anything until, gulp, sigh, she woke to find this. Mea culpa, mea culpa, but not really . . .

Damning, damning, damning, the words rattle over page after page.

Shuff-shuffle. The bald pate, the watery blue eyes. "Sketching a new sculpture?" Rich is oh-so-supportive of her work. He needs the money for his lifestyle.

"Sketching," Jeannie manages as she snatches up the pages.

Rich turns on the television. It's Thursday. *Survivor* is on Thursdays. Rich never misses *Survivor*.

"What's for dinner?"

"Salmon." Perfect but for the incriminating compulsion.

The osterizer: olive oil, pesto, onion.

"Dinner is served."

"Lover Girl, the salmon smells funny. Did you get fresh?"

"Fresh."

"The pesto is great. Happy tummy."

Over subsequent days Jeannie drips acid on brake lines and writes, melts off the tips of his épées and writes. Osterizes and seasons and serves.

And Rich lives. Thrives. Like the cat who came back the very next day. Jeannie cannot get her hands on an atom bomb.

Damn.

Nothing.

Damn.

Rich is hunkered on the sofa eating lasagna of hamburger, cheese, and the pages detailing how she greased the feet of the extension ladder before asking him to take a look at the chimney, when Jeannie realizes that, as a murderess, she's a bust. Rich is protected by angels. Or demons. Or stupidity.

Suicide returns as an option. She can't love. She can't leave. She can't live.

Damn.

Guns are too messy. Hanging too painful. Pills. Being with Rich for eight years has driven her to a veritable cornucopia: Ambien, Effexor, Desyrel, Xanax—all good traceable drugs. Surely if she takes them all at once . . .

The nagging of *Big Brother* on the forty-two-inch TV whines into the bedroom, where Jeannie, tuna sandwich untouched, sits in bed, sixty-two pills in pink, white, and yellow cupped in her palm, bottled water on the nightstand. Usually she sleeps nude, but tonight she has put on a nice pair of pajamas: discreet, modest. Lord knew how she might sprawl and froth. Better to be on the safe side.

Suicide.

So be it.

Rich had won.

Jeannie tips all sixty-two pills into her mouth and reaches for the water.

"Lover Girl?" Rich stands in the bedroom door. He looks peaked, as Jeannie's mother might say.

"What?" she mumbles around the deadly sleep in her mouth.

"Unhappy tummy," he moans.

He runs for the bathroom. Jeannie spits out the pills.

"Haven't taken a dump in days," he calls genteelly through the open bathroom door. Rich never closes the bathroom door. In fact, he makes deposits while she showers, brushes her teeth, suffocating, stifling deposits.

"Oh," she calls with mechanical sympathy.

Two days later Rich is dead. Jeannie dials 911.

"Impacted bowel," the coroner tells her. "Was your husband eating anything unusual?"

"Murder," Jeannie might have said, but she didn't.

The House of Deliverance

Christine Matthews

First it was food.

To hell with all the psychiatric logic from Dr. Phil and suffering looks from Butch. A bag of Chips Ahoys or a plate piled high with meat loaf, mashed potatoes, gravy and biscuits, a slice or two of chocolate cake for dessert, were the only things that comforted Opal. Potato chips with lots of onion dip. Ice cream sundaes, barbecue ribs, cheese in a can, popcorn with lots of butter and salt. It took more and more to help her get over what had happened to Brenda.

And she was getting there. In her own good time, in her own way. But soon she couldn't button her blouses, so she got stretchy T-shirts. Big ones. And pants with ten percent spandex, elastic waistbands—all in dark colors. She was fine with it.

Hamburgers with extra cheese, king-size orders of fries, pizza, fried chicken—anything fried—Twinkies, Oreos, and doughnuts.

She was getting better . . . until her blood pressure sky-rocketed, which led to migraines, shortness of breath, and backaches.

That's how she started taking pills. Diet pills from the drugstore, not the real ones the doctors prescribe. And she started losing weight. *There,* she thought, *is everyone happy now? Will you all leave me alone?*

But Timothy Bridgeman was out there somewhere having a life. Last she heard, he was interning down at Children's Hospital, and Brenda, sweet, beautiful Brenda, was still suffering so.

After a month her clothes got baggy. Another month and little lines around her mouth deepened, skin on her neck sagged, and she swore, if there was anyone around to swear at, that her knees had dropped close toward the floor. Looking in the mirror made her depressed. What had been the point? She'd forgotten. Besides, Butch never took her anywhere. It didn't matter what size she could squeeze into or even if she bought all new clothes.

"You're no good to anyone anymore," Butch shouted one evening during a commercial break from his basketball game. He shouted all the time; it was his normal tone with her now.

"What am I supposed to do? The police still haven't arrested that bastard. We've given them—"

"It's been more than three years. Stop waitin', 'cause

nothin' ain't never gonna happen. Never! Get over it, will ya⸮"

"For your information, Mr. Smart-Ass, it's been two years and three months. Shows how much you care about your own daughter. What kind of a man are you, anyways⸮ Our only child was violated by some punk who thinks he's better than us. He has to pay for what he done. Any normal parent, any parent who loved their kid at all, would want to kill Tim Bridgeman."

"Brenda's fine. Stuff like that happens in college. First time a kid's been away from home, booze, parties, hell, it happened to—"

"Rape's rape. It don't matter if you're on a date, or drinkin'—none of it matters. Brenda said she told that son of a bitch to stop. She swore she screamed for him to stop. Over an' over again, but he wouldn't listen." Why couldn't Butch get it through his thick skull that the law had been broken the moment Tim Bridgeman had turned into an animal⸮

"Yeah, well, all I know for sure is it come down to his word against hers. There never was no evidence. How do you figure that one out, Einstein⸮"

Their arguments always brought them back to that question. Truth was, Opal didn't know how to explain the absence of any semen or bruises on Brenda's body. And in a town, especially one as small as Atlas was, no one put up much of a fight against the family who ran the whole damn place. Certainly not her loser husband.

Butch stood in the doorway holding his beer can in one hand and a cigarette in the other. "Now listen up 'cause I don't wanna have to talk about this no more, woman. Your daughter needs you even if she ain't livin' here now. An' I'm sick an' tired of bein' the husband an' father of them poor Decatur women. I need you to straighten up. Do somethin' with yourself. Stop embarrassing this family. Get off your fat ass and go see Dotty. Or call up Rita—it's Thursday— play some bingo like you used to."

Opal sat in her chair across the room from Butch. The double-wide had been used when they bought it, but the furniture was new. Well, it had all been clean and pretty six years ago—before all this shit started.

Opal reached for a pill and studied her sorry excuse for a husband. "Just like that. You want me to get up and act as though nothing happened to Brenda. Geez, Butch, if only I could be as cold an' uncaring as you. Wouldn't that be dandy if the whole world could be as carefree an' happy as you? Tell me how to do that, Butch, an' I'll do it. For Christ's sake, just tell me how you manage to get up every day, go to work, an' not think about what Bridgeman done to your daughter? Your only daughter? Your little girl!"

He walked over to the ashtray on the end table next to her chair and put out his cigarette. Then he looked at her long and hard. After a moment he shook his head as if she were too pathetic to spend any more time with.

As he walked out of the room, Opal figured that the twenty pounds she'd lost with those big pills she'd been swallowing weren't making her feel any better about anything.

And that's when she found religion.

It hadn't come all at once like in some flash of silver, with Jesus standing in front of her wearing a robe trimmed in blue. It hadn't even come in a dream or a vision. No angels appeared at the foot of her bed like they had to Dotty, her neighbor on lot number six. The psychic at the fair she'd gone to years ago when Brenda was in sixth grade told her she'd never have any other children. She'd been right, Opal had known it the very instant she heard the words. But this wasn't nothing like that either. It happened in that quiet way life has of unraveling while you're working so furiously to tie everything up all neat and pretty.

And it happened at the House of Deliverance.

There it stood, but you had to look hard to find it. An old, run-down wooden building, off of Highway W, near a creek. Opal, who'd been living in Atlas for more than half of her forty-four years had never even noticed it before. Until that day—that beautiful, glorious, sunlit day when she made a wrong turn.

"I have half a mind just to call the sheriff sometimes an' have him repossess your license," Butch was always threatening. "What are you thinkin'?" he'd ask if she got lost. "Hell, Opal, you never go anywheres to get lost. Take your head out of your ass sometimes, will ya?"

So it wasn't unusual, even though she was alone in the car, that she winced at the realization she was lost. But later, after much reflection, it became clearer than a glass of Stoly that destiny had been steering her Buick.

Sunflowers bloomed everywhere. Big flowers, standing as high as a grown person, and as she walked through the field they seemed to nod at her. Guiding her toward the front door.

There were no other cars around and it wasn't until she got closer that she noticed a small gravel-covered parking area in the rear of the building. Golden letters on the door were worn, the *L* in DELIVERANCE missing altogether. A small side window was broken, frosted over with cobwebs. But there didn't have to be anything fancy here, it was in the air. In the ground. Opal could feel it. This was a place where the Almighty Himself visited from time to time. She was sure of it.

There were eight rickety stairs; she counted each one before starting to turn the rusted door knob, wondering all the while if she was trespassing.

"No, this is meant to be."

"Can I help you?" a man with movie-star-blue eyes asked as he opened the door.

"I'm . . . I was just drivin' . . ."

"And you got lost? Ain't that what you're going to tell me, my child?"

"Well . . ."

He slicked a piece of hair behind his ear and she could see the gold pinkie ring shine. That had to be a real diamond, she thought. Why, a man as handsome as he was surely had to be one of God's chosen.

His laugh made her feel giddy. "Why, if I had a dime for every person who come to my door askin' directions, I'd have enough money to put a new roof on this old place."

"But I don't think I'm lost. Not really," she said. "In fact, now that I'm standin' here, I think I was meant to make your acquaintance on this particular day."

"And in this particular way?"

She wasn't sure if he was making fun of her or just being friendly, so she didn't answer.

He didn't seem to notice her confusion. "Well, Miss . . ."

"Mrs. Decatur."

"Well, Mrs. Decatur, care to have a look around? Since you made the trip anyway . . . on purpose or not. The Lord is always workin' out there in His mysterious ways, ain't He? We just have to relax and go along for the ride. Watch that step there."

For a moment Opal thought about saying no, getting back in her car, hightailing it home to . . . Butch. Oh yeah, Butch. Picturing him sitting in his big ol' recliner, spewing advice at her. No, she realized in that same moment, this was a better place for her to be.

"Thank you," she said, and walked through the door.

She hadn't expected much and the inside of the building met her expectations. There were no stained-glass windows, no golden trim anywhere. Not even a piece of carpet on the floor. Plain. Everything was so plain. Which made it all seem truer. Truer and more real than anything she'd known during the last few years.

As they stood in the middle of the large room, he introduced himself. "I am Reverend Hempel and I welcome you to the House of Deliverance." His hands waved through the air gracefully, like one of those magicians on TV who made whole airplanes disappear.

She nodded, glad to meet him.

"We're a small but close-knit congregation."

"Baptists?" Opal asked.

"No."

"Lutheran, then?"

"No. We're what you might call . . . seekers. The Johnsons

were Catholic and the Quick family were Methodists, once upon a time."

"And now?"

"Just like the Bible says, Genesis 37:15: 'Behold he was wandering in the field—' "

"Just like me . . ."

" 'and the man asked him, sayin', What seekest thou? And he said, I seek my brethren.' They've all come to us because they were disillusioned, either with their faith or their way of life. Lookin' for others like them, lookin' for something more."

"Seekin' the truth."

"Exactly, Mrs. Decatur."

"Opal. I prefer Opal, if you don't mind."

"Now, Opal, why would I mind you treatin' me like a friend?"

He guided her to one of the pews and she expected to feel the roughness catch her skirt as she slid across the seat. But instead it was smooth, worn from years of use. Reverend Hempel walked across the wooden floor to the front of the room, climbed the single step, and reached behind a worn tapestry to flick a light switch.

The room was suddenly awash with the most comforting glow Opal could remember ever experiencing.

"There now, that's better," Reverend Hempel said. "Now you can get a real good look at our little church."

As he walked back toward her, she was able to see—really see—a crudely carved cross hanging in front of the tapestry. The contrast of reds in the fabric against deep mahogany made her feel calm. As she took in the entire room, there seemed to be enough space to seat maybe fifty people at the most. The windows, four along each wall, had been painted over with some sort of yellow glaze. The whole place felt holy. She wondered if she was having one of those epiphanies like Bobby Jo Winkelbauer was always talking about every time Opal went into the Kroger.

"It's glorious" was all she could say.

Reverend Hempel slid across the pew in front of her and stopped when he was positioned to her left. Then he turned around, rested his right arm across the top of the wooden bench, and put his feet up. "So you feel it, then?"

Suddenly Opal wanted to pour her heart out to this man. "If you're talkin' about the Holy Spirit, then I truly do. I felt Him while I was sittin' in my car and I'm sure He guided me up those steps and—"

"Right into the House of Deliverance."

Opal nodded so vigorously her glasses almost shook right off her face.

"So," the reverend began, "tell me, Sister Opal, what are you seekin'?"

That was all she needed. Someone to ask and be prepared to listen to her. And everything came tumbling out. She told him about her sweet, beautiful, smart Brenda and how that fuck—only she didn't actually say the F-word—Tim Bridgeman had ruined her sweetness. She cried when she got to the part about how crazy it was making her, but when he asked how her husband, Brenda's daddy, was handling everything, well, she got mad. Real mad.

"He acts as though nothin's happened. Like Brenda was askin' for it or somethin'. Are all men like that, Reverend? Because I pray God they ain't."

He nodded. "Yes, I'm sorry to say, it's been my experience most men react with anger. I try to counsel 'em, point out how all that rage just hurts their family even more."

"Well, it sure ain't that way with women. Every single one of my girlfriends want to go after Tim Bridgeman an' cut off that prick of his—pardon my French. But it's the God's honest truth, Reverend. I can't live with all this bitterness churnin' through my insides an' I can't live with my husband who won't hear me. He plain don't care."

"Now, I'm sure that's not true. He's just tryin' to be strong for you an' his daughter. You know, the reason men get so angry is because they think it's their job to protect their women. Mr. Decatur probably feels he let you all down."

Opal considered the idea and then dismissed it. "No, sorry, Reverend, you just don't know Butch."

"Well, that can be fixed. How about you two come back for Sunday services an' we'll all have a talk after the sermon. When everyone's gone home. Private. How does that sound?"

"Real good."

"What's wrong with our church? We belonged to Good Shepherd since before Mama died. I like it there. We know everyone. I feel comfortable—"

"You say hi to maybe four people, grumble, sit in your seat, an' fall asleep during the sermon. Every single one of 'em. You been doin' it for years, Butch."

"An' I like it that way. The Lord an' me, we got a deal, I give him an hour on Sunday and he keeps the devil away from me the rest of the week."

"Well, He sure did a piss-poor job of keeping the Bridge-man kid away—"

"Hey!" He pounded his fist on the table. The ketchup bottle tipped over and dropped to the floor. "I don't never wanna hear you talk about the Almighty with such disrespect again. Understand?"

"Sorry. But how can you sit there, actin' like everything's fine with the world. 'Cause it ain't, you know?"

"Don't you never let up, Opal? I'm sick an' tired to death of this. You got one song an' sing it mornin', noon, an' night."

"Come to the House of Deliverance with me, Butch. Meet Reverend Hempel. You'll see. It's different there."

He stopped chewing his dinner. "An' that will get you off my back?"

She nodded.

He gulped down the last of his sweet tea. "All right, you win. But just this one time."

Sunday finally came. Opal had told Brenda all about the church and Reverend Hempel, going on and on about how the Spirit had touched her in that little wooden house surrounded by sunflowers. How maybe if Brenda came with them, she'd feel it, too. But no amount of talking could persuade her daughter. Maybe next time.

She rushed to the bathroom, where the light was better, making sure her makeup was just right for the second time in ten minutes. The Mary Kay lady had shown her how to apply Bewitching Bisque foundation, but she could never get it to look like it had the day she purchased the products now stashed under the sink.

Butch came around the corner dragging his feet. He heaved a long sigh. "Let's go. The sooner we get outta here, the sooner we can come back."

Opal stopped what she was doing; after twenty-four years of marriage, she knew enough not to leave the house without looking her fashion reject of a husband over—real good. From his John Deere cap down to that Kmart plaid shirt he insisted was his favorite color, to his grass-stained boots, Butch wasn't fit to be seen.

"You're not wearin' those clothes. I laid out your gray suit on the bed. Go put it on."

He stood there, all dumb and disgusted like an overgrown ten-year-old. "Do I hafta?"

"Wasn't it you who got all mad at the thought that I might be disrespectin' the Lord? Well, how do you think He's gonna feel if you walk into His house without givin' one tiny thought to your appearance? Cleanliness is next to godliness, Butch. You standin' there, lookin' like that, puts you next to a garbage man, not our Heavenly Father."

He didn't have an argument for that one. Slowly, grumbling as he went, he returned to the bedroom and put on his suit.

The church seemed even smaller than she remembered. But then there were sixty-one people crammed inside—Opal had counted. The windows were open and a cool breeze brought in the fragrance of wildflowers as Reverend Hempel preached his sermon. Several times she looked over at Butch, just to make sure he was still awake, and each time was surprised to see his eyes not only were opened but actually focused. And she couldn't help wondering, as she followed along with the hymn, if she was witnessing a miracle.

After he finished, Reverend Hempel turned the floor over to some woman named Alma Monroe. This was usually the place where Opal expected to hear an announcement of a prayer meeting or bake sale. At least that's the way it was done where she came from. But instead, the elderly woman just stood there. Gathering her thoughts? Opal wondered. But after two minutes passed, there was no witnessing, no speaking in tongues, just this woman in her very pink floral dress (with matching hat) standing there, smiling peacefully.

The longer it went on, the more uncomfortable Opal got. "What do you suppose is goin' on here?" she whispered to Butch. When he didn't answer she nudged him in the ribs.

He shushed her. Just like he did when he was all involved watching one of his football or baseball games.

She couldn't believe it.

Trying not to turn her head too much—heaven forbid she appear rude—Opal pretended she was checking the shoulder of her dress for lint. This maneuver enabled her to catch glimpses of most of the people near her out of the corners of her eyes. They, like Butch, sat mesmerized.

Opal was confused. Hurt. A little angry. What the hell was she missing?

The silence hummed in her ears. No one moved. Not the baby in her little seat propped up next to her mother, not the teenager who had been trying to get the attention of a brunette across the aisle. No coughing, no shuffling of feet. It was downright creepy, that's what it was.

Then the woman smiled. A big grin that made everyone respond with a smile of their own. Butch sat there, happier than she'd ever seen him in . . . never! She'd never seen him like that. Opal joined in, not knowing why but wanting to feel what everyone else was feeling. Needing desperately to feel something.

Reverend Hempel stood beside the woman the whole time. He was smiling now, too. A few more minutes passed, and then at last—at long last—he put his arm around her and bowed his head. She followed his lead. The congregation took their cue from her, and a prayer, like thousands of others Opal had heard or recited, was offered up.

There was no collection plate passed around. No woeful tales about the church needing this or that and how everyone had to dig deep and help. It was all about feelings.

At first Opal worried she didn't have any. That maybe she wasn't this caring, kind person she'd always told people she was. Especially when Butch wouldn't stop talking on the drive home.

"I ain't never experienced nothin' like that. I felt it, Opal. Right down to my sorry soul. I felt the Spirit in that church, just like you said. Hey, wanna go to the Waffle House?"

"What about your game?" she asked.

"Everythin's different now." He took his right hand off the steering wheel and squeezed her knee. "Everythin'."

Butch had meant what he said. Everything was different from that day forward. He was kinder, sweeter, more thoughtful about Opal's feelings. He hardly ever watched TV; all his spare time was now spent at the House of Deliverance, talking to Reverend Hempel privately or sitting in on Bible groups. He couldn't get enough.

At first Opal was thrilled. She'd have dinner waiting for him after work—they actually ate together now!—he'd help her clean up, and they'd drive down to the House of Deliverance together. Oh, she never told him she hadn't felt what he had that first Sunday. Why would she? He had never been happier.

Or more talkative.

"It's not like that bein'-born-again crap," he told her. Again and again. "It's like the Lord is swirlin' around inside me. Liquid gold, lightin' up every part of me. Warm. Peaceful. Hell, you know what I mean. I don't hafta tell you, do I?"

She'd shake her head every time he asked. "You sure don't."

After a month or so of going to that place every single night, Opal asked why they couldn't just go on Sundays. When he made a face, she added, "And maybe Wednesdays for Bible study? Isn't two nights a week enough?"

The old Butch would have told her *he* was the boss. *He* was the one who went to work every day. *He* was the one who paid the bills. All she had to do was obey *him* and she was doin' a piss-poor job of it. Instead he told her, "Whatever you feel is right for you, sweetheart. Go with your heart an' you can't go wrong."

Who was this man? How could there be such a complete change in such a short time?

"But if you don't mind, I'll probably go visit with Reverend Hempel by myself sometimes. Or we could have him over here to supper now an' then."

Ah, there he was. She was relieved to see Butch was still in there, that he hadn't been possessed or turned into some kind of robot like the women in those Stepford movies. Still getting his way, only now he was taking a more Christian route.

She replied in kind. "Whatever makes you happy, darlin'."

The next Sunday she invited Reverend Hempel to come for supper on Thursday night. Butch had "suggested" she do it three times during the preceding week. "Could you make that meat loaf of yours? An' a cherry pie for dessert?"

When the reverend shook her hand after services, he accepted her invitation gladly. "Nothing I like better than to visit with my flock in their homes. It makes me feel like family."

When Thursday came she had set the alarm to get up earlier than usual. It would take all morning to clean, find and then wash the good dishes, buy groceries, and vacuum. The afternoon was spent making that damn pie Butch was so set on, throwing a meat loaf together, ironing her blue dress, and fixing her hair. She had just finished making the iced tea when Butch drove up with Reverend Hempel.

Dinner went well. Compliments flew; Opal was happy that all her efforts had been appreciated. While she cleared the table, the menfolk strolled into the living room and patiently waited for her to make coffee. As she scooped up vanilla ice cream and plopped it on top of the warm pie, she felt ashamed of herself. Well, just a little bit. Looking around the corner, she caught a glimpse of the reverend and his kind face. Why had she felt so threatened? she wondered. She peeked over at Butch, who sat smiling, softly conversing, and she thought what an ungrateful woman she was. Here she had what every woman in America wanted—or so she'd been told in thousands of articles and *Oprah* shows. Here she had a man who loved her. Who cared about her. Who always came home to her every night after work, except when he was at church. Church. How in the hell could a person be jealous of God? Maybe the devil was getting ahold of her soul. Maybe she had better start trying to change, like Butch had.

She loaded the silver tray saved for special occasions and holidays, and proudly carried it into the living room.

"And so, Butch, that's why—" Reverend Hempel stopped short when he saw Opal. She thought she would drop everything from the abruptness.

Guilty. That's how they looked at her.

Butch jumped up as if he'd been caught doing something nasty. "Here, let me help you with that."

All she could say was "Thank you."

Something was different. She'd suddenly gone from being the gracious hostess, wife of Butch, to the intruder. The outsider. She resented feeling unwelcome in her own home.

They ate the pie, drank coffee, but within ten minutes of taking the last bite, Reverend Hempel looked at his watch and said, "Opal, this has been a truly delightful evenin', but I'm afraid I have an unfinished sermon layin' on my desk back home. Butch, could I impose upon you one last time to drive me back?"

Butch jumped up like he'd been sitting on a spring. "No trouble. My pleasure." He kissed Opal on the cheek and the two of them were out the door before she could even stand up to say a proper good-bye.

After the car had pulled out of the driveway, all she could do was shake her head. "Now what was that all 'bout?" she asked herself.

"I don't know, but I'm sure as hell gonna find out," she answered.

It took about two weeks. But when Butch came home from church especially late one night, Opal knew the time was as right as it would ever get.

"Okay. What's goin' on? Between you an' the reverend, I mean. Whisperin' that way when he come for dinner. You got secrets you're keepin' from me, Butch, an' I don't like it. Not one bit." She stood with her hands on her hips, strong. "Just look at yourself. Always in such a damn hurry to get down to the House of Deliverance that you run straight from work. No time to change into clean clothes. What kinda respect are you showin' the Lord by enterin' His house lookin' like a bum anyway? None of it makes any sense."

He'd barely managed to get through the door. Tossing his jacket in the corner, he slumped down into his chair. "Are you talkin' about sex here? Is that what's goin' round in your crazy head, Opal?"

"Don't be stupid, Butch! I noticed somethin' fishy goin' on that night the reverend come for dinner. It's that church. It's done somethin' to you and I don't like it. Not one bit."

He cocked his head. "I ask you to come every time I go—"

"Listen to me now. I am referrin' to that dinner weeks ago. I walked in an' you clammed up soon as you seen me. It was downright weird. Like you two had some big secret."

"We was talkin' about seekers. You know how he goes on."

"No, he never talked to me in whispers like he done you. So . . . are you gonna tell me or not? What did he say?"

"He told me somethin' that stuck in my head, Opal. It was so powerful I couldn't talk to no one about it."

"Not even me, Butch? Hell, I'm your wife. Been for more than twenty years. You can tell me everything."

Butch thought it over and then, suddenly, started to cry. All she could think to do was go to him, hold him, and tell him everything—whatever those things were—was all right.

"I've been so uncarin' to you. To Brenda. My own daughter! I'm so ashamed, Opal. Reverend Hempel told me that in Isaiah, the Bible says: 'Learn to do well; seek judgment, relieve the oppressed.' "

"I'm sure it does, darlin'." She patted his shoulder and could feel his body shaking.

"I've turned my back on my beautiful Brenda when she needed me most. I didn't relieve her of any pain and I didn't even try to seek judgment by gettin' that bastard Bridgeman hauled into jail for what he done to our baby."

Opal wanted to fall to her knees and give thanks. Finally! At long last, hallelujah, her prayers had been answered!

"But I fixed everything, Opal. You'll be proud of me now.

Brenda's gonna respect her daddy again an' the Lord will forgive me. I know He will."

She pulled back from him, squinting to get a good look into his eyes while she asked, "An' just how'd you do all that?"

"I wasn't at church tonight, or last night. Or even last week. I been plannin'."

"Plannin' what, Butch?" She was afraid to know the answer and yet she felt her heart race, excited to hear more.

"First I had to get me a gun. Wallace down at work had one he sold me real cheap. Then I had to watch Bridgeman till I was sure I could get him alone."

"An' just where were you tonight, Butch?"

"Out in the wood, buryin' his sorry ass."

Opal fell back. "He's dead?" she whispered.

"As a possum all stiff by the side of the road. An' you know what, honey? I feel like celebratin'. I feel born again."

The Lord certainly does work in mysterious ways, Opal thought.

The sunflowers had long since gone to seed since that first time she'd driven out there and found religion by mistake. As she walked up the stairs now so familiar to her, she could hear someone inside.

"Reverend? Is that you?" she shouted through the locked door.

The bolt turned and there stood the man who was going to set her free. Free at last!

"Why, Opal Decatur, what a nice surprise. Come on in."

She shuffled toward the front of the room. "Reverend, I've come to confess somethin' an' I need you to hear me."

He followed her but then stopped and sat in the front pew. "Now, Opal, you know we're not that kind of church. There are no confessions here. Jesus loves you. Pray to Him. You don't need no one else."

"Oh, I guess I didn't—"

"Come sit next to me. I can see you're upset about something. What is it?"

She sat down but kept a bit of distance between them. "So, if I tell you somethin' in confidence, just to ease my own soul, you might have to pass it on? I can't count on you to keep it private?" she asked.

"Depends, I guess."

"On what?"

He pursed his lips. "Well, I guess on the seriousness . . ."

"Butch killed Tim Bridgeman."

Reverend Hempel looked like he was the one who had been shot. Stunned is what he was. Sitting there dazed until she asked, "Are you all right?"

"I . . . well . . . I . . . are you sure about this?"

"Positive." He'd never know how sure she was. No one would ever know that she'd gone out after Butch left for work that day and looked for herself. Yep, right where he'd told her it was. A sloppy grave, just the kind Tim Bridgeman deserved.

"Well, I'll have to call the police. Yes." He stood up, walking quickly toward the back of the room. "That's what I've got to do. Can't have this black mark on my church. No, sir. Can't have this. Not while I'm in charge." He was still muttering when he got to his office. Forgot all about Opal and her husband. Just like she'd hoped he would.

———

Maybe she should try traveling next. See the world, well at least Disney World, and get away from all her busybody neighbors. For a while there they had so much to talk about, Opal couldn't blame them much. What with the police coming for Butch, hauling him away like that. Then there was all the business about digging up Tim Bridgeman's body and, of course, lots of juicy stories about Reverend Hempel and the House of Deliverance. Like he was a saint or something when all he did was make one phone call. Attendance was up so much there was a building fund to pay for an addition. And she'd even seen a commercial for Sunday services on Channel 10.

Religion had never really taken hold of Opal Decatur, but still she had to admire how the Lord had managed to clean up all the dirt—make things right. Of course, getting rid of Butch and Bridgeman couldn't make up for all her suffering . . . Brenda's, too. Nothing could. But it was a start.

Lawn and Order

Carole Nelson Douglas

I. Grass Widow

The ultimate unkillable plant with good resistance to insects. Growth is comparatively slow, but it lasts for many years.

"Here, Mom," Madison said. "Nothing like a touch of greenery to make a room homey. I'll just set one pot on either side of the window. So clean and sculptural."

"I don't want to fuss with keeping plants alive," I said. "Those look more like dinosaur quills than plants anyway. And my name is Celeste."

"Now, Mother Hubbard!" Madison knows I hate that predictable play on words. "Moving here to Dallas from Indianapolis is a huge change, but William couldn't leave you alone in that awful inner-city neighborhood. And think of the winters! Besides, these plants are in the succulent family. All they need is a bit of water now and then. You can't kill them."

Then she left me, at last, in the mother-in-law apartment over their three-car garage, alone with my Siamese cat, Cleopatra.

I stroked her now. There'd been nothing "awful" about my old neighborhood. It had been aging, yes, just like me, but the homes had been considered quite nice in their day. And why couldn't William be Bill? He was before he married one of those women named after avenues or institutions. "Mad" she went by with her friends, but Bill had to be "William." And never "Sonny," which had been his nickname since kindergarten. I still used that name to bug her, just as she called me "Mother Hubbard" from time to time, especially when she wanted to remind me to stay in my place. Which was not in her household. I was to keep my hands out of running the house, period.

"You and Cleo," she'd said when we moved in, "should have plenty of room up here."

"Cleopatra's used to roaming a whole house."

"Not mine." Madison had managed to sound both sweet and sour, like a Chinese dish.

She was skinny, thanks to endless hours at the gym and Pilates and yoga classes. With two children in school, you'd think she had time on her hands, but going to the French manicurist and community meetings kept her on the run.

I eyed her professionally blonded hair and meticulously made-up face. She reminded me of some hothouse orchid, decorative but useless.

I was used to managing a whole house, but I didn't say it. Her sprawling Texas minimansion was three times the size of my lost midwestern colonial, but she employed half a dozen slaves to maintain her domain. I'd managed to run my kingdom solo.

Cleopatra, crouched on the carpeted "window perch" I had bought her, yowled plaintively to hear her name invoked in nickname fashion. She was a chocolate-point Siamese with an elongated neck and delicate profile that recalled the head of Nefertiti and my cat's namesake, the Queen of the Nile.

Madison was what they called the Queen of Denial these days. She wanted to deny that Cleopatra and I were here to stay.

When she left it was with a last, disparaging glance. This house was her queendom and Cleopatra and I had been dethroned.

I sighed and began examining the apartment. The large living/eating/kitchen area overlooked the long pebblestone driveway in the front. A separate bedroom/bathroom suite overlooked the "automobile court" in the back. Darling "Mad" called everything by some snooty name like "automobile court" or "suite." At least the place had a window or two for Cleopatra to look out of. Me, too. Mad had made it clear that Cleopatra was barely tolerated. It reflected her unspoken opinion of my presence.

These quarters had been intended for a live-in housekeeper, but Madison had a Spanish cleaning woman come in twice a week. Everything here was beige. A no-color "scheme," as dear Mad would call it. I gazed at my new roommates. The two plants were bunched green spears about three feet tall. Mottled like snakeskin. Their paler green edges and pointed tips looked sharp enough to cut someone.

Did darling "Mad" think I didn't know that snake plants were also called mother-in-law's tongue? A daily reminder to keep my mouth shut?

We'd see about that.

"Mrs. Hubbard!" The sixtyish lady across the street who was tending the house-foundation plants on a knee pad stood up painfully to wave. All the houses here were hemmed around with shrubs. It kept the foundations from drying out and cracking from the heat, Sonny had told me. Such circling greenery also harbored slugs and snails and toads and—I'd been warned—the occasional scorpion.

"Nice to see you out." she said. "The neighborhood is as quiet as a tomb during the day."

I ventured onto her driveway. Lawns were sacred here; no walking on them . . . and God forbid if a loose cat or dog should poop on one. The thick St. Augustine grass was unpleasant underfoot anyway, so thick you could turn your ankle and maybe even break your neck. Its short blades were as thick and stiff as the snake plant's, not the pliable, soft grass that tickled your soles and soul up north, the kind that Walt Whitman had called "the beautiful uncut hair of graves."

"Where I grew up, or maybe I should say *when* . . ." I began. Mrs. Berwick smiled, her hair snow-white under a wide-brimmed straw garden hat. She wore a long-sleeved, pale blue T-shirt and long denim pants, looking a little like an Asian rice-paddy worker.

"You and I are among the few seniors in the community," she said. "Most of the neighborhood residents our age are housed in ritzy assisted-living facilities nearby."

"Assisted living is a fast track to assisted death," I replied. "You start by downsizing from a house to a small apartment with room for none of your favorite things, soon vegetate and move 'up' into assisted living, then daily care, and finally hospice. Not for me. I have plenty of energy and ability left, as do you, Mrs. Berwick."

"What were you going to say about where you grew up, Mrs. Hubbard?"

I eyed the two-story brick mansions surrounding us. *Massive facades* was the realtors' selling phrase. These homes all boasted winding Tara staircases, home theaters, pools with "natural" waterfalls. During the day, these sinuous, curving streets were deserted except for the battered, tacky trucks of lawn and pool services, or slight young mothers in huge SUVs shooting past, cell phones clamped to their ears, backseat kids unseen and unheard behind dark-tinted window glass.

"We had city blocks up north, laid out on grids that were easy to navigate," I said. "Kids used to play outside in my neighborhood, in the streets and yards, until twilight when their parents called them home. The mothers stepped out their front doors to call their names. Kids 'called' on other kids to play: stood outside in the summer and yelled the other kid's name until he or she came out. All the house windows were open to snag any cool breeze through the screens. No air-conditioning. The games kids played were active, inventive, thrilling as dark came on and their voices echoed from curb to curb. Red Light, Green Light. Frying Pan. Simple Simon . . . No. That's not right. Simon Says! Hide-and-seek in the dark. These suburban Fort Worth streets are beautiful but confusing and sterile. Hermetically sealed. Nothing happens here."

Mrs. Berwick bent to push an edging brick into more perfect alignment with the toe of her tennis shoe. "I remember summer days like that, too. But everything's air-conditioned now, and no one wants their kids out of sight. Sexual predators, you know."

"Who even knew about them years ago? Poor kids today! They're all being driven everywhere. Their little limbs will shrivel."

"Hardly. There's soccer and baseball and football practice and dance and violin lessons. It's the mother-chauffeurs who will shrivel, but they have their Pilates classes and gym routines."

"I wish I could garden as you do. Or keep house. I'm used to being active, but my daughter-in-law won't hear of my lifting a finger around the house."

"It's a point of status here, dear. Everyone can afford servants. But I do sympathize with your restlessness, Mrs. Hubbard. Oh, yes. Virgil and I are hangers-on in a much younger area. I so love working in the yard, and my doctor says it's good for me. Oh, will you look at that!"

Her tennis shoe toe pointed to a small island of thick-bladed St. Augustine grass. Three brown clumps. "Even here 'some people' will let their cats out at night to soil 'other people's' yards. It makes me so mad!!"

"My cat is kept indoors," I said hastily, watching my genial neighbor's face turn furious. "Usually it's dogs that leave things on lawns. Cats will bury their . . . leavings if they can."

"I picked up fourteen of these miserable little 'presents' from my yard last week. The cats claw up my garden trying to bury their offal, but the ground is too hard, so they leave it just sitting there on the lawn for me to deal with."

She pulled a plastic newspaper sleeve over one arm like an opera glove, then bent to pick up the sun-dried turds, turning the sleeve inside out to bag them.

"Are those there to discourage the cats?" I pointed at the creatively colored rubber snakes sunning on the edging stones between the zinnias and lantana.

They were quite cleverly molded into various sinuous positions. Their fanged, open jaws even sported tiny rubber threads of tongue. Turquoise and white, green and lavender, yellow and red, black and green, they almost resembled exotic flowers.

"I've tried everything—mothballs, commercial repellents. I'm told the snakes are my best bet. And you think that children never play on the streets around here? I've found several balls crushing my blooms and leaves, so some little devils must get out once in a while."

"Good luck with your lovely garden. I'd best be off on my walk."

"The park and green space are that way."

"Oh, I like to walk the neighborhood streets. Get to know my new neighborhood."

And I did.

I grew to know it as no one else could, because they all sheltered behind their plantation shutters and air-conditioning and attached garages.

Sonny's street was named Meandering Lane. Streets in the sun belt all seemed to be named "lane," though they were a world away from the shady unpretentious paths that word implied. Things here were never what they seemed. And that applied to people as well.

The Merediths' young son, Dustin, for instance, was hired to mow a few neighbors' lawns as a gesture of neighborhood solidarity. (The Merediths were rumored to have lost it "all" in the dot-com crash and to have sold their French Provincial furnishings on eBay.) Hence poor Dustin labored like an ordinary teenager.

He was a tall, well-built boy with an athletic scholarship to a major university in the fall. And when he tended the Cathcarts' lawn, front and back, he spent far longer in the back than seemed necessary. There was, I heard from Mrs. Berwick, a splendid Infinity Pool, spa, sauna, and steam-room environment there, but not much grass.

There was also likely a fanatically sunbathing Mrs. Cathcart, who needed expert shaping, trimming, and hosing. I'd seen her racing about in her Lexus SUV: a stringy, brown-skinned, highlighted, over-made-up example of contemporary suburban female who daily drove a Datsun Z to Nordstrom's and/or Neiman Marcus like a bat out of hell. Young Dustin was looking decidedly pooped, but was no doubt getting lots of college-freshman spending money, not to mention dating tips.

All the women along Meandering Lane were in their frantic thirties or early forties, maintained as meticulously as racehorses, domestic goddesses with both too much and too little to do. Now, if Madison had a job, *I* could handle the house and the children . . .

But she never would have any job except controlling Sonny, pushing her children out of the nest and ladying it over me. I really couldn't conceive of all these women being so *useless* yet spending so much time and their husbands' money celebrating that state.

Of course I was pretty useless myself at the moment. All I could do was walk the neighborhood, peering past the massively false facades into the hidden realities. And there were plenty.

II. Evil Growth

Mother-in-law's tongue is so common and easy to care for that few people, even plant lovers, give it much thought.

Cleopatra and I used to peer down from our one window that overlooked the street.

My little Neon was parked far behind the driveway, out of sight, looking like a marooned golf cart. So tacky for the neighbors to see, you know.

Cleopatra always purred as I stroked her bony form in its smooth coat of beige. Her fine points were her chocolate-brown ears, so keen. She always heard the d-in-law coming up the spiral staircase to our quarters before I did. Devil-in-law. Cleopatra's blue eyes were clearer and brighter than any flower in Mrs. Berwick's garden across the street.

And her tail twitched like an annoyed metronome whenever Madison was within sight and hearing. So when she began to droop, I began to worry. Cleopatra was elegant and strong, only seven years old. She took to lying down, rather than crouching on her sole window perch. My fury grew. Madison knew perfectly well we'd been exiled to her vacant servants' quarters. But Sonny! He said nothing, living in a spreadsheet world, very well remunerated but isolated by the gap between office and home.

Their son, Kyle, was twelve. Off at a military school! Their daughter was Kinsey. Named after a sex researcher! Only eight and already on such a fast track that she had no time for family dinner.

So it was often Sonny and Madison and I. Dinner for three.

The expensive asparagus was overcooked, the main dishes were served half-raw, but Mad occasionally allowed me to "help" with the cooking. At first I was pleased, although the huge kitchen with a granite-topped island long enough to serve twenty made for many extra steps. Then I discovered that this cooking invitation was an exercise in disparaging and humiliating me.

"Not canola oil, Mother! Extra-virgin olive oil. Must you use that crude cheap grater you brought from Indiana! This is from Chef Jean-Paul's cooking school. Much finer. Believe me, even you will notice the difference . . ."

Even my Cleopatra had wilted like the spinach leaves in Madison's corrosive French vinegars.

I stroked her and she no longer purred. Madison called me hysterical when I decided Cleopatra needed a 7 P.M. vet run. Sonny hid behind his *Wall Street Journal* and murmured meaningless encouragements. "She'll be fine. A little indigestion."

———

"Has she been exposed to anything toxic?" the lady vet asked after whisking Cleopatra from my sight into that strange country behind the examination rooms.

Only my daughter-in-law, I wanted to answer. "We moved from the Midwest a month ago. She was fine there."

The vet grimaced a smile. "I hope she'll be fine here. We'll do some tests."

The waiting room was clean and clever. Glossy pet magazines lay fanned on low coffee tables like women's magazines at a doctor's office. Bulletin boards featured photos of happy feline and canine clients and a few heartbreaking notices of found dogs and cats who needed homes. An espresso-machine-and-microwaved-chocolate-cookies setup reigned side by side in a niche with a designer water dispenser. Lots of people brought dogs and cats in and out. And . . . no word on Cleopatra.

I was finally called in again, where the vet set her clipboard on the examining table and asked me to sit down.

"She's very ill. I have to advise you to put her down."

"But she was in perfect health when I had her looked over before the move a month ago! May I see her?"

"Of course. But we've had to put her in an oxygen chamber."

The vet led me back beyond the examining room, where I found Cleopatra gasping for breath in an oxygen chamber, her blue eyes unfocused and the usually invisible inner lid clouding their sky-blue brightness.

I felt my own heart seizing. "Can nothing be done?"

"Nothing." The young vet's brown eyes brimmed with tears.

"What is it? What happened?"

"We think it's some domestic intoxicant. Check your residence for anything a cat could get into."

"My place is so small, there's barely room for Cleopatra and me."

"Look for lethal chemicals, cleaning items, sprays, plants."

Plants.

"I received a . . . gift when I and Cleopatra moved here. A housewarming gift. A snake plant. Mother-in-law's tongue they also call it."

"Oh, good God! Lethal. To cats. I'm so sorry. We can do an autopsy to make sure."

The white-coated young female assistant clasped my hand as I watched Cleopatra's sides labor in and out in the death throes of toxic destruction.

"Get rid of that plant," the vet urged.

"I will," I said. Swore. "Now that I know."

III. Tea for Two

This plant is called Mother-in-Law's Tongue because of the liquid this plant contains. Given in a small dose in coffee or other drink, they paralyze the vocal cords of the person drinking the concoction.

My long walks now became brooding sessions. Cleopatra's ashes were in a vase that a five-toed dragon figure guarded on her sunning shelf. I kept the plants, of course. I found it soothing to stare at their stark lancelike stalks rather than agitating. Had Madison murdered Cleopatra? Did she hope losing my beloved cat would make living in the mother-in-law apartment we'd shared too painful? Did she assume I'd then move to the senior-care apartment she'd always urged Sonny to provide for me? Or hadn't she known the plant was lethal to cats?

I asked her up for tea, after having driven in my little Neon to the library and consulted several books on distilling tinctures.

"Tea, Mother? How quaint."

"It's herbal."

"Green, too," she said approvingly. "Supposed to be very good for the immune system and the complexion." She sipped hers, then said, "I hope you won't annoy William with plans to acquire another cat. He has much more important things to think of."

"It wouldn't bother anything up here."

"Still, it might live a long time, and of course it couldn't accompany you anyplace else."

"Like an assisted-living facility?"

"Exactly. We must face facts, Mother. You won't be here forever."

"The women in my family are very long-lived."

Her face turned slightly green, like the color of the tea.

"Really . . ." Her voice was a bit hoarse. She coughed. "I don't want to argue with you. I think, uh . . . Kyle has an animal-hair allergy."

"But he's so seldom here."

"The hair remains and gets in the vents and poisons the

whole house. If you have any consideration for us at all, you'll forget about getting another cat."

I nodded. She cleared her throat.

"I'm glad we had this talk," Mad said, standing. "Now we know where we stand."

The next morning she complained of having contracted a horrible cold at the gym. She complained in writing at breakfast because she had completely lost her voice.

It was some comfort to know that the snake plant was living up to its legend and could bite Madison as well as Cleopatra, but I was looking for something a bit more effective.

I had given up making another acquaintance in the neighborhood besides Mrs. Berwick. Then someone made mine.

I was walking on the park sidewalk alongside the shallow excuse for a creek that puddled alongside it when a young voice hailed me.

"Lady! You got a handkerchief on ya?"

Of course it was a boy, squatting on the back of the putrid creek, squinting up at me.

"No handkerchief."

His ten-year-old face fell. I wasn't used to seeing emotion reflected on faces in the neighborhood.

"But I do have some plastic newspaper sleeves I carry to pick up . . . litter."

"Dog poop? Yeah, that'd work. Can I have one?"

"May I."

He screwed up his face. "You already have it. I only need one. Or two."

"Come and get them, then."

He scrambled up the bank, his tennies gray with mud, T-shirt and baggy shorts sopping wet. A moment later something wiggling between his clasped hands slid down the throat of the plastic bag I held open.

I screeched a little.

"It's just a baby garter snake, lady. Musta got lost from the bunch."

I examined the grass next to the sidewalk.

"Won't hurt you. Not that kind. I know. I have lots of snakes at home." Since I must have looked impressed at this information, he went on. "And toads and turtles and tortoises, which are different from turtles, and hamsters and ferrets. A whole wall of my bedroom is terrariums with reptiles."

"Lovely. And why are you Snake Boy?"

"It's my hobby. I study 'em."

By then we were walking back to Meandering Lane. "Which house is yours?"

He pointed with the snake bag.

Oh. The home-school house: 4329. A big brick colonial whose mater familias I had never even glimpsed. None of the neighbors knew much more than that about the Effertz family. They had two kids seldom seen. Snake Boy was named Ethan, he told me. Mr. Effertz drove vehicles much despised for bringing "down" the neighborhood tone: huge, boxy, reconditioned Checker cabs painted Virgin Mary blue and canary yellow. Mary Ann was a harried-looking faded redhead who dared to be forty pounds overweight and shop at Sack 'n' Save instead of Tom Thumb or Central Market.

The Banes of the Block, in other words.

"Well, young man," I said fondly to Ethan, "I am most interested in your collection. Do you suppose you could show me where this little fellow will find his new home?"

Of course I understood that it was in just such isolated home-school families as these where desperate housewives could suddenly drown all their children and everyone would puzzle and try to figure out why.

"We'll have to sneak back in," he warned me.

"Fine. I haven't had a good sneak in years."

I continued to walk ferociously as Halloween came and went and the weather remained hot. No one else did. Walking was for umbrella-carrying ladies of the African persuasion who were leaving the minimansions to catch phantom buses back to the vague distant neighborhoods in which they lived.

Nothing growing slackened, except for a few fallen leaves from deciduous trees. The trumpet vine along the backyard fence still sent out aggressive runners. My own snake plants were thriving at their window-side quarters, growing even taller and more sharp-edged.

I stopped, on one of my walks, to admire Mrs. Berwick's now fully mature foundation plantings. "What is that tall, leafy plant, with the golden-orange blossoms?" I asked.

"Ah. My calla lilies. Excellent around pools. Very dramatic. But I don't think that they'd thrive indoors."

I smiled tightly. Mrs. Berwick well understood that the only world I commanded was a sparse eight hundred square feet above my son's garage.

"These irritating kids!" she added, wading into her perfect flowers to pluck out a lime-green fuzzy tennis ball that reminded me of a moldy green apple the Wicked Queen might have doled out to Snow White. "Keep tossing their balls into my garden, even though they're not allowed to play outdoors. Even though they might be my *near* neighbors' children."

I lifted an eyebrow, about all I was allowed to do on Meandering Lane. "You're not saying that my daughter-in-law, Madison, would allow her children outside privileges when at home from school?"

"Probably not," Mrs. Berwick admitted. Madison was too totally controlling to accuse of supporting anything amusing. Mrs. Berwick sighed. "I wish it was so simple. Between the kids themselves and their awful projectiles, my life is a nightmare."

IV. Domestic Hiss

Mother-in-law's tongue gets its nickname from the long, pointed shape of its leaves. Perhaps the plant's stubborn tenacity has something to do with it as well, but I could find no further explanation in all my books.

And would Mrs. Berwick want my dreams? I wondered. My lovely, lost Cleopatra crouching on her carpeted window shelf in the moonlight, the loathsome snake plants shooting tall and straight to either side of her delicate, ghostly form. Gross, green blades as thick as putty knives. And outside that very window, a peephole on the suburban perfection that covered treachery and corruption the way a good ground cover hides slug- and bug-ridden soil. I'd never been much for digging in dirt.

When Sonny was home from a business trip over the Thanksgiving holiday, I volunteered to cook a pot-roast dinner to welcome him back.

"Pot roast?" Madison wrinkled the skin between the bridge of her nose and her waxed and colored eyebrows until she resembled a Ferengi from the *Star Trek* universe. On earlier visits I'd used to watch television with young Kyle before he'd been shipped off to a military academy. I doubted it was a *Star Trek* academy.

"A midwestern dish," I said. "Takes time to achieve the tendernesss. We don't have specialty butchers beating our beef to death before we buy it."

"Sounds quaint, Mother Hubbard." Mad produced her supercivilized smile. "Be sure to scour the pots when you're through. My girl won't touch a copper pad. It ruins her manicure."

So even the hired help is ritzier than me.

I cooked all day. Young Kinsey and Kyle came tagging along, asking about the strange ritual of using the oven for hours. I set the children to chopping parsley and slicing carrots into the zigzag shapes of french fries. There were rosemary red potatoes. Green beans with sliced almonds and bacon bits. A banana cream pie for dessert.

The house smelled like a church supper, redolent with the incense of sensible food.

Sonny joined us in the kitchen, plucking lids off pots and inhaling as if he were fighting a ten-day cold. The kitchen was hot, steamy, filled with voices and laughter.

"What a fatty piece of meat," Madison said the moment

she put a toe of her Cole Haans over the threshold. "Roasted potatoes! Really, William, what wine will you serve with this, this . . . mess-hall assemblage."

"A cask of Amontillado," I suggested smoothly.

The ignorant fool merely frowned. "Spanish wine would be a disaster with American pub food. Look up some beer, dear." I read the subtext. *Preferably canned. Possibly lite. Obviously piss-poor.*

V. Child's Play

The succulent varieties seem to be extremely thick-skinned. You can press the leaves hard between your fingers and nothing happens. One especially tough customer, Sansevierea halli, *is nicknamed "baseball bat" for obvious reasons.*

November in Texas can still be warm, but warm weather had the advantage of sending Madison into the shopping malls for a pre-Christmas shopping orgy. After all, she was shopping for two: her gifts to the children and Sonny, and also all the luxurious things Sonny would "give" her.

I unbagged the Louisville Slugger I'd bought for Kyle and the Christmas tree. Nothing like a preholiday workout. The after-school streets were deserted until the workaholic husbands came home around six or seven. The women were out shopping until five or six. That gave us two hours.

I'd coaxed Kyle into rounding up some neighborhood boys and girls his age for an oddly enthralling new game that long Thanksgiving weekend. Stickball in the street. I insisted they use poison-green tennis balls so no one could get hurt if a line drive hit someone.

Even Ethan removed the screen from his first-floor bedroom window and managed to join us, watching his house nervously over his shoulder and the windows with all the miniblinds tightly closed. That was another thing Madison had against the Effertzes: miniblinds, not expensive plantation shutters. I'd heard her rant. It brought the whole neighborhood down!

No, I'd thought. *Just you.*

Of course the tennis balls went astray and landed in nearby yards. Ours. Mrs. Berwick's.

I made sure the kids scattered before their unfettered shouts penetrated the windows, closed and shuttered to keep the air-conditioning in and street life out.

Of course I vanished around the curve of our driveway when Mrs. Berwick charged out to order the kids away, pulling tennis balls from her front flower beds as if uprooting weeds, and threatening to keep them.

"I don't know what's got into you kids," she railed. "Acting like street gangs. Playing all over everyone's yards."

"We stay in the street," Kyle said. "It's just the balls that bounce out of bounds. And we don't dare go in the yards to get them back."

"I should hope not, young man. This St. Augustine takes a lot of time and money to get looking so nice. And I'm not your ball boy! Your mother is not going to like seeing you tossing nasty old tennis balls into her foundation plantings. Why don't you go to the clubhouse and play?"

Because play is meant to be part of a neighborhood, I answered her silently. A real neighborhood, where childish squeals were treasured, not quashed. Where games like Frying Pan and Simon Says and hide-and-seek were still going strong as the sun went down. Where there weren't bad-air days and where the sharp smoky smell of the first fall fires being lit was something you stood outside to savor, not something never noticed while dashing from house to garage to street and back to garage and house.

Neighborhoods were meant to *breathe*.

That night I made my move at 2 A.M. Dressed in black like a cat burglar, I tiptoed down the spiral stairs of my aerie. It was right off the kitchen. I collected two never-used oven mitts and a set of sterling-silver salad tongs. I would have preferred grocery-store steel, but one can't have everything. I put them in a black canvas tote bag I hitched over my shoulder. CARPE DIEM, read the letters on one side, which I turned against my body so they wouldn't be visible.

At the door leading to the backyard I turned off the security system, unlocked it, and eeled through. This was the tricky part. I was too old to climb the brick and lumber fences isolating every house. I'd have to ease down our driveway to the street, my black sneakers making no sound. I was more worried about triggering the outside security lights at the corners of every house.

Soon I was strolling up the empty street in what could have been Stepford. No cars in sight, no sign of life. I turned in at the Effertzes' driveway and finally stepped on their grass. Not Bermuda. Another cardinal sin on Meandering Lane, where adultery was preferable to loitering and littering children having simple fun. Ethan's bedroom window was down the house's sidewall, next to the droning air-conditioning unit. Sonny at that age had slept like a hibernating bear.

I lifted aside the screen the clever home-schooled Effertz boy had made into an easy exit. I don't approve of home-schooling. It strikes me as a way to brainwash children, to insulate them from stimulating social differences. In this case, home-schooling had done me a favor. The Effertz parents had not put their funds into yards or decor, but poured them into any enthusiasm one of their children showed. Ethan's fascination with reptile life had produced a pet store ambience I wouldn't care to lay me down to sleep in every night. Soft, purple-toned night-lights lit his wall of terrariums holding bats and toads and lizards and snakes, oh my.

I knew just the fellow I had come for. I had recognized him at once during my earlier visit. Luckily, he was a Texas native. Ethan, of course, knew what he was and had taken precautions. I lifted the cover, donned my oven mitts, and maneuvered the sterling-silver tongs over a two-foot-long rope of scaled skin draping a dead twig.

The job's most ticklish part was pressing firmly enough to extract the snake without crushing or riling it. In a moment its colorful body was coiling into one of the soft velvet sacks in which Madison's high-end holiday brandy bottles had come. I had seen it in a kitchen drawer and found its royal purple color worthy of my reptilian friend.

I made my way out, retraced my steps, and left the bag in the front plant bed of Madison's house, along with three dirty and lurid tennis balls, one on the grass, one on the brick edging, and one on the soil.

In minutes I was back in my "quarters," out of my sneak-thief outfit and into my nightgown. I slept as fast and hard as young Ethan.

I usually rose the earliest and went outside to collect the paper. The thick St. Augustine was wet, how or why in this dry climate I wasn't sure. This morning I had clattered around the kitchen first, the surest alarm clock that control-freak Madison would respond to.

"Mother Hubbard!" Madison stood in the front doorway in her thick terrycloth robe with THE GREENHOUSE SPA embroidered on it, triumphant at having caught me misbehaving like a naughty child. "Get off the grass. Your slippers will get all wet and track it inside. That stupid woman who delivers the paper is supposed to throw it on the dry *driveway*. Why they let her do the job if she's too feeble to manage it, I don't know. There goes her Christmas tip."

I gestured to the front plantings. "I was just going to pick up those unsightly tennis balls."

"Tennis balls! Why are these kids suddenly playing in the street when they have every place else to do it! And who lets those dogs and cats roam at night to fertilize our lawns?"

"They may be homeless."

"Not in this neighborhood, unless someone is dropping them off. Honestly. You get back on the driveway! Look at these awful things. Look like they've been in dog's mouths, or worse."

She was leaning over the plants like a fury, picking up tennis balls, brushing leaves and twigs aside to search for more in the brightening light of morning.

"And here's one of Mrs. Berwick's cheap, silly Technicolor

rubber garden snakes! They so trash up a yard. What's it doing—*oh!*" she screamed.

She dropped what she'd caught hold of. "It bit me."

Rings of primary color—red, yellow, black—vanished back into the green leaves. Poor fellow. He'd have to make his own way in the world now. Maybe he'd find a lady friend.

Madison had fallen to her knees. "I can't believe I touched that loathsome thing! It was all cold and dry. It didn't look real."

Snakes come in all colors, some a dust-dull hue to camouflage them against desert and dirt, some leaf green to live in trees, some ultrabright to warn possible predators that they are not worth messing with.

Madison was amazingly ignorant about anything beyond her own selfish circle of interests. I knew the old saw, of course. *Red against black is a friend of Jack. Black against yellow will kill a fellow.*

Or an outlaw in-law.

Madison tumbled over on her side, moaning and looking very unwell. Her face seemed to be bloating. That would look so tacky in the casket. I collected the empty purple velvet bag and shuffled around to the back driveway, as ordered, leaving the newspaper lying on the lawn with the scattered tennis balls.

No one would be up or out for at least an hour or two. And by then it would be too late.

The snake plants will look quite nice on either side of the two-faced fireplace that serves the great room and family room/kitchen behind it. They'll add a clean and sculptural touch. Also a hint of something living. They won't require any work at all. Being virtually unkillable.

And, oddly enough, I've grown strangely fond of them.

VI. Snake in the Grass

The coral snake found in Texas is the only black, red, and yellow crossbanded serpent whose red and yellow bands touch [and is] locally common in suburban neighborhoods. Coral snake venom is largely composed of neurotoxically destructive peptides and is, therefore, more deadly than the venom of any other North American reptile.

—Alan Tennant

Unless it is an out-of-work mother-in-law. I shut the library book and checked the return date. Plenty of time, and I had laundry and supper to do. A mother's work is never done.

Joy Ride
Nancy Pickard

Marianne Roland would have been the first to admit that, of the two of them, the Other Woman was much the nicer person. Her husband's mistress was a sweetheart. Everybody who knew her said so, even if they didn't realize they were saying it to his wife. The Other Woman was kind and generous as well as being sweet and affectionate. She was good-natured as well as being thin, blond, and young. Marianne knew herself to be none of those things. Not thin, not blond, not kind, or generous, or sweet, or affectionate, and certainly not good-natured or young. It was no wonder that her husband, Lee, had taken up with Jennifer Ludlow instead of remaining loyal to Marianne. Given the choice, any half-wit might have done the same, she thought, and Lee was no half-wit. Lee was the male equivalent of Jennifer, only older. In spite of the age difference, Lee and Jennifer were a natural match, and everybody who Marianne had tricked into saying so, said so.

Really, she thought as she filled out an index card with certain pertinent information, as befitting the female half of a match made in heaven, Jennifer Ludlow was an angel.

Or soon would be.

Marianne, who could at least claim a sense of humor, smiled.

The index card she was filling out, in a handwriting that slanted left where hers normally slanted right and that crossed *t*s in ways that she never did and dotted *i*s straight up instead of off to one side, and capitalized where she never would, said: *2005 Mercedes ML 350 SUV. Black. Fully Loaded. Under 5,000 Miles.* She listed a price well below its Blue Book value and added, *Private Owner Must Sell Fast.*

Irresistible, she felt sure.

When she finished, she laid the card flat on her dining-room table.

She removed the rubber gloves she had worn to do the job, walked them over to her trash bin underneath the kitchen sink, and threw them in.

Then she picked up the card between the pincers of some blunt-end eyebrow tweezers and carried it with her to her car—which was *not* a 2005 Mercedes ML 350, but rather a gleaming silver 2006 Infiniti FX, which was ever so slightly more expensive.

The phone number she had listed on the card was also not hers.

With the afternoon free to finish this last task before the main event, Marianne took her time driving all the way across the state line from her home on the Missouri side of Kansas City to a prosperous suburb on the Kansas side. Once there, she found an ordinary, L-shaped mall with a coffee shop. She walked in and ordered a tall latte. As she waited for the barista to call her order, Marianne lingered by a bulletin board where dozens of people had left their calling cards, want ads, and sales notices.

Child care. Lawn mowing. House repairs. Cars, vans, and trucks for sale.

Her own sales notice and the tack in the top of it was in her left hand, hidden by a paper napkin that also kept her fingerprints off of it when she lifted the napkin to the bulletin board and pressed the tack into the cork.

"Tall latte for Susan!"

Marianne whirled around, checking to see if anybody was looking her way. As she expected, no one was—because who would pay any attention to a plain, stocky, middle-aged woman in drab slacks and blouse? Satisfied that she was as good as invisible to the mostly younger, hipper crowd, Marianne walked confidently over to pick up the coffee she had ordered under the name that also was not hers.

"This isn't right," she complained to the barista. "I ordered a mocha latte."

The words popped out of her mouth before she grasped the paradox of calling attention to herself when the last thing she wanted to do was make people remember her. Unfortunately, some habits—like demanding service she didn't deserve—were hard to break.

Marianne attempted an apologetic smile.

"Sorry," she murmured, aiming for a sweet tone.

Maybe the barista would confuse *her* with a nice person.

The young man behind the counter frowned and took the cup back in order to stare at the order written on it. Regardless of the fact that it said exactly what Marianne had ordered, he did what she knew he was trained to do, "I'm really sorry. I'll make you a new one. Mocha latte? you said."

Normally she would have promptly demanded, "With whipped cream, and I already paid for it!" but this time she said meekly, "Yes, please."

"No problem," he told her.

When he handed her the new, more expensive drink, he also handed her a card entitling her to a free drink the next time she visited the franchise. It often worked that way. When it didn't, she raised hell until they gave in.

Jennifer would never do such a greedy thing, Marianne knew.

As if stealing another woman's husband was not greedy!

So far, so good, she thought as she left the shop, sipping her caloric coffee.

Jennifer probably drank only nonfat lattes.

If she was even addicted to caffeine at all.

Jennifer probably drank only herbal tea, as Lee started to do soon after he'd hired her.

It hadn't taken great deductive powers to figure out *that* Lee was having an affair with somebody. Late nights, missed suppers, always "too tired" to have sex. Two weeks of that was all it took; down from three weeks the time before and way down from the whole damned year it had taken Marianne to finally catch on the first time, many years before. As always, finding out *who* was the tricky part. Once she'd accused the wrong woman. That was humiliating and required a change of jobs on Lee's part. He hadn't been happy about that, but he was never one to complain all that much about anything—not with Marianne's millions to persuade him, time after time, that she was, when all was said and done and all the money counted, infinitely more attractive to him than any other woman could ever be.

But this time felt different to Marianne.

Maybe the difference was just that Lee was old enough now, had worked long enough and done well enough and made enough money on his own, to feel freer than he ever had before in their marriage.

Sweet, nice Jennifer looked like trophy-wife material to Marianne.

But she was one potential trophy wife who was going to get her brass peeled off.

The index card Marianne left at the coffee shop had little strips cut along the bottom of it, and each little strip had a phone number, so all a prospective Mercedes buyer had to do was tear a strip off.

Call 6 to 7 P.M. weekdays, Marianne had put on the index card.

Lee was always gone then—shouldn't be, but was.

So she was free to park in the lot of the grocery store

where the pay phone was and hang around the entryway reading free newspapers and bulletin boards until it rang. On the second night, it did ring and she reached for it.

"I'm calling about the Mercedes?" a young female voice said.

"You've got the right number," Marianne assured her.

"Can we come see it?"

"Sure. When did you have in mind?"

"Tonight?"

"Tonight's good. How about eight-thirty?"

"Okay. Where are you?"

"Meet me in the church parking lot at a Hundred and Fourth and Oak; you know where that is?"

"We can find it. Are you a minister, or something?"

Marianne laughed. "No, I just don't want people coming to my house. You understand, I'm sure."

"Yeah," the caller said. "I get it."

"Okay. Eight-thirty. Church parking lot, a Hundred and Fourth and Oak. You'll recognize me because I'll be the one with the black Mercedes, but what will you be driving?"

If the caller had said something light and compact like a Mini Cooper, Marianne would have come up with a reason why she couldn't meet her after all. But when the girl said, "We're in a truck," Marianne smiled at the wall behind the pay phone.

"I'll be watching for you," she said.

When she hung up, her heart was pounding. A truck! How lucky was *that*?

It was going to happen. She was going to do it. This was *it*.

———

At first, Marianne had suspected his secretary.

Lee wasn't, she knew, all that imaginative and clichés had never bothered him. Give him a little pulchritude right under his long and handsome nose and he'd take it, saving himself the trouble of going farther and looking harder.

But then she heard a rumor that the secretary was a lesbian. Marianne decided that even if the woman swung both ways, it would be far too complex an affair for Lee to bother with. It wasn't that Lee was lazy; it was merely that he was beautiful and so things and women came easily to him when he wanted them to. Too easily to have to work for them or to have to put up with complicated circumstances. She and all her money had come easily to him, too, and she knew perfectly well that if there had been a prettier girl with just as much money anywhere in the vicinity, he would have grabbed her instead. But none of the prettier girls were as rich as Marianne, or else they were already taken, and so Lee had grabbed the plain but extremely golden ring.

She had wanted him desperately then and she desperately wanted to keep him now.

To find out who the woman was this time, Marianne had ended up resorting to a maneuver that had worked once before.

"Hi, this is Tracy down in personnel," she said, calling the extension of one of his more junior people who had never met or talked to the boss's wife. "Are you the new girl up there, or am I thinking of somebody else?"

"Not me, honey," was the answer. "I been here since God created staples."

"Well, then, who's new?"

"You probably mean Jennifer Ludlow."

"I probably do," Marianne had said, a bit of a growl to her tone.

"She done something wrong?" the employee asked, responding to that tone. "I'd be surprised, you know, 'cause she's really nice."

"Is she?"

"Oh, yeah; you wouldn't think somebody that good-looking would also be so nice, but she is, she just is."

"Everybody loves her?"

"Oh, yeah. Who wouldn't? She's a sweetheart. You want her extension?"

"Please." And Marianne had written it down: 1121.

One one two one. Added up to five. And five was the loneliest number that Marianne had ever seen.

Sometimes Marianne was aware that having been born wealthy had given her a self-assurance that other people didn't have, but most of the time she took her own self-confident style for granted. It allowed her to look as if she belonged when she did things like walk up to the front door of her vacationing friends' home, unlock it with the emergency keys they had left with her, and then walk through the house as if she owned it and march down the stairs into the garage. Once there, she climbed into their 2005 black Mercedes ML 350 SUV, used their automatic opener to raise their garage door, and then backed the car out as if she owned it, too.

When a neighbor watering his flowers looked up, she waved at him.

And then she closed the garage door, backed into the street, and drove away.

If a question arose when her friends came back from Aruba, she would tell them, "I had to borrow the Mercedes while the Infiniti was in the shop. Good thing you were gone so I could use it."

At the grocery-store pay phone, when Marianne heard such a young voice, she had wondered about it. What were kids in a truck doing looking at a Mercedes? But when their headlights approached and they pulled up beside her, she knew it was going to be just fine. Their vehicle was no beat-up farm truck, but rather a small, powerful, shiny thing that must have cost nearly as much as the car they had come to see. And when a girl stepped out of the passenger's side and a boy from the driver's side, they turned out to be good-looking and dressed in the kind of sloppy-chic clothes that the sons and daughters of Marianne's friends all wore.

Somebody has Daddy's money, she thought as they walked up to her, giving her smiling glimpses of their perfect teeth. *And I ought to know.*

Privileged kids. Kids with bright and shiny futures.

Too bad about that, Marianne thought without regret or remorse.

Turning her smile up a watt to match theirs, she said "Hello!" with nearly as much warmth as she thought Jennifer might have done.

"Hi," they chimed back at her.

She had parked behind the church so they had to drive around it to find her.

"Looks like you've already got a nice truck," she observed.

"His," the girl said, and grinned.

"And the Mercedes?" Marianne asked them.

The boy also grinned and then he pointed. "Hers."

Even though the boy moved with a cocky air, it was obvious they were car-buying innocents. He made a show of popping the hood and looking under it, but Marianne could tell that he didn't know a dipstick from a driveshaft. Neither did she, but it didn't matter to somebody who had trust funds to foot the bills. *Some people,* Marianne thought as she watched the boy fuss, *are mechanics, and some people support mechanics.*

They were a little older than the girl had sounded on the phone. Marianne had half expected sixteen-year-olds to drive up, but these gorgeous kids looked to be in their late teens or early twenties. He had very short spiky blond hair. Hers was dark and glossy brown and hung like sable to her waist.

Marianne would have been jealous if she hadn't known what was in store for them.

They didn't ask why she was selling a practically new car. Either they didn't care, or such possibilities as bankruptcy had never entered their lives yet.

Marianne held out the keys.

"Test drive?"

The boy grabbed them. "Oh, yeah!"

"There's only one problem," Marianne said.

They both looked at her then, alert as sleek deer, listening.

"Just before you got here, I got a call. Kind of a family emergency that I've got to do something about. How about if we trade vehicles. I'll meet you back here in an hour. That'll give you more time to try it out."

The girl looked at the boy.

He looked back and forth from the Mercedes to the truck as if gauging comparative values. Maybe he was sharper than she'd thought, Marianne decided. Which meant he would come to the obvious conclusion.

"Sure," he agreed. "That'd be okay."

Of course it would, Marianne thought as she took the truck keys he gave her. *If the seller has your truck and you have her Mercedes, you know she's going to come back.*

Every weeknight, predictable as sin, Jennifer Ludlow went running in the cool night air after she got off work. After she got through "working" with Lee. After they had dinner together. After they did whatever else they did up in the office on the top floor after everybody but the cleaning crew had gone home, and while Marianne sat in her car on the street watching the lights in the executive suite.

She had Jennifer's schedule nailed.

Up in the morning at 6 A.M., off to work at 7:30, home again at 9. Back outside again in one of her adorable running outfits at 9:10. Most of her route was along safe suburban streets that were regularly punctuated with streetlights, porch lights, yard lights, headlights, even the little flashlights that some late walkers carried. But there was one stretch of a quarter mile that curved through a tree-lined darkness. Keeping up her steady, tedious pace, Jennifer entered the darkness every night at around 9:25 and emerged into the next streetlight a very short time later.

It took ten minutes for Marianne to travel from the church parking lot, draw near to the dark stretch, park in front of a home, put the truck in idle, turn down the headlights, and slouch down in the driver's seat. She found a baseball cap on the console and in a moment of inspiration stuck it backward on her head the way a boy would wear it.

Jennifer, thin, blond, young, sweet Jennifer whom everybody liked was right on time on this night, too. The moment her right foot stepped into the darkness, the black truck started up. It drove into the darkness behind her, picking up speed.

Jennifer Ludlow made a satisfying thud as she was struck full on her back, and then she made two more bumps as the heavy wheels rolled over her.

And then two more on the return trip.

Thud. Bump, bump. Bump, bump.

And there was a bonus: after one had struck her husband's mistress with the truck, Marianne's headlights picked up a surprise. Another runner was coming from the other direction and he had seen it all. She could tell by the horrified way the runner had his hands up to his mouth and how white his face was, how wide his eyes. He looked paralyzed on the other side of the road. Knowing he was blinded by her lights, she turned the truck around in the middle of the street so she could head back in the other direction. She slowed down a bit so he could plainly see her roll over the victim one more time—and so he could also see the letters and numbers on the lighted license plate.

All the way back to the church parking lot, Marianne tapped out the happy rhythm.

Thud. Bump, bump. Bump, bump.

Marianne knew the young couple would know to look for her behind the church, so this time she pulled the truck deep into the shadows at the far end of the lot, nose into the trees. She would be gone before they realized the spots on their windshield were blood, if they even noticed before morning, and long gone by the time they saw the bloody hood and grille.

They didn't know her name, not even the false one she had been ready to give them, because they were too innocent to ask. All they had was a tiny bit of an index card with a phone number that couldn't be traced to her, if they even still had that. Before the night was over, she would stop by the coffee shop to remove whatever was left of the card so the kids would never be able to prove it had ever existed. They would look like desperate people trying to lie their way out of hit-and-run homicide charges.

That was the plan.

Marianne checked the illuminated face of her wristwatch. Five after ten. They were a little late. No problem. It wasn't as if she would need an alibi for the time of death. Nothing could connect her to it.

Ten after ten.

Where are they?

She had to return the Mercedes to her friends' garage. God forbid they had been in a wreck with it. That was a contingency she had thought about but dismissed as highly unlikely. There were some things you just had to leave to chance, especially when the odds were in your favor.

At ten-thirty she stopped pacing and stood behind the truck willing them to come.

When, at ten forty-five, headlights turned off the street, she nearly sobbed with relief. She wouldn't even read them the riot act; she'd just tell them they couldn't have the car, and then she'd get the hell out of there and disappear from their lives forever.

The headlights picked her out of the dark.

Marianne, feeling like the star in a spotlight, smiled into it.

Maybe their daddy's lawyers could get them off.

Suddenly a third light beamed at her.

An actual spotlight . . .

Marianne raised her hands to her eyes to shade them.

She heard a car door open and shut, and then a second one.

"Ma'am?" It was a policeman's voice. "Is that your truck?"

"We scored this time, baby."

The girl with the long brown hair looked across the lush leather seats of the Mercedes at her spike-haired boyfriend. "Beats that fucking truck."

"What you got against trucks?" he joked. "That one got us from St. Louis to Kansas."

"Next time? I want a convertible."

"Sure. Why not?"

"Let's get one in Denver."

"Drive through the Rockies with the top down? Cool."

They were on their way to California, maybe. Or maybe to somewhere else. Transportation was no problem. She was the one who'd had the idea to begin with. Find ads for private cars for sale. Take them for test drives and leave their own car behind as supposed collateral. And then all they had to do was keep on driving.

They had pulled it off three times already between New York and here.

He started laughing.

"What?"

"I was just thinking about her waiting back at that church for us."

His girlfriend giggled, and soon they were laughing so hard he could barely see to drive and she was doubled over in hysterics in the passenger seat of the black 2005 Mercedes ML 350 SUV.

The Next-Door Collector

Elizabeth Massie

Life went downhill when the next-door collector moved in. She and all her writhing, wriggling pets, pressed against the window screens, mashed against the greasy glass, staring out, begging Anthea and all who looked their way to come in.

Come in.

Anthea Lonas's house on Riverview Road was perfect. Two-story Victorian with a finished attic, a wraparound porch, and a detached garage, on a half-acre lot along which Anthea had planted roses, birdhouse gourds, sunflowers, azaleas, and colorful annuals in tidy raised plots. Several mature maple trees straddled the Lonas property and the unsold brick rancher next door, making for a natural delineation between the two properties. Anthea, her husband, Paul, and their twelve-year-old son, Dylan, had lived in the south-side Richmond house for nearly a year, having moved there from a crowded neighborhood in Chicago. Chicago just hadn't worked out.

Things were fine throughout most of the summer. The sunflowers were nearly eight feet tall, their heavy, furry lion heads obediently scanning the sky for the sun. The gourds climbed the trellises to either side of the front porch, and the roses were only mildly infested with Japanese beetles. Dylan had made friends with twin boys, George and Gene Kidd, up the street, good kids from a good family, and they spent much of their vacation days at the local public swimming pool, watching television at alternating homes, and pounding on guitars-drums-keyboard in the twins' carport in an attempt to whip up a band good enough to perform in the middle-school talent show come October. Paul, who worked as a highly skilled software developer, was happy in his position, and was expecting advancement soon. Anthea gardened, worked out at the gym four times a week, and painted what the local art gallery called "brilliant, emotion-infused modern oils revealing nature on fire." She spent a good deal of time alone except for hours with her family, and enjoyed her solitude.

And then the next-door neighbor moved in.

The woman's name was Lisa Ferguson. She was in her late forties, newly divorced, with enough equity in her former home to put a down payment on the rancher. From the window in her art studio upstairs, Anthea had watched as the woman moved in. She studied the eclectic, shredded collection of furniture hauled out of the moving truck by the uniformed men, and the crates of animals Lisa herself carried into the house. Anthea tried to count the pets based on the number of crates, but it was hard to figure if each held one or more, and by the time Lisa was returning to her car for the fifth crate, Paul called from work and Anthea, who refused to have a phone in her gallery, had to leave her stakeout.

Then, Wednesday morning, when Anthea was laying down fresh mulch in the pansy plots along the property line, Lisa came outside. She was followed by three dagger-tailed, yellow felines with winking eyes and wrinkled noses. Lisa held out one hand and introduced herself with a big smile.

"Hi, I just bought the house next to you. You probably saw and heard me moving in yesterday. I'm Lisa Ferguson, and you're . . . ¿"

Anthea wiped a tickle of loose hair from her forehead and put down her rake. "Anthea Lonas. Hi." She shook Lisa's dry, scratchy hand. The woman could do with a bit of hand lotion and a serious makeover. She had short, slightly greasy brown hair going gray at the temples and round rimless glasses. Her face was angular, her teeth a bit crooked, and her breath smelled vaguely of coffee and chocolate.

"You have a family, Anthea¿ I see a bike in your yard. Children¿"

Anthea nodded. "A son, Dylan." Damn. She wasn't keen on telling strangers too much. That had happened before, sharing too much too soon, and it had led to very unpleasant results. Like the young mother back in her old neighborhood who found out Anthea liked a particular soap opera and so for a good six months called Anthea every single evening during dinner to rant over who was screwing whom and who would fall in love with whom and whether Joan would have her sex-change operation and if Marshall was the baby's father and if so, when the DNA test came back, would he stay and be a man or go off to Alaska and join the pipeline. Hopefully, Lisa Ferguson would not push the let's-be-buddies routine too soon. If they were to be friends, it would happen naturally and with time. Though Anthea already had serious doubts, just looking at the woman.

"I love children. Do you have pets, too?" asked Lisa as the cats intertwined one another and then Lisa's leg. "I adore animals."

"We used to have a dog," said Anthea. "A border collie. Unfortunately he developed such a bad case of arthritis we had to put him to sleep." *Too much information, Anthea.*

"Pound animals are the best," purred Lisa. She picked up a cat and draped it over her shoulders like a stole. "And strays. They are so needy. I love them all, I can't help it."

Anthea glanced over at the windows of the brick rancher. Cat faces and dog faces were pressed to the screens, watching Lisa. How many did the woman own?

"Excuse me, Lisa, but how many pets do you have?"

Lisa raised her brows and her eyes spun a little. "Oh, gosh, when did I last count? Twenty, twenty-two . . ."

Twenty-two pets? Good Lord. "That's quite a few . . ."

". . . cats. Dogs, hmm, I think there are nineteen last count. I have them spayed, don't you worry about that. How responsible would that be, letting them breed over and over?"

"Not responsible at all."

"I've seen those *Animal Planet* pet cop shows with all those crazy, inbred creatures." Lisa shivered, then immediately brightened. "You should come over and meet my babies sometime." She put the stole cat down and picked up another, cradling it upside down in her arms. "Not a grumpy one in the bunch. No fleas, either, though Lord knows I fight the good fight with that. Come for tea?"

"What?" Anthea realized she'd just been invited into a house filled with forty-one animals. For tea. To sit down on that scarred sofa or in an infested kitchen and try to sip at something as millions of pet hairs floated about her face. No way on this green earth would she do such a thing. "That's sweet, Lisa. But do you know? I'm so busy this week. I'm an artist, not just a lowly gardener." She laughed, and hoped it sounded apologetic. Sweat and gnats dribbled down the front of her blouse and she had the terrible urge to scratch her breasts. She didn't. "The painting, the house, my son, my husband. It's just crazy at times."

Lisa nodded, her glasses bobbing on her nose. "I never had children, so I can't imagine. I would have loved to, but the doctors declared this old garden to be sterile." She patted her tummy. Anthea found that incredibly crude. "Too late now. Too old. So I love my fur babies."

Fur babies. Give me a break.

Anthea excused herself, saying she heard the phone ringing although she didn't. She went inside and peeked through the curtains as Lisa puttered in the yard, the three cats at her heels, then went back inside.

Dylan got home just after five, his hair a matted mess from the pool and one of his shoes missing. "Somebody stole it while I was swimming," he complained. "I'd love to find out who took it. I'll kill 'im!"

"No, you wouldn't kill him," Anthea said as she put a

platter of baked chicken on the dining-room table. Dylan stabbed three pieces with the serving fork and dropped them onto his plate. Paul would be late tonight—eight or so—and supper couldn't wait. "We'll call the pool manager tomorrow morning and report your missing shoe. The lifeguards or somebody should pay better attention to what's going on there."

"That's not the lifeguard's job, Mom," Dylan said with a rolling of eyes. "Don't call. You'll embarrass me."

"Dylan," said Anthea, crossing her arms firmly but feeling a surge of love for her scroungy offspring. "A mother's job is to take care of her children. To protect them. To even protect their shoes if they go missing."

"Or stolen!"

"Or stolen."

"Yeah, whatever." Dylan waved his hands to change the subject. They ate in silence until it was time for one of Dylan's television shows. Anthea went to her studio and slapped red paints onto her newest painting, *Sunflowers at Dawn*.

Lisa put up a tall chain-link fence around her property. This was enough to keep most of the cats and dogs, newly sprung from house arrest, from running out into the road or into Anthea's yard. However, a few of the more athletic cats did climb the links and then take dumps—uncovered, no less; who did the cats think they were, dogs?—beneath the sunflowers. Anthea continued to dodge the invitations to tea and Lisa continued to be oh, so understanding.

Then Lisa began collecting plastic, lidded containers. She

brought them home and stacked them in the backyard, all sizes and all colors—gray, blue, pink, yellow—in several increasingly lopsided, spiraling towers near the trash barrel, lids stacked against the fence. Anthea was more than curious, but kept her questions to herself until one morning when she was watering the roses, Lisa parked her Toyota in front of her house and trotted around the side with yet another couple boxes.

"Hello, Lisa! What's up with all the boxes?" she called through the chain link.

Lisa stopped, smiled, and said, "Aren't they great?"

"Great? I suppose so."

"You never know when you'll need to put stuff in something, and keep the stuff dry."

"I suppose not."

Lisa continued on to the backyard and added her finds to one of the unsteady rainbow stalagmites. Four dogs followed her as if expecting a treat, while another good half dozen lay in the sun and wagged their tails at Anthea.

The neighborhood kids soon discovered Lisa's animal emporium. And they loved it. Nearly every morning, there was a collection of preteens playing with the pets in the yard. Anthea could only imagine the smashed feces the kids carried home with them on their shoes.

"I don't want you over there," Anthea told Dylan as he and Paul chewed on the French toast Anthea had served for breakfast. She sat in her chair at the table, her fork prongs pointing toward the ceiling, but she wasn't going to eat anything until she and her son had an understanding. "I don't believe it's at all safe, and certainly not sanitary."

"You don't know," said Dylan. "You never went over there. Lisa told me that she keeps inviting you but you never go."

"No, but . . ." said Anthea. Dylan was right. *But still.* "Somebody who collects animals like that . . . it just isn't . . ."

"Isn't what?"

"Sane," said Anthea.

"Now, hon." This was Paul. He wiped syrup from his lower lip with his folded paper towel. He was a handsome man with dark hair and a trim beard. "That's not really fair, do you think? I've spoken to her on occasion and she seems to have plenty of wits."

"Do you think?" said Anthea. Paul's comment was infuriating. He was supposed to be on her side with these kinds of things. "So tell me, what kind of wits?"

Paul shrugged. "She seems nice. A tad eccentric, but nice all the same. Harmless." He did a little flick of the eye and tip of the head in Dylan's direction. Clearly, Anthea's husband didn't want them saying bad things about the neighbor in front of their child. Anthea didn't care. Nice wasn't all it was cracked up to be sometimes.

"Nice, yes, fine, but that doesn't excuse all those animals," she said. "It's like a pack of vermin over there, all eyes and paws and claws and tails. It's a living nightmare. Paul, you're gone most of the time, you have no idea."

"She keeps them confined. They don't look dirty or mangy."

"No, but some have crawled over the fence and have shit in our yard!" *Oh!* Anthea glanced at Dylan, who had one hand to his mouth. He was grinning. "I didn't mean to say that, Dylan. You know I don't curse. I'm sorry."

Dylan giggled and said, "Yeah, right, Mom. That was no accident!"

Trying to ignore her blunder, she looked back at Paul. Out of the corner of her eye, she could see Dylan, still snickering. "Really, Paul. I wish she'd never moved in next door. All those animals, all those plastic boxes. What next? Old cars or concrete lawn ornaments? I'm certain there is a regulation in our city code of how many pets someone can own or how much junk someone can stash in their yard."

"I'm sure there is, Anthea." Paul sighed then put his hand on hers. She wanted to pull it back out but didn't. He had no clue. He was going to be patronizing; she could hear it in the lilt of his voice. It set her teeth on edge. "I don't want to be an ugly neighbor. And with the exception of a little cat . . . feces . . . I'd rather let it go. She's harmless, Anthea. Live and let live. Please. You want the same for yourself."

Anthea put her fork down. "Okay, I won't call anyone about her mess. Let her live in squalor if that's her choice. But, Paul, I'm ordering holly bushes to plant between the trees against her fence. I don't even care to see what goes on over there. And Dylan, you are to stay away."

"I like the cats and dogs. They like me!"

"The discussion's over."

"So is breakfast!" said Dylan. He slammed away from the table, kicking his chair over backward, leaving Paul to look at Anthea and Anthea to look at what appeared to be cat hair floating in the morning light and landing on her French toast.

Lisa Ferguson was up at two-thirty Sunday morning. Anthea usually wasn't, but she was still angry with Paul—God, but they had become so distant over the last three or so years—and couldn't sleep. She didn't want to watch television and she didn't feel like painting. She went to the bathroom and looked at herself in her purple satin robe. She was still beautiful, not even middle-aged yet, with a firm body, full hair, and eyes that used to turn Paul on in a heartbeat. Not now. It had all edged over, grown a crust that didn't seem likely to soften.

Anthea turned off the light and sat on the toilet in the dark, counting her heartbeats. Then she noticed a light burning down in what was probably her next-door neighbor's kitchen. Anthea put her chin on the windowsill and watched as Lisa moved back and forth, as energetic and busy as someone would be during the day. Anthea could see the edge of a table, a counter and sink, and a chair. There were cats on the table and counter, and a dog on the chair. There was a flurry of activity, shadows Anthea couldn't decipher, and then the light went out. A minute later, Lisa was in her backyard in the moonlight, collecting one of the plastic bins and a lid. She went back inside. Anthea waited another few minutes until her eyelids would have no more of staying open, and she returned to bed.

Sunday afternoon was surprisingly cool and pleasant, with lilting breezes and vague scents of impending autumn. Paul had taken Dylan to a game, leaving Anthea alone. Alone was all right. Alone was familiar. She shoved her studio window up as far as it would go, drawing in a long breath of sunlight, then slipped on her paint-covered apron and busied herself with *Sunflowers at Dawn*. Her next show was in November, and this was the fifth in her new series of flower portraits. It was the best so far, looser than any of the others, a four-foot canvas bleeding with yellows and browns and crossed with sharp, scarlet slashes. *Red sky at morning, sunflowers take warning.* Anthea smiled at the meaningless, random thought. She stuck the end of her paintbrush between her teeth and gazed at the work, deciding the next move.

"Hello!" came a cheerful voice from outside. "Anthea! I see you up there! I've made cake!"

Anthea went to the window.

"You're painting, aren't you?" said Lisa.

Anthea took the brush out of her teeth, though she could still feel the ghost of the hard wood on her enamel. "Yes, Lisa."

"I've made chocolate cake!"

"That's very nice."

"Want some? Come on, I've been living here a month now and you've yet to visit." Two dogs bounded at Lisa's sides while another popped his nose through a link and ran his tongue along the metal. Behind them, in nearly every square foot of the worn-down yard, lay or sat or rolled an animal.

There was a beat, then another, then, "Okay, sure. Thanks, Lisa."

All right, fine. I'll do this. This will give me concrete evidence to use with Dylan and Paul. I wish I had a hidden camera, like on Dateline NBC *or* 60 Minutes. *I do this distasteful task for my son. He's worth it.*

Anthea slipped out of her painting apron, went down to the street, and entered Lisa's yard through the gate.

"Come in," Lisa said, holding open the screen door.

Anthea had been inside Carlsbad Caverns when she was five and her family had taken a cross-country trip. The only clear memory she had was that of millions of bats loosening themselves from the walls and ceiling and flying out into the sky. Bumping, thumping, clumping, completely obliterating the fading blue of the sky. Chittering, skittering, their filthy leather wings cutting the air like fouled knives into delicate flesh. Anthea had screamed, dropped to her knees, and covered her eyes.

It was all Anthea could do to keep from covering her eyes in Lisa Ferguson's house. Every square foot of floor was occupied by a pet or slobbery pet toy. A front-hall bookshelf had two cats on top and one on a lower shelf, rubbing its cheek against the sharp edges of a hardcover. Another cat lounged in the glass globe of the hall chandelier, staring down with a contented expression. A spotted dog, clearly not neutered yet, sat in the center of the hallway, licking his balls. Lining either side of the hall were covered litter pans. She could hear digging in several of them. Anthea bit the inside of her cheek, tossed back her hair, and followed Lisa to the kitchen.

There were two cats on the refrigerator and several under the table. A dog with one eye was on one of the four chairs at the dinette. A Kit Cat clock with moving eyes and swinging tail hung on the wall next to a calendar showing children playing by a pond.

Lisa took a cake, covered in plastic wrap, out of the fridge. She pulled two small Fiesta plates from the cabinet and put them on the table. Anthea studied her plate without picking it up. It looked clean. She hoped Lisa didn't let the dogs lick stuff off the plates like some people did. But there *was* a dishwasher in here, and she could see no dust-covered feces balls in the corners or grass-laced upchuck puddles on the floor. The house wasn't completely filthy, as she had suspected.

Yet the air was stifling in spite of the breeze through the kitchen window. And Anthea detected some sort of strong chemical in the kitchen, an unfamiliar cleanser, perhaps, or an insecticide. It made her nostrils burn and her head uncomfortably light.

Lisa removed a large knife from a lopsided drawer and cut two thick pieces of cake. She put them onto the plates then sat. She ate. And talked.

And talked.

She talked about her ex-husband and how he had never wanted pets or children. She talked about the job she used to have working in a children's clothing store and how she would give each good child a sucker before they left. She talked about the next cat she planned on adopting if nobody claimed it within the week, a tabby that had been hanging around the gas station over on Brindel Street. "I should open my own shelter," she said as she ate her piece of cake. "I would if I had enough money."

Anthea nodded and forced herself to swallow bite after bite of her own slice. There was no pet fur she could detect with her tongue, no trace of urine.

But still.

But still Anthea's breath felt tainted in her lungs, and the hairs on her arms prickled like seaweed in a strong current. Her mouth was dry. She did not want to be there. She did not like Lisa's house or Lisa's pets. She did not like the woman herself.

The moment Anthea took her last bite of cake, she thanked Lisa and excused herself to leave.

"Oh, no, already?" implored Lisa, taking off her round glasses and inspecting them for smudges. "But we're having such a good time."

"Well," said Anthea. Then: "I do have things to do. Thanks for the cake."

As she stood, she heard strange noises from behind a closed door that she guessed led to a pantry, or basement. It sounded like children's hushed, urgent voices.

"Lisa, are there kids here?" Anthea asked.

"Hmm, what? Oh, no, I don't have children, just my fur babies." Lisa picked up a cat and rubbed her face against its body. "I probably told you I couldn't have kids, though I wish!"

"No, I asked if there are children here?"

"Where?"

"There." Anthea pointed to the door.

"Oh. Why would children be in my cellar?" Lisa put her cat down and ran her fingers through her hair, pushing it back behind her ears. This made the sharp angles of her face sharper. Almost witchlike. *Anthea, that's not fair.* "There's nothing down there but boxes and—oh, I don't know, other odds and ends I couldn't fit upstairs."

Anthea paused, her head tilted, listening. She no longer heard the voices.

Maybe it was only cats or dogs, or even hissing water pipes.

"Okay, then," said Anthea. She thanked her hostess for the cake then waded out through a mobile maze of mutts and felines. Back in her own house, Anthea took deep, cleansing breaths. "That's over. That's good. And in spite of the animals the house itself wasn't a toxic-waste station. I won't need to call the CDC. Yet."

But I'm still not going to let Dylan play over there. That's just the way it will be. I'm the Mom and I don't like what I feel when I'm in that woman's presence or in her house. I think something's wrong.

Something's quite wrong.

September brought several things: the beginning of school, more pets and plastic containers in Lisa Ferguson's yard, more frequent and shadowy late-night business in the Ferguson kitchen, and Anthea's first real argument with Dylan.

She had gone to the store a week before and had picked out a wonderful new wardrobe for her son. Jeans, T-shirts, polo shirts, new shoes and socks. He was growing so fast, it was hardly a frivolous purchase. But Dylan hated all the clothes. The jeans weren't baggy enough, the T-shirts were plain and the wrong brand, polo shirts were for morons and geeks, and nobody, *nobody* wore shoes like that anymore. Anthea screamed at him and threw the clothes in his face— she'd never done that before and felt like a bitch afterward— and told him he could just wear his old clothes until they fell apart. She didn't mean it, but Dylan had no trouble with that whatsoever, and so the new clothes went back to the store.

The summer flowers in Anthea's yard faded and went brown. Early autumn mums popped open in warm golds, reds, and oranges. The gourd leaves shriveled and the gourds were picked and taken upstairs for still-life models. The sunflowers were droopier, nearly seed-bare, and ready to give up the ghost.

After school, children still stopped by Lisa Ferguson's yard to play with the animals, though the numbers were dwindling. Perhaps other mothers had the same concerns as Anthea. Anthea caught Dylan in Lisa's yard once in late September, and she threatened to ground him for a month. Dylan was furious and punched the walls and bruised his fist, but then reluctantly agreed because with a grounding, he'd not be able to practice with the band he, George, and Gene had going. "We're going to kick major ass at the talent show!" he boasted with a preteen sneer. "We're the River Rats, and we're gonna get gigs and make money and burn a CD! Just wait."

That was the plan.

Until the twins disappeared.

The first Tuesday in October, right after dinner, Cathy Kidd knocked on the Lonases' front door. Paul invited her in, but she was too flustered, too upset. "No, I just wanted to ask if you have seen Gene and George. Aaron is at home calling around, but I thought it best to go myself and look, not to just sit at home, you know?"

"I know," said Anthea, touching the other woman on the arm. *Poor, poor Cathy!* Anthea's heart clenched.

"The boys got off the bus at the regular place at the corner, but some of the other kids said they headed off this way instead of home."

"Did Aaron call the cops?" asked Anthea.

"Of course we called the cops! They said give it an hour or two, the boys are probably just goofing off somewhere!"

"That's wrong," said Anthea.

Paul nodded sympathetically but added, "They probably will show up soon, Cathy. Try not to worry too much. Kids do stupid things all the time, but they'll come home."

Cathy Kidd sniffed and ran her hand under her nose. "Nobody's seen them since four. I was wondering, was hoping, Dylan . . . ?"

Dylan, standing behind Anthea and Paul, shook his head. Cathy Kidd wailed. Then she left.

The interneighbor phone calls began then, mothers and fathers and children sharing their fears and agonizing over the fact that two boys were missing and wondering aloud all the possibilities of what might have happened. Anthea tucked Dylan in bed for the first time in four years, and he didn't complain.

At midnight, she and Paul both went to bed. He fell asleep immediately. Anthea went to the bathroom and sat on the toilet to look at the window of her neighbor's kitchen. The light was on. There were furtive, brisk movements, shadowy forms flitting in and out of the light. Then Lisa went into her backyard in her robe in the moonlight and selected two large plastic containers. Oh . . .

The woman went back into her house. After a few minutes, the kitchen light went off.

Oh, my God. That's impossible. She only collects pets. Cats and dogs.

And plastic, lidded boxes.

Anthea's fingers dug into the wood of the windowsill. Blood pulsed noisily at her temples. Her heart froze for several painful counts then kicked into high gear. "Impossible," she whispered. "I know Lisa, she's lived here for two months now."

You don't know her. You don't know shit about her. You've always sensed something wrong. But this?

She said she always wanted children.

Her first thought was to awaken Paul, but then he was

such an ass these days he'd just tell her to fix some green tea and get some sleep.

Please, God, let me be wrong.

Anthea put on her shoes. And her gardening gloves.

Come in.

With gloves on, it wasn't very hard to pull out the screen on the kitchen window. Anthea eased herself up and through, coming down on top of the dinette table in the dark. Cat eyes winked at her, little glowing globes of distrust and disdain. The Kit Cat ticked more loudly than it should have. The chemical scent was there, stronger than before. Anthea climbed off the table and stood with her hands clenched to her chest, listening.

Listening.

Then she saw the streak of light beneath the door to the cellar. And she could hear the soft children's voices, muffled, fearful.

For a moment, Anthea could not move. The backs of her arms were flushed with ice water. Lisa was in the basement. What if she had a weapon of some sort? Anthea held her heart, counted to five, then quietly opened the lopsided drawer where Lisa kept her knives.

She tiptoed to the basement door and eased it open. It did not creak. A cat came up to her, sniffed her leg, and hissed. Anthea licked her lips and her tongue came away with cat hairs.

Holding the knife like a baby, she moved down several steps. *George, Gene, be safe! Dylan, thank God you obeyed me!*

The cellar was completely unfinished. A fluorescent light

in the ceiling tossed bluish light along the stone walls and lumpy clay floor. Anthea eased down another step, and knelt, and it was then she could see Lisa at the far side of the room. She was chipping at the floor with a shovel. There was already a large hole next to where she was now digging. Two large plastic bins with lids in place were against the wall. Several cats sat by her feet, watching the progress. Other soft spots were visible on the floor, where other holes had been dug and then filled back in. A chewed pair of boy's sneakers lay against the water heater.

Anthea gasped.

Lisa looked up. And for the first time since Anthea had known her, the woman scowled.

"What are you doing here?" she demanded.

"George and Gene," Anthea managed. "What have you done to them?" She looked at the containers, just the right size for two twelve-year-old bodies to be folded and stashed. Anthea's head reeled, and she grabbed the railing to keep from toppling over.

"Who?" Lisa took several threatening steps in Anthea's direction, holding the shovel over her shoulder. The woman's hair was wild and tangled, and there were several dark streaks along her bony, witchish cheeks.

"Where are George and Gene? I see the shoes, the bins. The . . . holes."

Lisa kicked one of the sneakers. "What? These old things? They're dog toys, for heaven sake! Now get out of my house! I didn't invite you this time!"

"Let me see what's in the containers." The knife shook violently in Anthea's grip, but she did not let go. "Show me!" From under the steps, she heard soft crying. *More children? Dear God!*

"You don't want to see. It's ugly."

"I'm sure it is!"

Lisa moved to the bottom of the stairs. Anthea backed up three but then held her place.

"Leave me in peace! Leave me with my pain!" Lisa shouted. "You could never understand what I've been through, what I'm going through. Go!"

"Show me!"

"Bitch!"

The children under the stairs cried more loudly.

"Show me!"

Lisa lunged up the steps then, the shovel poised to swing into Anthea's head, but Anthea ducked and brought her elbow up into Lisa's jaw. Lisa squawked like a hen, dropping the shovel, flailing for the barest second then tumbling downward. The shovel bounced off the step and dropped beneath the railing to the dirt floor. The back of Lisa's head bounced off the stone wall with a sharp cracking sound. The woman fell to the floor, her neck bent at an impossible angle.

The children beneath the stairs screamed.

Anthea put her hands over her eyes. She counted as fast as she could, *One two three four five six seven eight nine ten eleven twelve thirteen . . .*

The children stopped screaming.

Slowly, Anthea put her hands back to her sides. She walked down the steps, removed a glove, and tested the woman's pulse. Lisa Ferguson was dead.

Anthea turned and looked beneath the steps. There were no children. No sign of children.

She looked inside the plastic boxes. There were dogs inside, folded neatly, and stiff with rigor mortis, tongues lolling.

———————

She painted throughout the night. *Finish a new one for the show. A new one will be good. A new one new one new one new one.*

It was black against white, this painting, furious and wild strokes that cut the canvas like the blades of night. Ebony pigment splashed Anthea's apron and the drop cloth.

Morning dawned, red. Paul was audible in the hallway, shuffling, coughing, moving toward the bathroom. Anthea could hear his footsteps stop short, and then he called, "Anthea? You up already?"

She said nothing. His footsteps moved closer.

"Anthea?"

She held the paintbrush in her teeth, studying the angry, jagged image. She heard Paul as he moved into the open doorway. And then: "Oh my God, Anthea, you're painting in black again."

The paintbrush went back to the paint and then to the canvas with a *whoosh, whoosh!*

"Anthea."

Anthea said nothing.

"Anthea, who did you kill?"

Anthea said nothing.

"Anthea!" Anthea jumped and the paintbrush went flying. "You've killed another neighbor, haven't you? Did you kill Lisa?"

Anthea could smell the chemical smell again, cloying, thick, overwhelming. The floor beneath her seemed to shift. "She fell and hit her head on the wall. She wasn't sane, Paul. Not sane at all."

"Damn, Anthea," he said, his voice filled with anger, regret, resignation. "I thought it would be better here. I thought you would be better here. A new place, the pace slower, less stress."

Anthea stared at her black painting. Black sky at morning. Who should take warning?

"In Chicago, you thought the man ran a white slave trade, but he just liked to party. In Atlanta, you thought the woman belonged to a sleeper cell, but she was only a Southern Baptist with dark hair!"

I have to protect my child from danger.

Paul put his wife to bed, saw Dylan off to school, and went to work, knowing very well that to stay home would be to arouse some kind of suspicion. Let Lisa be discovered by someone, sometime. Thank God it would appear to be another accident. But they would have to move again, get out of Richmond, find a place even smaller, out in the country perhaps, if Paul could even find work in such a location.

Damn.

It was getting old, Anthea's delusions.

As the real-estate agent hammered the For Sale sign in the yard of the Victorian and as the coroner hauled Lisa Ferguson's week-old corpse out of the cat- and dog-filled brick rancher to the fascinated stares of the neighborhood kids, good news circulated throughout the street. George and Gene Kidd were home again, having run off and having run out of money after eight days.

Anthea sent a note to the art gallery, apologizing for bailing on her November show, but she sent along a stirring black-on-white painting to the patrons as a thank you for their thoughtfulness.

Acid Test

Sara Paretsky

I

She hadn't known her life could unravel so fast. Yesterday morning, her biggest worries had been the phone calls from Ruth Meecham, complaining about the noise ("Are you running a hippie commune in there, Karin?" "Yes, Ruth." "I'm complaining to the alderman: you're renting rooms without meeting the building code for separate entrances." "Fine, Ruth") and Clarence Epstein's threats to sue her for harassment. In fact, when the cops arrived—all thirteen of them, at midnight, with enough cars to run Indy right there on the spot—she'd assumed it was because Clarence had made good on his threats.

Hyde Park was filled with people she'd known since first grade. Ruth Meecham was one of them—they lived side by side in the same outsize houses where they'd grown up. Clarence was another. In high school, he'd just been another grade-grubbing faculty brat, but when Karin got back from her time in India, he'd turned into a power-grubbing economist.

He and Ruth and Karin had all lost their parents relatively young, and they'd all inherited their childhood homes. Clarence Epstein had donated his family's brick home to the Spadona Institute. Of course, their main offices were in Washington, but so many of their fellows were on the University of Chicago faculty—most in economics or business, some in law—that Spadona needed a home near the university.

Ruth had inherited a portfolio along with her house. She lived alone in eighteen rooms, and kept them up with a meticulous round of repairs, gutter cleanings, and tuck pointings. Gardening was her acknowledged hobby, but meddling ran a close second.

Ever since her parents' death brought Karin back from India twenty-six years ago, Ruth had been monitoring her. She'd even noticed Karin's pregnancy before Karin admitted it to herself, admitted that the nausea she'd suffered since coming home wasn't due to changing back to Western food, or even grief at the loss of her elderly, remote parents, but a souvenir of the ashram in Shravasti.

She so missed life in the ashram that she turned her parents' mansion into a kind of co-op. Unlike Ruth, she hadn't inherited money to keep up the house, and the co-op helped pay the bills, besides giving her a chance to practice the nonviolent activism of Shravasti. She usually had three or four tenants, usually young activists who stayed a year or two before moving on. Right now the most intense was a young environmentalist with a toddler who'd shown up at Karin's door when the baby was only a month old. Remembering her own trials as a young single mother, Karin took her in, adopted Titus as an honorary grandchild, and tried to keep peace between young Jessica Martin's volatile moods and the rest of the co-op.

Jessica had made Clarence's Spadona Institute her particular project, writing about it for the blogosphere, staging sit-ins, helping a group of nuns with prayer vigils, and inviting a lot of police surveillance of Karin's home—which had increased since Clarence's death Tuesday morning.

Karin sat cross-legged, palms up, thumbs and forefingers forming an O, trying to chant, but she couldn't empty her mind. She'd been arrested before, but for demonstrations against wars, or the kind of trespass that Clarence had been so exercised about. She'd never been alone in jail, though—it had always been with friends, and never for a charge like murder. She couldn't comprehend it, even though she was choking on cigarette smoke and gagging on the other smells—stale urine, vomit, the iron stench of drying blood.

Empty the mind. Swami Rajananpur used to say, "Karin, caught between hope and fear, the spirit is like a trapped bird frantically beating its wings, and going nowhere. Empty the mind, join yourself to the great Now."

"*Eka leya,*" she chanted softly, *harmony.* A woman rattled the bars of the cage and screamed for a guard. A trapped bird, let it out, let it fly away. "*Eka leya, eka leya,*" she kept repeating, trying to set free all the birds whirring in her head, but last night's interview with the state's attorney kept flying back in.

"We know you had a major fight with Dr. Epstein two nights before his death." The state's attorney had been a young man, wearing navy pinstripes even at two in the morning, and trying to intimidate her by leaning over her and talking in too loud a voice.

"We didn't fight," Karin had answered, trying to explain that even if Clarence was angry, she, Karin, was too committed to nonviolence to fight with him. Nor would she add that everyone in the house had been angry, because it was also against her principles to shield herself at someone else's expense.

Had it been only five days ago? Clarence had come over in person—usually he'd sent a student or an intern with his complaints—and he'd seemed angrier with young Jessica Martin than with Karin herself. That wasn't so surprising, given Jessica's protests at the Spadona Institute. Conversation had been heated but civil until Jessica's little boy, Titus, toddled in, moving uncertainly on his chubby legs. Clarence tried picking him up, and Jessica snatched Titus away, shouting, "Don't touch my child. I won't have him covered with the blood that's on your hands."

Clarence had turned white with fury. "At least everyone knows what I stand for. I hate to see a child raised by a hypocrite."

Titus was usually a sweet and happy baby, but the angry voices made him start to howl.

"You two know how to calm down," Karen cried, taking Titus from Jessica. "Don't you see, if two smart grown-ups can't talk calmly, there's no hope for the world?"

"Karin, don't tell *me* what to do, you overgrown hippie. You never had a sense of values and you haven't got them now, letting anyone and everyone camp out here, and using your father's house as a base for violating my privacy!"

Jessica started to shout something, but Karin shook her head. "Insofar as I can, I run this house on principles of nonviolence. That means nonviolent verbal reactions, too, Jessica. If someone comes in here who's out of control, it's his problem, not ours. So I won't allow you to shout at him in here or call him names. You can take it outside if you have to do it, but think how much happier you'll be if you can stay calm."

"Oh, be as sanctimonious as you want, Karin, but keep this in mind while you practice your heavy breathing: if you let this flip-flopping radical stage a protest out of your father's house one more time, I will be suing you for intent to injure me and my institute. I came over to tell you I've been getting legal advice on this matter and my attorney is prepared to act."

Karin laughed. "It's my house, Clarence. Are you trying to say my dad would have supported your institute if he were still alive? Maybe so, but I bet your mom would hate to know what you do in there."

And then she'd felt ashamed, because in one second all her training, all her values, had gone out the window at the chance to score on him. Jessica had given a harsh laugh and yelled, "Right on, Karin," which made Karin leave the room abruptly, still holding the baby. At least she'd defused the encounter—Clarence had stayed another half hour, and Karin hadn't heard any shouting coming from the big common room where he and Jessica were talking. That was the last time she'd seen him, and she'd been shocked, even if not grief-stricken, when she learned of his death two days later.

The state's attorney hadn't believed Karin. He thought the threat of Clarence's lawsuit was enough to make her drop all her principles, figure out how to make a bomb, and how to set it off just when Clarence and his crony, the Spadona constitutional scholar Thomas Antony, were having an early-morning meeting on Tuesday.

"I don't know anything about explosives," she'd protested.

"But your daughter does, doesn't she?"

"Temple?" Karin had been astonished. "She's an engineer. She knows how to calibrate things, and wire a house, and make heating and cooling systems go. She doesn't know bombs!"

"Anyone could have built this one."

Karin shook her head. "Not me. And I'm sure not Temple, either."

Although, really, where her daughter was concerned, Karin was sure of nothing. How could you love someone and know so little about her? She had raised Temple in the relaxed, accepting atmosphere she herself had longed for in her own rigidly controlled childhood—and Temple had grown up tidy, precise, so compulsive she changed her answering-machine message every day—as Karin realized when she'd made a frantic call to her daughter as the police were arresting her. Listening to Temple give the date, her whereabouts, when she'd return calls, Karin had moaned, "Darling, please, just answer, just answer," and, when the beep finally came, had time only to cry out, "Temple, come as soon as you get this message—it's urgent!" before the cops snatched the phone from her.

II

Temple had been in the water lab at the Probit Engineering labs when the Spadona Institute blew up. She was conducting tests on a grooved end-fitting that had come loose in a water-main break to see whether the fitting was defective or had simply been improperly installed. She was covered in waterproof gear, happily reading gauges and jotting down notes to take back to the computer, and didn't hear the news until later.

"Isn't that the place where your mom leads protests?" Alvin Guthrie asked when Temple got back to her desk. "I thought I saw her on TV when Abu Ghraib hit the news, because she said that some of the Spadona fellows were training torturers, or justifying them or something."

"Your mom is totally amazing," Lettice announced. "Still living the hippie life after all these years. My mother is, like, obsessed with her body, you know, getting into a size two instead of a size six. I like how your mom just enjoys life, and eats what she wants."

"It would be better for her health if she worked out, and didn't eat so much dal and curry," Temple said—although her suggestions along those lines to Karin had made her mother tilt back her head, with its rope of graying blond hair, and laugh. (She'd stroked Temple's cheeks an instant later, because she hated cruelty in herself as much as in others, and said, "Darling, I can't be the kind of woman you see at your health club. I do yoga every day, you know, and even if I'm twenty pounds overweight, that doesn't stop me from making a tree vrksana." And she flipped onto her hands, knees against her elbows, while little Titus clapped his own hands and tried to imitate her.)

"Anyway, I don't have enough memory in my BlackBerry to keep track of all the places Karin goes on protests," Temple added, when Alvin went back to his original question. "I think I was born at a rally or protest of some kind."

She could picture her mother, giving birth in the street, wrapping Temple in a banner, and continuing to march. Temple's earliest memories were of painting signs for protest marches, or the marches themselves. Whether the cause was peace, farmworkers, or reproductive rights, Temple's childhood was spent waking to a house full of strangers, tiptoeing around throwing out beer cans, and scraping leftover curry into the garbage while the activists slept until noon.

She told her coworkers this, and Lettice once again exclaimed in envy about how open Temple's mother was. The idea of a house full of empties didn't make them gag, the way it did Temple herself. She'd gone to engineering school as the logical culmination of an obsession both with order and with making things work properly, but Alvin and Lettice were both good engineers with a high tolerance for mess—as Temple knew, since they'd all roomed together in engineering school.

"If you'd grown up in my family, you'd welcome your mother's open-house outlook," Alvin said. "My parents only entertain once a year, when they have my father's family to Thanksgiving, and that is an evening in hell, let me tell you."

While Alvin and Lettice argued which one of them had the more neurotic family, Temple slipped into the hall to call her own mother. "You weren't at the Spadona Institute today, were you?"

Karin laughed. "You don't think I blew it up, do you? We had a gazillion fire trucks on the street; Titus was in heaven—you know how little boys are with loud machines. But we had a teen reading circle at the house this morning, so I couldn't go. Jessica was there with the sisters, and I hope you don't think a group of pacifist nuns could blow up a building. Thank goodness none of them was injured—they were kneeling out front when the place went up."

"Temple!" Her boss, Sanford Rieff, had suddenly appeared behind her. "I hope that conversation is about the threads on Rapelec's pipe valve, because we need a report for them by the end of the day."

Temple felt her cheeks grow hot and fled back to the office. While she wrote up her results, her office mates kept up a running commentary on the Spadona bombing, which the news sites were covering with an orgiastic glee.

TERRORISM STRIKES CHICAGO, and AL QAEDA IN THE HEARTLAND, they trumpeted. A few hours later came the reports that police had discovered the bodies of Clarence Epstein and Thomas Antony in the building rubble. This seemed to pin the blame securely on Al Qaeda: the two men had been heavily involved in the interim government in Iraq, Epstein as an economist, Antony giving advice on how to draft a new constitution. The FBI figured that Epstein and Antony were targets of the blast, since they often met early in the morning before any of the administrative staff arrived.

The news reports expressed astonishment at the institute's location, but the *Herald-Star* did a sidebar explaining that the University of Chicago had taken over a lot of mansions on Woodlawn and Kimbark Avenues to house some of their auxiliary activities; the Spadona Institute, from its beginnings among the economists of the Nixon era, had always had close ties to both the university and the Republican Party.

When Sanford Rieff came in at three to see whether Temple had finished her analysis, she was glad she had Rockwell hardness charts up on her screen—it was to Lettice and Alvin that Rieff said drily, "Have you been assigned to the Spadona bombing? I didn't realize anyone had retained Probit Engineering on that case yet. Temple, are you finished? And, Alvin, don't we have anything productive for you to do? You can go assist them in the crash lab."

The bombing was a three-day wonder. Whatever clues the FBI's forensics team had picked up in the building, they were keeping as secret as possible, although they did concede it wasn't a typical bomb—something more homemade, which made people think about Oklahoma City. On Thursday, Temple, egged on by Alvin and Lettice, went down to see what Karin knew, and to inspect as much of the damage as the police barricades allowed.

They stopped at the Spadona Institute first. Like Karin's house, and other homes along Woodlawn, it was an outsize brick mansion, with some twenty rooms, standing on a double city lot. Set well back from the street, with a couple of old maples and an ash on the front lawn, it had done nothing to attract attention to its activities, at least until it blew up.

When the three engineers got close to the house, they could see that a number of windows had shattered; behind the glass they could make out charring from the fire. The main destruction was on the roof and third floor of the building, but they could see black scarring underneath the second-floor windows, as if the house had been tied up in a giant black ribbon.

"Odd kind of destruction pattern," Alvin said.

The two women nodded, and moved cautiously around the building to the back, which looked much like the front. Although all three were engineers, none of them had training in explosives; Lettice, a chemical engineer, came the closest, but she had never looked at a bomb site. Temple was a mechanical engineer, which meant she knew a lot about furnaces and heating/cooling systems; at the Probit forensic lab, she'd mostly been working with pipes and valves.

"Have they said where the bomb was planted?" Lettice asked. "Because it looks as though it was under the roof, which would be really weird if you were trying to kill someone. Maybe whoever set it off just wanted to disrupt the institute—maybe one of your mom's nuns didn't know enough to realize she'd got hold of something powerful."

Temple shook her head. "It can't have been set under the roof, not with that burn pattern around the second story. Fire goes up."

"Duh," Alvin said. "I missed class the day they talked about fire."

Temple swatted him with her briefcase. "It wouldn't burn downward, at least, not along that very precise route—you'd see fingers of charring. This looks like it followed the pipes."

"So maybe it started on the second floor and traveled upward," Alvin said.

"Along what route?" Lettice asked. "Temple's right—the burn pattern doesn't make sense."

A police car pulled over; the man at the wheel didn't bother to get out, just broadcast over his loudspeaker that the area was off-limits. He waited at the curb until the three engineers went around the block to Karin's house.

The front door stood open: so many different people used the common rooms of the house for meetings that Karin never locked up during the day. When Temple and her friends walked in, they heard a woman shouting.

"You and your stupid protests. You *look* stupid with all this adolescent behavior, your marches, your prayer vigils, wearing your hair as if you were still twentysomething instead of fiftysomething. You hated Clarence so much you'd let anyone into this house who was ready to hurt him. You never thought to ask any questions, but believe me, he did, and I did."

The young engineers couldn't make out the murmured response, but the first speaker shouted, "You made his last days on earth miserable! Don't tell me to calm down."

"Ruth Meecham," Temple said. "She lives next door; she and Karin and Clarence Epstein all grew up together. Karin hates people shouting, but when she says 'calm down,' it sometimes makes you want to hit her."

Temple led the way into a large common room, where her mother stood, a toddler in her arms, facing her neighbor. Temple suddenly saw her mother through strange eyes: she did dress like an old sixties hippie, in her Indian pajama trousers. Her graying hair hung unbraided to her waist. She was barefoot this afternoon, too.

Almost as if she were deliberately accentuating their differences, Ruth Meecham had dyed her hair black, and wore it severely bobbed around her ears. She was wearing makeup, and the open-toed espadrilles showed she had polish on her toenails.

"Hi, Karin; hi, Ms. Meecham. Hi, Titus," Temple added as the little boy squirmed out of Karin's arms and toddled over to her. "Where's everyone else?"

She bent to pick up Titus, but he wriggled away and made a beeline for a chest in the corner where Karin kept toys—not just for him, but for all the children whose parents brought them to the many meetings held in the house.

"Jessica Martin left as soon as I came." Ruth Meecham bit off the words as if they were cigar ends. "She knew I'd let her have what for, the way she treated Professor Epstein."

"Clarence had so many resources," Karin said. "The president, the Congress, all those billionaire Spadona donors. Was Jessica really more than he could handle?"

"Not even letting him touch the baby!"

"And how do you know that?" Karin asked.

Ruth Meecham hesitated, then muttered that it was all over the neighborhood. Karin didn't reply to that; after an awkward silence, Ruth started to leave. She paused in the doorway long enough to say, "Do you ever investigate the people you give house room to?"

Karin laughed. "I hope you're not suggesting Jessica is a fugitive from justice. She's a little aggressive, it's true, but she's still very young."

"Oh, grow up, Karin!" Ruth Meecham stomped down the hall to the door.

"Did Jessica and Mr. Epstein have a fight?" Temple asked. "Oh—Karin—you remember Alvin and Lettice, don't you?"

"Of course." Karin gave them a warm smile. "Jessica is too hot-tempered; she wouldn't let Clarence hold the baby. But Ruth was lying, wasn't she, on how she knew."

"I bet she was listening under the window," Temple said. "She does, you know. At least, when I was a kid, I sometimes saw her with binoculars, studying the inside of our house."

"That's a little different from listening under the window, Temple!"

"She might have a remote mike," Alvin suggested. "Something with two-point-four gigahertz could pick you up from next door without her leaving the comfort of her home."

"If she wants to listen in on our pregnant-teens book group, she's welcome," Karin said. "Maybe it'll make her want to volunteer. I suppose, though, Clarence told her. She always had a crush on him and he knew she'd see his side of things, no matter how crooked that side might seem to me."

Lettice and Alvin started asking her questions about the explosion. Temple wandered over to a battered coffee table whose surface was covered with flyers and books, old mail and unread newspapers; she started sorting them.

"Leave those alone, Temple," Karin called out. "Whenever you tidy up, it takes me forever to find my notes."

Temple bit back a reply. She wasn't going to argue with Karin in front of her friends, but really, how could anyone stand to live in this kind of chaos? Karin had never been a typical mother, and she certainly had never been a typical housewife. Temple controlled the urge to pick up the papers that had drifted to the floor and looked at Titus, who was trying to fit a rubber ball into a plastic jug. The jug's lips and handles were misshapen—from being put on the stove, Temple imagined—in her mother's haphazard home, the kitchen always was the site of small catastrophes.

"That's quite an engineering problem you've set yourself, little guy." She squatted next to him to watch, then said sharply, "Where did you get that?"

When she pried the jug from his grasp, Titus began to howl—at which moment his mother appeared in the doorway.

"What are you doing to my child?" Jessica demanded.

She was a tall woman; Temple, who was barely five-two, always felt invisible next to Jessica. She craned her head back and said firmly, "I was taking this from him. It's had something nasty in it, and I think it's pretty irresponsible to let a baby play with it."

Karin interrupted her own description of Clarence Epstein as a high-school student to say guiltily, "Oh, dear: I found that in the trash and meant to put it out with the recyclables. Titus must have picked it up from the kitchen table before I got around to it."

"Oh, everyone around here is so fucking pure! Couldn't you just leave it in the garbage for once? I picked it up in the backyard and threw it out!" Jessica grabbed Titus, who howled even more loudly.

"Sorry, sweetie." Karin smiled at Jessica. "Sometimes we're myopic, putting recycling ahead of the baby's curiosity. And the recycling—oh, dear—I promised I'd look after that along with the seedlings, and I completely forgot to take them out last week. Sandra and Mark will be so upset when they get back."

"I'll take it out to the recycle bins." Temple picked up the container, giving her mother a level glance that stated her unspoken opinion of the sloth that let the container stay in the house.

Karin pursed her lips and turned away. Temple knew what she was doing—a minimeditation, a mini–letting go of anger with Temple herself, not with Jessica, who couldn't look after her baby and then got pissed off with someone who was paying attention to his welfare.

She walked through the house to the kitchen, which as usual had pots and papers and bags of organic granola on every surface. A blender was on the floor, where Titus could conveniently slice off his fingers; Temple put it next to a precarious mountain of bowls in the sink. Karin had never appreciated her tidiness, even when she was eight, and making the chaotic house livable. Maybe Jessica was the daughter Karin had always wanted—an activist, the daughter who could tolerate mess—unlike Temple, in whose stark white apartment every pen and paper clip was in a tidy accessible drawer.

She blinked back self-pitying tears and went out to the recycle bins, where she removed newspapers from the bin for glass. Who knew what the papers had been used for—they were streaked with white powder. Surely no one was using cocaine in Karin's house. Temple rubbed a little of the powder in her fingers, which began to burn. She quickly wiped them on the grass.

A few minutes later, Alvin and Lettice joined her. Alvin wanted to see the greenhouse where Karin grew herbs, in case she had any medicinal marijuana. The greenhouse sat in the back of the garden, next to a compost heap where wasps were hovering.

"Knock it off, Alvin; if my mom was breaking the law she wouldn't be doing it where people like you could barge in on her. Anyway, the greenhouse is the responsibility of one of

the other house members who's big on organic gardening—
she starts all her seedlings out here."

Temple was annoyed with all of them, with Jessica for
being such a dimwit, with her mother for running such an
idiotic household, and with her friends for treating Karin
like a sideshow in the circus. Her annoyance made Alvin
clown around more, pretending that the oregano he plucked
in the greenhouse was reefer. He staggered up the sidewalk
past Ruth Meacham's house, and Temple's anger increased
to see that the neighbor was watching them all with a kind
of voluptuous malevolence.

It was six hours later that the police came for Karin.

III

"What's she doing in handcuffs?" Temple demanded.

She had found Karin in a side room, where prisoners were
held after their bond hearings until court ended, when they
would be put on buses to Cook County Jail.

The sheriff's deputy bristled. "It's the law, and if you
want to talk to her, you won't carry on in here."

Temple sized up the deputy, the gun, the attitude, and
squatted next to her mother, who gave her a wobbly smile.
Temple was overcome with shame: she had heard her mother's message when she got home at one, and decided if there
was a crisis, it had something to do with Temple's visit earlier in the evening. She didn't feel like hearing a lecture on
why she needed to treat Jessica with more consideration, so
she'd erased the message and gone to bed.

It was only when she was dressing for work with the radio on that she'd heard the news: her mother arrested for murder. Traces of the explosive used at the Spadona Institute, a common household cleaner, mixed with fertilizer, had been found in the greenhouse at the back of the garden.

"I don't believe it, any of it," Temple announced to her kitchen. "This is insane."

She had called the house to try to find out where her mother was. The phone rang a dozen times before Jessica answered it. She was surly, as if annoyed that Temple wanted to talk about Karin: the police raid had totally freaked out Titus, she said; he'd cried until three in the morning. "I don't know where Karin is and she's not my responsibility. If she blew up the Spadona Institute, then I am out of here—I am not getting involved in her crimes."

"Sheesh, Jessica, after all my mother's done for you, all the babysitting, letting you run off when you need your own space, or whatever sob story you lay on her. What happened? What grounds did they have for arresting her?"

Jessica bristled at Temple's criticism, but she did confirm the news reports, that the cops had found what they were looking for in the greenhouse.

Temple frowned. "I was in that greenhouse yesterday afternoon, and didn't see any buckets or bottles of cleaner. And you know Karin doesn't use that kind of product, or let anyone in the house use it—didn't you tell the police that?"

"It was the middle of the night, the baby was howling, what was I supposed to do, give them a lecture on nonviolence and green gardening?"

Temple snapped her phone shut. In her head she could see a spreadsheet with a to-do list, the items filling in as if written with invisible ink. Number one, evict Jessica, had to be moved to number four, she decided: number one had to be to find a criminal lawyer for Karin. Number two was to find out what evidence the state had and number three was to see if Karin was guilty.

Since Probit Engineering was a forensic lab, her boss, who'd testified in a gazillion or so criminal cases, surely knew a good criminal lawyer. She caught him on his way to a meeting. He thought for a minute, said that Luther Musgrave was the best, if he was available, and that Musgrave could also find out exactly where Karin was. Musgrave wasn't in when Temple called, but his paralegal traced Karin and told Temple that Musgrave or one of his associates would meet her in bond court as soon as possible.

Temple was still squatting in front of her mother, rubbing her cuffed hands and sniffing out an apology for not responding to Karin's SOS last night, when Luther Musgrave arrived. He was such a model of the corporate attorney, from the bleached hair cut close to his head to the navy suit tailored to his tall body, that Temple was sure her mother would reject him. She was astounded when Karin got to her feet, awkwardly because of the cuffs around her ankles, and held out her chained hands to Musgrave.

"Luther, of course! If I hadn't been so rattled last night, I'd have thought of you myself. Bless you—that is, I assume you've come for me?"

"Of course, I should have known it was you." Musgrave turned to Temple. "Our parents had adjoining cottages in Lakeside when we were growing up. I knew your mother before she went to India and changed her name to Shravasti. Let's get you out of here."

"They set bail at a million dollars," Karin said. "Even if I take out a higher line of credit on the house, I can't come up with that much money."

"That's why you've hired me. Or why your daughter has. Million-dollar bonds for felons are just part of our complete service."

IV

"I won't pretend that I'm going to wear black and sob at their funerals, but I didn't kill Epstein and Antony," Karin said.

"I don't want any hairsplitting here," Luther Musgrave said sternly. "If you placed an explosive device in the house, intending to blow it up before the guys got there, you're still liable for their deaths."

"Luther! I don't know word one about explosives, and I am utterly and completely committed to nonviolence."

"That's really true," Temple said. "And besides, she's totally green, you know. They're saying she mixed ammonia with fertilizer from the compost heap, but Karin wouldn't buy a cleaning product with ammonia in it."

"But they found her gardening gloves in the greenhouse and they're saying they had traces of the ammonia and some fertilizer on them," Jessica put in.

They were sitting in Karin's private parlor. When she turned her house into a co-op, she'd kept a suite of four rooms for herself at the back of the second floor. Normally at a meeting like this, all the housemates would have taken part, but Jessica—and Titus, happily banging away on a drum improvised out of old milk cartons—were the only ones at home. Three were trekking in Uzbekistan and the fourth, an elderly civil-rights lawyer, was visiting his daughter in northern Michigan.

"But I don't garden," Karin said. "Maybe I have some old work gloves, I guess I do, but Sandra—one of our housemates—looks after the greenhouse, and she's one of the ones away trekking right now. In fact, it's been on my conscience that I haven't looked at her seedlings to see if they've been watered."

"It's impossible to prove, Karin." Luther held up a hand as Karin and Temple both began to protest. "I'm not saying I doubt you, but I can't prove it in court, which is where it matters. If you're innocent, someone planted your work gloves in there, coated with ammonium nitrate. Who could have done that?"

"Anyone," Temple said. "Karin keeps an open house. Doors are locked at night, but I bet you never lock the gate leading to the alley, do you?"

"Of course not, darling, why would I? It just makes twice as much work. It's bad enough that people are always losing house keys, without worrying about the garden, too."

"Are you sure it was an ammonium bomb?" Temple said. "I'm surprised it behaved like this one did."

"What do you mean? How does an ammonium bomb *behave*?" Jessica gave the word a sarcastic inflection.

Temple saw Karin mouthing *Let it go* and took a deep breath before she answered. "Ammonium-nitrate bombs leave a big hole. The house would have fallen in on itself if the bomb had been set inside, and if it was outside, the front or the back would be missing. The Spadona building just has roof damage and a pattern of burn marks around the second floor."

"Are you an expert?" Luther asked.

"No, but that's the kind of thing everyone knows," Temple said. "What about the samples from the house? Where was the bomb set? What was it made of?"

Luther jotted a note. "I'll see what the feds are willing to say. Going back to who could have planted this on you, do you have any ex-tenants, or old enemies in the neighborhood, who might have it in for you?"

"Just Ruth Meecham," Jessica said. "She's always calling the alderman's office about the number of people living here."

"Oh, Ruth," Karin said dismissively, when Temple interrupted her.

"There's something I need to check on. I'll talk to you later, but get some rest, go to the Buddhist temple, do something for yourself, okay? Today isn't your day for being Titus's babysitter."

She darted from the room without waiting for anyone's reaction—just as well, Karin thought, given Jessica's furious expression. A moment later, they heard the clatter of metal lids. Jessica and Karin went to the window, followed by Luther. They looked down to see Temple rummaging through the recycling bins. A flash of light made Karin look across the yard. Ruth Meecham also had her binoculars trained on Temple.

V

Alvin and Lettice had spent the whole morning discussing Karin's arrest, and how she'd managed to plant the bomb. When Temple finally arrived at the lab, a little after noon, they pounded her with questions.

"My mother did not put a bomb in that building," Temple snapped at them.

She pulled a couple of specimen bags from her canvas briefcase and laid them on Lettice's desk. One held the distended plastic jug, the other a newspaper. "Can you analyze these?"

Alvin came over to look down at the bag. "Hmm. Small print, lots of words, a screed about liberals in the media, must be the *Wall Street Journal*."

"Please don't joke about it, Alvin—these might help with Karin's defense."

"What are they?" Lettice asked.

"The *Wall Street Journal* and an empty water jug," said Alvin, unrepentant.

Lettice picked up the specimen bags. "What am I looking for?"

"Yes, what is she looking for, and why are you giving her the assignment?" It was their boss, Sanford Rieff, who had materialized in the doorway.

"Oh, sir, it's—you know, the Spadona building, my mother was arrested, they planted false evidence in her greenhouse, I'm sure of it, and I want—"

"Slow down, Temple. I can't follow you. Give me a step-by-step picture of what this is about."

Temple shut her eyes. Where Karin chanted for harmony, Temple saw her to-do list, laid out in her head like a spreadsheet. It was so clear to her that she had trouble putting it into words, so she went to her computer and typed it all out.

Sanford Rieff looked at it and nodded. "And who is the client? Who is going to pay for time on the mass spectrometer, and for Lettice's time?"

Temple swallowed. "I guess that would be me, sir."

Sanford looked at her for a long minute, then walked over to her computer and typed a few lines. "Okay. I've added you to the client database. You can finish Lettice's tests on the water in the Lyle township pool—you know enough chemistry for that, right? And do you know what you expect Lettice to find?"

Temple took a deep breath. "I don't know if these are connected to the explosion, but—I'd look for ammonium nitrate, to see if the stuff they found in the greenhouse is on these, and check for acetone in the jug. I knew it smelled funky when I took it away from the baby yesterday, but it was only just now I realized it was nail-polish remover, I mean, I never use it, and I'd forgotten, I had a college roommate who was always doing her nails, but what I ought to do is go back to the Spadona building and get samples."

"You're not making sense again, Temple," her boss said, "but what you ought emphatically *not* to do is go back to a closed-down explosion site to get samples. You could be arrested, or even worse, injured. Someone has taken samples and we'll see if we can find their reports."

Sanford Rieff pushed her gently toward the door. "You have the makings of a forensic engineer, Temple, but we need the swimming-pool analysis this afternoon. Alvin, what are you doing, besides trying to best Temple's time at Minesweeper? Get me all the reports that are available on the Spadona bombing, then go back to the electronics lab to give Dumfries a hand with the timing problem he's working on."

It was six before Lettice was able to get time on the spectrometer. Temple, who'd finished her work on the swimming pool an hour earlier, stood next to her while Lettice read the bar graphs into her computer.

Temple pointed at a peak on the graph. "Would C_3H_6O spike there?"

"Temple, I swear, you are hovering like a bumblebee, and if you don't stop, I am going to swat you. I'm not going over these with you—I'm taking them to Sanford first, and he's left for the day, so get out of my hair!"

"I'm the client," Temple objected.

"And you're like every other annoying client, trying to run the investigation for us. Can't you do something useful? A yoga headstand or something?"

Temple stepped away, fiddling with her watchband, and looked at the samples she had brought in. Lettice had returned the *Wall Street Journal* to its protective bag, but the jug was just standing open on the counter. Come to think of it, who at her mother's house read the *Journal*? They got their news from *The Nation* and *In These Times*. And if she was right, if that was acetone in the jug—well, that came from nail-polish remover, and she was sure no one in Karin's house used polish or remover—Karin didn't approve of environmental toxins, whatever use they were put to.

But Ruth Meecham—that was another story. Temple had seen the polish on her toenails earlier this week, and Ruth, supporter of Clarence Epstein and the Spadona Institute— she surely read the *Journal*.

She walked over to her desk and called her mother. Jessica answered the phone and told her Karin was resting. "Do you want me to give her a message?"

Temple hesitated, trying to balance her jealousy of Jessica with her need for information. "Where did you get that jug, that one that I took away from Titus yesterday?"

"I told you—I found it in the backyard! Did you call up to give me another lecture on child safety? Because I don't need it."

"Don't yell at me, Jessica. I'm trying to figure out how to clear my mom's name, and I think that whoever planted the ammonium nitrate in her greenhouse made a bomb out of something different, probably out of acetone. I don't know how it worked, but if a fire had gone up through the air-conditioning vents, it would have left the kind of burn pattern you can see on the outside of the house, following the track of the vents around the perimeter, and acetone would be a really good fast-igniting agent. We're waiting on the test results, but I'm wondering if Ruth Meecham might have tossed the jug into our—into Karin's yard."

Jessica paused before answering, then said, "If she did, what motive could she possibly have for blowing up the Spadona Institute? She adored Clarence Epstein, she talks about him as if he were a saint. I think they were lovers or something back in college and she kept mooning over him even when he obviously had moved on to bigger and better things. He was a star, but she was only a moon." She laughed at her own pun.

"I don't know motives," Temple said impatiently. "Ms.

Meecham hates the way Karin uses the house as a commune, she hates the causes Karin supports—maybe she's deranged and figured if she could plant a big crime on Karin and send her to prison, the house would shut down. But I need to go through her garbage and see if I can find any traces of the ammonium nitrate before she gets rid of it, or even worse, dumps all of it in Karin's trash. I think I'll come down tonight and have a look, before it's too late. Don't tell Karin—she doesn't like people thinking vengeful thoughts."

Before leaving, she checked back at the spectrometer lab, but Lettice had disappeared. She wandered back to Lettice's desk and looked at her computer. Lettice probably used her cat's name as a password. Temple's fingers hovered over the keyboard, then withdrew. She knew it was acetone in the jug; she bet it was some kind of dried acetone compound on the newspaper that had burned her fingers yesterday afternoon. It was more important that she get down to Ruth Meecham's house and go through her garbage before Meecham decided to move it. And despite what Sanford Rieff had said, she'd go through the basement at the Spadona Institute and get some samples there. She had a hard hat in her trunk, she had a briefcase full of specimen bags, and she had a disposable camera in her glove compartment.

The late-summer dusk was turning from gray to purple when she reached Hyde Park. She left her car on a side street and came up behind her mother's house through the alley—other neighbors were probably just as nosy as Ruth Meecham, and she was less visible in the alley. Ruth Meecham's back gate was locked, but Karin's—naturally—stood open to anyone who wanted to come in that way.

Temple came through the gate as quietly as she could.

The fence that separated her mother's and the Meecham property ended at her mother's greenhouse; there was just enough space behind the greenhouse for her to squeeze past. When she reached Ruth Meecham's side of the yard, someone tapped her on the shoulder and she almost screamed out loud.

"Temple? Sorry to scare you." Jessica's face loomed over her in the dark. "Something worrying has happened."

Temple could still feel her pulse thudding against her throat.

"Right after we talked, Ruth Meecham called Karin, and Karin went over to Ruth's house and—I don't know. If Ruth was really crazy enough to blow up the Spadona Institute just to get back at your mom, I'm worried what she might be up to now."

"We should call the police," Temple said.

"To tell them what? That Karin has gone to visit a neighbor and we don't like it?"

"I guess I could go in and see what's going on," Temple said uneasily.

"I'll wait here. If you're not back in ten minutes, I'll call the police and tell them I saw someone breaking in," Jessica said.

"Where's your little boy?" Temple suddenly remembered Titus.

"He's asleep. He's okay by himself for a few minutes. Don't worry about him—you're as bad as your mother, fussing over me!"

Temple shut her eyes briefly: let it go. Jessica was a major pain in the ass, but she was helping, don't waste valuable energy fighting her. She didn't say anything else, but walked around Ruth's house to the front door and rang the bell. Jessica stayed behind her at the bottom of the steps, squatting so she couldn't be seen from the front door.

After she'd rung twice, Temple cautiously tried the knob. The front door was unlocked. She turned to wave at Jessica and moved inside. Her heart was still beating too hard, so she stood inside the doorway for a minute, picturing a decision tree: where she would look for Ruth and Karin, what she would do, each decision with its "yes" and "no" forks visible in her mind.

She'd been in the house only a few times and didn't know the layout, but she moved quickly through the ground floor without seeing anyone. Stairs to the basement led from both the kitchen and the front hall. Since she was right by the kitchen stairs, she went down those, but the house was so quiet she was beginning to worry that Ruth might have persuaded her mother to drive off with her somewhere.

She pulled a small flashlight from her canvas bag. She was in a small laundry area, with doors leading out of it to other parts of the basement. She swept them with her light. An instant later, she heard her mother call for help.

"It's me, Mom, it's Temple, I'll be right there."

The voice had come from her left. In her haste, she tripped over a basket of towels, but when she got back to her feet she managed to find a light switch. At first she saw only the furnace and other mechanicals, but when her mother called to her again, she found her in the back of the room, by the water heater, bound hand and foot. Next to her was Ruth Meecham, also tied, but unconscious.

Temple knelt next to her mother and started to undo her

hands; her own were shaking so badly she could barely use them. "Karin! What happened? I thought Ruth—"

"Temple, look out!" Karin shouted.

She turned and saw Jessica standing over her, a piece of firewood held like a club. She tried to roll out of the way, but shock slowed her reflexes, and the wood hit the side of her head as she rolled.

VI

She blacked out for only a minute or two, but when she came back to a nauseated consciousness, she found herself lying bound on the floor next to Karin. Jessica was placing a wrinkled copy of the *Wall Street Journal* on the floor next to the water heater, her motions as precise as a temple goddess laying out a sacrifice.

"Jessica, what are you doing?" Temple knew she was slurring the words: everything was blurry—the lights, her voice, the giant standing over her clutching the *Wall Street Journal*.

"I'm solving the Spadona bombing," Jessica said. "Poor Ruth—her hatred for your mother had grown to such outsize proportions she brought the two of you here for a funeral pyre."

"But, Jessica, why? Why do you need to kill all of us? We don't wish you any harm, or at least, if it was you who blew up the Spadona building, why do you want to harm us on top of killing Mr. Epstein and Mr. Antony?"

"Because you were meddling!" Jessica spat. "You had to go taking my supplies to your stupid lab. This way, it won't matter what they find, because all the evidence will point here! To the jealousy between Ruth and Karin."

"My God, you're foul!" Ruth had regained consciousness and now tried to sit up. She fell over again but said vehemently. "You thought no one would pay attention to your harassment of Clarence, but I saw it for what it was. I tried to warn Karin, but she's too holy for warnings and doubts."

"Let it go, Ruth, let it go, it doesn't matter."

"Let it go?" her neighbor said. "For five cents I *would* leave you to blow up here if I could, you and your sanctimonious chanting. Jessica worked for Clarence in Washington. Titus was his baby. She came here to Chicago to taunt him with it, and you let her use you as a dupe! If you ever asked the questions I'm prepared to ask, you'd never have given her house room!"

Temple felt a bubble of hysterical laughter rising in her, like a bubble floating on a fountain in a child's water experiment. She still felt dizzy, dizzy and ditsy; she thought, *What a way to go,* and she laughed helplessly.

"So you think it's funny?" Jessica snapped. "You're little Miss Perfect, aren't you, living your life according to so many rules you're like a walking computer, so I don't suppose you've ever even thought of having sex with a married man. Professor Conservative, the economic saint of the neo-cons, tried to force me to have an abortion. He didn't want a child on his résumé, at least not one belonging to one of his interns, not when he has a perfectly respectable wife in their Potomac mansion. When he was here last week, he threatened me, threatened to take Titus away from me, he said he could prove I was an unfit mother, and get me put in prison."

"But, Jessica, I would have helped you," Karin said. "You

didn't need to kill him. You can stay calm, I know you have it in you, we can work this out together."

"Oh, *fuck* you and your calm!" Jessica screamed. "Read the newspaper—it'll forecast the end of the world for you."

She ran from the basement. Karin began chanting softly, *"Eka leya, eka leya." Harmony.*

Ruth told her to shut up, she didn't want her last minutes on earth to be filled with Karin's hippie crap. Overhead, Temple heard water running in the pipes.

"Is someone in the house? Who's running water?" she demanded, opening her mouth to scream.

"No one, I'm not like your idiot mother, running a commune in my parents' beautiful—"

The newspaper. That was it, Jessica had made explosive paper, soaked it in acetone, left it to dry, made a perfect torch. She was running hot water somewhere upstairs, and when the water heater pilot flicked on—it would at any second—the paper would go up like a napalm bomb. Temple rolled over painfully and flung herself at the heater. The drain tap, she needed to open it, she couldn't get her hands in front of her, dammit, seconds not minutes. She clenched her teeth around the tap and jerked hard, again, a tooth cracked, again, and a stream of hot water flooded her, the paper, and Ruth Meecham, lying in its path.

VII

"You're going to be okay, darling." Karin stroked Temple's bandaged head. "You got burned on the side of your face, but not too badly, and the surgeon says there will only be a faint scar, once they operate. You were so brave, my darling, so clever. How did you know what to do?"

"I'm an engineer," Temple said. "They teach us that stuff."

"But what was on the paper?" Karin asked.

"Acetone, with mineral oil and something called PETN, that's kind of a detonator," Alvin said.

Lettice and Alvin had come to the hospital to see Temple. They had brought a video game that they assured her was impossible to solve so she'd have something to do while she waited for her surgery. "Now the feds are agreeing it's what Jessica used in the Spadona building—anyone can get the details from the *Anarchist's Handbook*—you don't have to be an explosives engineer. It was smart of you to guess how the fire went up the mechanicals—Sanford says you did well for a beginner, even if you stuck your head in where you shouldn't have."

"I didn't know," Temple said. "She made me think Ruth was behind it all."

"Oh, Ruth, she's just a confused and angry person. She got us out of there—once she saw you use your teeth to open that valve or tap or whatever it was, she used her teeth to pull the knots apart on my wrists. Even though she was still woozy from the blow to her head, she got upstairs to phone for help."

"Jessica must have been totally insane," Lettice said. "How could she imagine she'd get away with it all?"

"Poor Jessica: she's going to have a hard time in prison. I didn't do well, with all my years of training, but unless she starts wanting to find a place of balance, she's going to have an angry hard time of it."

"Poor Jessica!" Temple said. "Can't it ever be 'Poor Temple,' or even 'Poor Karin'? Don't you care as much about me as you do about her? She was a murdering bully, and I saved your life!"

Karin knelt next to the bed and put her arms around her daughter. "Darling, I love you. You're the moon and the sun goddess in my life, but you're never 'Poor Temple.' You'd never be so weak and so scared you'd have to kill someone to make yourself feel better. How could I insult you by feeling sorry for you?"

"See?" Lettice said. "My mom would never say something like that to me. It'd be, 'Lettice, get out of your hospital bed to bring me a glass of water.' Your mom is the coolest, Temple, get used to it!"

Trailer Trashed

Barbara Collins

Tanya—nineteen, blond, petite, and pretty—sat at a gray Formica table in the tiny kitchen of her mobile home and poured whiskey into a Wile E. Coyote glass. She took a swig, then almost choked on an involuntary sob. So far, the Southern Comfort hadn't given her much comfort.

Jake, her husband of two years, padded in from the single back bedroom, wearing faded NASCAR boxer shorts, his brown hair flattened where his head had hit the pillow. He was fairly handsome when cleaned up, but had gotten too thin for Tanya's liking, unloading heavy boxes at his Wal-Mart job.

He took one look at her and groaned. "Ahhh, hon, you're not *cryin'* again . . ."

That only made the tears flow harder.

"It's that stupid MTV program, ain't it?"

Tanya, sniffing snot, managed to snap, "It *ain't* stupid!" Then she added in a pitiful voice, "You know bein' on that show meant the world to me." And Tanya broke down again.

He said indifferently, "Well, get over it. Them guys didn't want us. Move on."

But she couldn't. "I don't know why Sheila and Rick got picked for the *Trailer Marvelous Makeover Show*," she sobbed. "I'm *way* prettier than her, and you're better-lookin' than that doofus." Tanya slammed a small fist on the table. "She's *fat,* and he's a *drunk!*"

"Darlin', it ain't the *people* they was after . . . it's the *trailer*. Sheila and Rick got a double-wide. Besides, those Hollywood types probably thought by them pictures you sent that our place looks just fine. We didn't *need* no damn makeover."

"Didn't *need* no makeover?" she shouted. "Just *look* at this place!"

He spread both hands defensively. "What?"

She jumped from her chair, hands fluttering. "This stuff ain't even *ours!* We didn't pick it out, some stupid strangers did! It come with the repossessed trailer."

"So? It's ours now."

"So I want nice things, Jake . . . things that don't have pee stains from somebody *else's* pitbull, not ours."

He sighed. "I don't have time for this . . . I gotta go to work. Where's my lunch?"

She gestured dismissively toward the Dale Earnhardt lunch box on the counter, where a stale peanut-butter sandwich and an overripe banana languished inside.

"Okay. Thanks, sugar." He lingered, wearing a goofy smile.

Tanya thought, *If he's waitin' for a good-bye kiss, he can forget it.* She went over to the sink and pretended to be busy.

After a moment, the flimsy aluminum screen door banged shut.

Tanya, fresh tears welling in her eyes, watched out the dirty kitchen window as her husband climbed into his pickup truck, then left in a cloud of dust.

She crossed over to the other small kitchen window and peered out. At the end of the gravel road of Happy Trails Trailer Court she could see the *Trailer Marvelous* film crew's long, shiny, old-school Airstream camper parked near Sheila and Rick's large mobile home; the camper had arrived a few hours ago, and people wearing T-shirts with the show's logo were scurrying back and forth between the two, getting ready for tomorrow's shoot.

Tanya felt sick to her stomach, like she had to throw up a bad fast-food meal.

The kitchen wall phone rang. She wiped her eyes with her fingertips, then answered it.

"Tanya!" The voice on the other end was breathless with excitement. "Do ya see 'em?"

"Yes, I see 'em," Tanya said flatly.

"I wish me and Rick didn't have to go bowlin' tonight so I could stay round and watch . . . but I guess they're gonna be leaving here soon, anyways—just checkin' the place out today, before comin' back first thing in the morning to shoot."

Wish they would shoot you, Tanya thought.

"Tanya?"

"Yeah."

"You're comin' to the Big Expose when they're done decoratin', aren't ya? They want all the neighbors to see the unveiling, right along with us. It'll be a riot!"

Tanya said sullenly, "I dunno."

"You'll get to be on TV!"

Yeah, in the background, she thought, but said, "Maybe I'll be there."

"Okay. Well . . . I'll let ya go," Sheila said, sounding hurt, and hung up.

With a dejected sigh, Tanya took a few steps into her narrow living quarters and plopped down on the sagging sofa. All of the crying and turmoil had made her exhausted.

She'd closed her eyes for only a minute when there came a sharp knock at the door.

"Jesus Christ," Tanya muttered, getting up. "Why don't people just leave me the hell alone?"

"What?" she snarled, flinging the screen door wide. Then both hands flew to her mouth, covering a gasp.

Standing on her very own portable steps were Bart Brooks, host of *Trailer Marvelous,* and the show's star designer, Johnny Hardy!

"Oh ma God!" Tanya squealed. "I don't believe it!"

Had they come personally to ask her to attend the Big Expose? If so, she'd swallow her pride and attend.

"Is this the home of Tanya and Jake?" Bart asked politely.

The former country-western star was tall, clean-shaven, and cute as a hound dog . . . but his clothes were *weird:* striped yellow golf shirt, plaid hat, wingtip brown shoes.

Like that old geezer her grandmother (bless her soul) used to be so crazy about—the one who smoked a pipe and sang "Ba-ba-ba-ba-boo" (but younger, of course!).

"Yes . . . yes!" Tanya sputtered. "This is them . . . I mean, we is us."

Johnny asked, "May we come in?"

The show's designer, decked out in torn blue jeans and a heavy-metal T-shirt, was a hunk, with streaked blond hair and cool dragon tatoos on both arms. Johnny was the kind of guy she would just love to pick her up at the Lonely Bull Tavern some night Jake was working late shift.

Barely able to contain her excitement, Tanya stepped aside.

"The kitchen is best," she suggested as the TV stars hesitated just inside. "The couch ain't so hot, as you might notice."

Spotting the whiskey bottle left on the table, Tanya dashed ahead of them, grabbed it, and stashed the booze in one of the lower cupboard drawers that worked. She didn't want them thinking *she* was a damn lush, like Rick.

The men pulled out worn vinyl chairs.

"Can I get you something to drink?" she offered. "We got Sam's Cola."

Bart grinned easily and said, "Some of that Southern Comfort would be nice."

"Ditto." Johnny smiled.

Tanya smiled back shyly and retrieved the bottle, along with three glasses. Then she joined them at the table.

Bart began slowly. "As you know, we're supposed to film up the road tomorrow at Sheila and Rick's . . ."

Tanya, pouring the drinks, nodded.

". . . and I have, say, between you and me and the lamp-post . . ." He paused while Tanya handed him a glass.

"Lamppost?" she asked. "We don't got none. Wish we did 'cause it gets awful dark out here at night."

The two men exchanged glances and laughed. And Tanya laughed. It always amazed her how funny she could be sometimes, like she was some kind of comedy-club ge-nius.

Bart looked down at his glass, swirled the whiskey. "What I'm trying to say is we're beginning to think we made a mis-take in picking those two for the show."

"Really!" It came out too happy, so Tanya tried again. "Really?"

Johnny belted back his drink and set the glass down with a clank. "Yeah, *big mistake*. I mean, what audience is gonna care if some jerk with a porky wife gets a shelf made to put his beer-can collection on?"

Bart leaned forward, interjecting, "But a sexy little gal like you could help ratings."

Tanya felt herself blush.

Johnny smirked. "Which are in the toilet right now."

Tanya frowned, said, "But I thought the show was popu-lar. All my friends watch it."

Bart sighed. "We're up against *Extreme Full Body Tattoo Bik-ers' Mud Wrestling* this season, and our slice of the pie just got smaller."

She wasn't sure what pie had to do with it, but Tanya wanted to help if she could. If the program got dropped, she'd lose a lot of good decorating tips, like making a picture frame out of macaroni (but she wished they would have had the common sense to say not to cook it!).

She dared to ask, "If you don't want Sheila and Rick, why don't you come here to our place?"

Bart sighed. "Darlin' we'd sure love to . . . but unfortunately, the producers have already signed a contract with them."

"So?" she said. "Why can't you sign another one with me?"

Johnny said, "Because Sheila and Rick would sue us."

Tanya asked, "Can they do that?"

Bart replied, "Oh, yeah. And *that* kind of publicity we don't need."

Tanya thought hard but couldn't come up with a solution. Finally, she asked despairingly, "Then what *can* we do?"

The men, drinks finished, stood. Bart said, "Pray for a miracle, I guess."

"What kind of miracle?" asked Tanya.

Bart laughed humorously. "Like maybe a tornado or earthquake hits . . . Or a fire breaks out over there and we can cancel with them and film over here."

Johnny had stepped into the living area and was surveying it, hands on hips. "Ya know," he said, "this place really has possibilities."

Tanya was at his side. "Like what?"

The designer spread an arm out, fingers splayed. "Like maybe a leopard-covered contour chair over there . . ."

Tanya squealed, "Could it have heat and vibrate?"

". . . and in that corner? One of those hanging cages with cherubs . . . You know what I'm talking about? Where liquid beads slide down the wires while it plays 'You Light Up My Life.' "

"I've always *wanted* one of those!" She stuck out her lower lip. "But we could never afford it. Jake won't let me work 'cause men keep hittin' on me. He just wants a damn housewife."

Bart said, "Well, you'd have fifteen thousand dollars to play with."

Tanya smiled. That's what each featured trailer owner got to spend on redecorating. Practically a fortune! Her mind began to whirl.

Then she frowned. But the kind of "miracle" Bart mentioned didn't seem likely to happen between now and tomorrow morning. She'd never even *heard* of an earthquake around these parts . . . and it wasn't tornado season yet. As far as a fire breaking out at Sheila and Rick's trailer, what were the chances of that?

At the dented screen door, Bart said, "Well, thanks for the drink. You should know that you and Jake were our second choice, but you should've been our *first*."

Tanya managed a weak smile. "I guess second just ain't good enough."

Johnny, at the bottom of the steps, turned to Tanya, framed in the doorway, "I don't know . . . look at what happens if Miss America gets dethroned . . ."

"What?"

He shrugged. "The runner-up steps in."

The two men climbed into a black Mercedes and, with gravel crunching under its wheels, drove off.

Tanya watched until the dust dissipated, then went to find the gas can.

A cool night breeze flapped the American flag that hung on a short pole attached to Tanya's mobile home as she slipped outside and down the steps, gas can in hand.

She had seen Sheila and Rick drive by her trailer earlier in their rusted-out Camry, happy grins on their faces—which would soon be wiped off, she had thought. Jake's shift at Wal-Mart had already ended, but Tanya could always count on him going out for beers with his low-life friends and not coming home for hours.

Dressed in black sweats, Tanya crept confidently along the back sides of the trailer homes, making her way slowly toward Sheila and Rick's. Occasionally, a mangy cat hissed or a penned-up dog growled, stopping Tanya in her tracks; but that was nothing out of the ordinary, so no one looked out.

With only a distant yard light to guide her, Tanya searched quickly among the short weeds by the steps of the double-wide for the spare key Sheila kept hidden in a piece of fake rubber dog poop Tanya had once given her friend for a Christmas present.

Finally, Tanya spotted it, reached down, and picked up the brown swirled thingie, which looked real in the dark. It squished in her hand. Yuck! It *was* real! Disgusted, she wiped her gooey hand on the weeds and tried again . . . this time with results.

Inside the trailer—they'd had tacos for dinner—Tanya set the gas can down and risked turning on a small table lamp made out of an armadillo. She'd never torched a place before and didn't know where to start. The fire should look like it broke out naturally (helped along with the gas, of course). Tanya looked toward the kitchen area, remembering a late-night movie she'd caught about a woman who was going to lose her house to her husband and his mistress. The wife turned on all the kitchen appliances, which caused an electrical fire, then left.

Tanya went over to the kitchen, where a blender sat on the counter. Sheila had once used it to make her a really wretched margarita after Tanya got her house-arrest ankle bracelet removed. Tanya made sure that the appliance was plugged in, then tried to get it going, but the thing was broken. She crossed to the microwave, punched in ninety-nine minutes, pressed *start,* and . . . nothing. Busted.

With a determined sigh, Tanya returned to the living room. She stared at the couch. One time, her uncle Bob had fallen asleep with a cigarette in his hand while watching *All-Star Wrestling* and started a fire in his pants. Maybe the sofa was the best place to begin . . .

Carefully—because once this guy next to her at the pump had spilled gasoline all over himself, then flicked his Bic and lighted himself—Tanya sprinkled the pungent petrol all over the couch, then did the same to the ugly recliner (maybe Sheila and Rick's trailer *did* need a Marvelous Makeover).

Satisfied, Tanya stood back and surveyed her handiwork.

Now, how to start it.

This could be tricky, because she had to get herself out before the fire took hold. She remembered another movie about this couple who wanted to collect some insurance money, so before they flew to Tijuana, they left a candle burning that caught the curtains on fire.

This idea seemed perfect because Sheila always had a candle or two going whenever Tanya and Jake came over, to cover the septic-tank smell.

In a drawer in the kitchen, Tanya found a small tea light, which she took back to the living room and placed on the gas-soaked couch. It should give her plenty of time

to get back to her trailer. Maybe *she* could even be the one
to call the fire in. Sometimes the local news played the 911
call over the disaster they were covering. Wouldn't *that* be
cool!

Tanya lit the tiny candle, then picked up the gas can and
left, making sure the door was relocked and the poop key
put back in the weeds.

It took about a half an hour before Tanya saw flames lick
at the sky. Watching from her kitchen window, she was
amazed how fast the blaze spread; in a matter of minutes
the whole double-wide was engulfed.

Tanya dialed 911, but was too late; somebody else had
beaten her to it. Oh, well. With Sheila and Rick now out of
the picture, the *Trailer Marvelous* show would be coming to
her place, and she'd get to be seen on TV, which was way
better than just her voice.

Six months later, Tanya's dream came true.

Latrisha, tall, slender, dressed in a cotton denim shirt and
slacks, yelled, "Hey, everybody! Tanya's gonna be on!"

The other women, dressed the same, stopped playing
pool and cards and gathered around the single small set in
the recreation room of Joliet Women's Prison.

Latrisha patted the seat of a plastic chair directly in front
of the television. "Sit here, girl! You gonna be famous . . . You
in the pre-mirror show."

Excitedly, Tanya sat, and soon the program's title, *The
World's Wackiest Criminals,* filled the screen. When the host of
the program, Bart Brooks, came on, all the women (except

for Tanya, whose eyes were glued to the TV) whooped and hollered.

One the inmates said, "I thought he was on a different show."

Someone else said, "Yeah, but that went under."

Bart's face filled the screen.

"*Tonight, we have a tale of jealousy and greed, a betrayal by a best friend—*"

Tanya said, "She weren't my best friend," and got shushed by the other women.

"*—who wanted to be on* Trailer Marvelous, *our former series, so badly that she burned a contestant's home to the ground, not realizing that our film crew had set up small cameras inside and a feed was already going, capturing her entire movements.*"

As Tanya watched the ten-minute footage, she heard laughs and snickers around her. And when it was over, some of the women seemed disappointed as they got up and returned to their previous activities.

Latrisha asked, "Girl, what's the matter? You don't look happy."

Tanya, still seated, said, "They was laughin' at me."

"Oh, they wasn't," Latrisha told her. "They was laughin' *with* you."

"But I weren't laughin'."

Latrisha put an arm around her. "Never you mind . . . they's just jealous 'cause you got on tee vee." She paused, then added, "You gonna get *respect* now around here, you'll see."

A female guard clanged the butt of her nightstick against the steel bars of the rec-room door.

"Fun's over," the woman announced, her voice high and shrill. As the inmates pissed and moaned, the matron singled out Tanya and Latrisha, who were apart from the others. "You two . . . you're on latrine duty in the morning."

Tanya, shuffling back to her cell along with Latrisha, said thoughtfully, "Ya know, I think that Bart guy knew all along I was gonna set that fire."

Latrisha gave her a wide-eyed look. "Girlfriend, that's jus' silly."

Tanya shrugged. "I dunno . . . why else would he have them tiny cameras going?"

Latrisha stopped her with a hand. "Honey, it don't matter . . . 'cause millions of people saw you. You're a TV star now!"

"That's right," Tanya said firmly. "I'm a TV star. I got on TV."

"So it was worth it, girl."

"Yeah, it *was* worth it."

Tanya entered her cell. The bars slammed shut.

She was sure it was worth it.

Anyway, she was pretty sure.

An Invisible Minus Sign

Denise Mina

Moira sipped her last-ever gin and tonic and looked out over the immaculate lawn. This afternoon, before the roads got busy with the school run, she was going to take the car out and drive herself off a bridge.

The state of their lawn wasn't down to her; Mr. Toppy did that. She hardly ever went into the garden. The boys used to play cricket out there in the summer, but now they spent their time masturbating in their rooms, looking at pornography on their computers—she wasn't stupid. Both doors had mysteriously developed locks. When she did get into tidy them, the rooms were ankle-deep in hankies.

The boys had been her life, but they were never home

anymore. When they did meet her, in a hall or the kitchen, both were so disinterested they could hardly see her. She was an empty space. Invisible. An invisible minus sign.

Moira was invisible to herself. She no longer knew if she liked strong cheddar or the boys did, whether France was somewhere she wanted to go to on holiday or David's choice. And she didn't even think she liked the hidden Moira enough to send out a search party.

She sipped again and the bitter tonic pleased her, making her tongue flinch. She wished vaguely that she had some lemon to slice into it. Knowing it was the last drink she would ever have, she had made it indulgently strong, but still she stood over the kitchen sink, the cold metal pleasant in the well of her flattened hand, a chill seeping through her trousers, cooling the silver stretch marks on her stomach. She was over the sink trying not to make a mess. She always ate her lunch there. When she realized what she was doing, the timidity of her life had appalled her. Her eyes brimmed with hot angry tears as she wiped imaginary crumbs from the work top. She never left traces of herself anywhere, no crumbs or mess or dirty cups. Whether dead or alive, she didn't leave a ripple in the world.

The most intense connections in her life had been with people who were looking the other way: crying over her dead mother's body; watching her husband sleeping after the first time they made love, when he was handsome and didn't smell of offices; watching her eldest son in the incubator when he was born, panicked tears dripping onto the thick plastic, the weight of milk in her heavy breasts crushing her heart. Never reciprocated, never witnessed. She might never have been there.

When she realized, she had tried to make her mark. She'd taken on part-time work in a small business but gave up because the other receptionist made everything sticky with food.

She took up exercise, step classes and jazz/tap, but got an injury, a bad ankle, and was told to stop it by the doctor. She folded the pastel tracksuits up, one pink, one blue, and stacked them in the back cupboard in the fug of mothballs, knowing that another desperate attempt to connect was over.

She started a catering company for friends' and neighbors' parties, making quiches as small as a thumbnail, but grew bored. It took fifteen minutes to make each one and the pastry was so delicate that they often broke.

She had an affair, with a man called Brian, desperate fumbles in hotel rooms that left her wishing she had gone shopping instead. She observed him like a scientist: Brian's passion was damp, his erection fragile, his orgasm loud and red-faced. They said good-bye sitting in her car in a county council carpark and he cried. She watched him, feeling nothing, and wondered what was wrong with him and then, later, what was wrong with her.

Moira tried these and a hundred other suburban redemptions, but still no one could see her. She couldn't stop herself dressing discreetly, speaking softly, and never divulging a secret. She listened to Classic FM and knew the names of many flowers. David, her husband, had become so bland to her that she had trouble remembering his age, his job, and recently his name.

And always the endless shuffle of objects from one room to another, the boys' clean clothes taken upstairs, laundry baskets brought downstairs, plates to cupboards, cups to mouths, cleaning, cleaning, an eraser swiping back and forth across all traces of her presence on the planet.

Finishing the gin and tonic, she unthinkingly rinsed out her glass and left it on the draining board. Without stopping to consider it, she picked up a handbag that matched her white rain mac, beige with a white piping trim, and transferred her wallet, keys, and a small packet of tissues. She turned on the alarm and locked the front door carefully behind her.

As she walked around to the driver's seat she brushed two loose leaves off the bonnet, scanning the car for splattered bird droppings to wash off when she got back. Bad for the paintwork.

She'd chosen the road already. It was out of the way, two miles out of town, a small bridge over a deep gully. If the impact against the low stone wall didn't kill her, the fall to the river would. It was a very quiet road. No one would see her or be upset by the mess. She hoped the first thing anyone would notice was the break in the wall or the car on its roof, the wheels spinning slowly and a curl of smoke from the riverbed.

She approached the spot far sooner than she had expected. It was three hundred yards ahead, around this next corner, but she was resolved, glad to be going, looking forward to an eternity of nothing.

She turned the corner, thinking about her wedding, labor pains, a summer party a hundred years ago when she felt popular and beautiful, her father's heart attack, even Brian's red face straining over her like a tortoise doing the toilet. She shut her eyes and spun the wheel.

A piercing scream and she flew forward half a foot, stopped suddenly by the restraining band across her chest. She'd put her seat belt on. Why had she done that? She wanted to die, but it was too late. The air bag burst in front of her, squashing her face and upper body, releasing a nasty smell of plastic.

Noting that the car hadn't fallen any distance, she realized that she was still on the bridge. And there was something else: her throat wasn't raw from screaming. She had no resonance in her nose. She hadn't made any noise as she crashed, just shut her eyes and breathed in. If the scream hadn't come from her, it must have come from someone else.

Moira opened the door. A breath of warm afternoon country air engulfed her, picnic weather. She uncoupled the seat belt and wrestled her way out of the insistent air bag, hanging on to her like a drunk at a party, as she climbed out of the car.

Staggering slightly, finding her feet and knees unsteady, she looked back at the car. It was pressed tight against the stone bridge wall, paintwork scratched on the bonnet but otherwise untarnished. It looked badly parked but nothing more. She stepped back and it was then that she saw it: there was a body underneath the car.

Little-legs navy nylon trousers were topped with sensible red lace-ups, both pressed to the side like the Wicked Witch of the West's. One foot, the left foot, twitched as if to kick her, if only it wasn't so sleepy.

She skirted the car, bunny-dipping down to look underneath. The woman was slim and elderly, had a white perm. The shattered lenses on her glasses obscured her eyes, making it bearable to look at her. In the shade of the car, next to the dead woman's hand, was a small gift-wrapped parcel and a sensible navy handbag, a little scuffed but good leather nonetheless.

Moira knelt down on all fours and looked underneath. The front wheel of the car was planted on the woman's chest, crushing her heart flat. Mora felt past the cheap watch with a leather strap for a pulse, but there was nothing.

She had killed a woman. A nice woman. A woman who gave gifts to people, cared about people. She had been a good girl, too, going about her good-girl business, until Moira crashed into her and parked a car on her heart.

Moira grabbed the gift and the sensible leather handbag out from under the car and scrambled across the road. She ripped purple paper off in a mad burst of energy. A ceramic picture frame, the shop picture of a square-jawed man still in it. A cheap gift, not for a special friend or family member, not unless she was tightfisted.

Light-headed, she unzipped the woman's handbag and found a large brown purse. She unclipped it and found a photo of three sweet children, sitting side by side, smiling for granny. Moira had murdered a grandmother. She stuck her hand in the bag again. Deep inside a side pocket was a packet of cigarettes and a plastic lighter. She ripped the packet open and put a cigarette in her mouth, lighting it. She hadn't smoked since she was at college and had never inhaled before, but now she sucked in the smoke hungrily until she was able to think clearly.

She had killed a woman and then gone into her handbag without permission. She'd stolen. And she was openly smoking a cigarette.

She looked across at the car. She could clearly see the little nylon legs underneath and the jaunty angle of the car resting on the good granny's rib cage. The police would be here soon. Someone would pass the bridge and see what she had done, they'd phone 999, and the police would come and get her.

Moira looked up at the glorious trees around the bridge, heard birds singing in the sunshine, and watched her gray stinking smoke climb into the blue sky and spoil it for everyone else. She'd done it now, though: it was a hell of a big ripple.

She smoked five cigarettes and waited until the sun went down. No one came. Eventually, not knowing what else to do, she got into her car and backed carefully off the body and drove home.

Jason sat down at the kitchen table without greeting her or speaking or acknowledging her presence in any way. He picked up his serviette, shook it, and lay it across his lap. There was a pause during which Moira would usually have slipped the plate under his nose, quizzing him, asking questions about his day and being rebuffed. He touched his knife and fork, letting his hands fall to his lap again, filling the moment.

Neither food nor questions came. He knew she was up at the sink. If he bothered to look at her, he'd see that she was looking at him and her arms were crossed.

His eyes flickered to the cooker, finding it bare, then to the oven, over to the microwave. "No dinner?"

Moira didn't answer. She did what he did when she asked

him questions: shrugged and grunted. Jason frowned at the table and made himself look at his mother. His nose twitched.

"Does it smell of *cigarette smoke* in here?"

Moira shrugged. "Dunno."

He sat up straight. "It does. Has a workman been in today?"

"No." She was leaning against the work top, bad posture, and seemed to have some food spilled on her top, a drip down her front.

"Well, why does it smell of smoke in here?"

He could see the change in her and it startled him. He sat up straight. "Where's the dinner? What's happened here? Why are you wearing a dirty top?"

His voice had cracked five years ago. Last in his class, but it was a whinging high-pitched voice, like his father's when he was younger. "Mum?"

"Jason," drawled his mother, standing up straight, "stop bloody whining, would you?"

It was a crisis. She hadn't done a wash in four days and everyone was running out of underpants. They had plenty, pressed and stored in bottom drawers, but their favorites, the ones they didn't need to look for, were dirty and no one knew how to run the machine.

Moira was sitting on the sofa, the remote tucked under her thigh, ashtray balanced on the arm of the chair, overflowing onto the white linen cover. Empty plates were scattered around the sofa, stacked messily on one another over the floor. They'd had satellite television for four years, but she'd never realized before this week that *Jerry Springer*–type shows were on for ten hours a day. She was starting to recognize episodes.

The living-room door was glass. She could hear them telling the doctor about her. Jason, junior medic, kept saying "head injury" and "personality change." She could tell by the paucity of "uh-huhs" from the doctor that he didn't believe it.

"She doesn't usually smoke," said Gerald, her younger son. His voice was whiny, too.

"We've been married for eighteen years and she's *never* smoked." Definitely an inheritance from their whiny father.

The doctor knocked gingerly on the door and slipped in as though he were approaching a sleeping bear. He pulled the door closed behind him. His were the first eyes she'd met since the bridge. He had little-currant eyes and a fat nose that sprawled across a jaundiced face. His haircut was cheap.

He asked if she was all right and she said she was, she was fine, just going through a bit of a change of lifestyle. What did she mean, he asked, by "lifestyle"? She shrugged and looked back at the television. He married his stepmom but loved his stepsister. They were fat, all of them, and shouted rude words so they had to bleep them out.

"And you've recently taken up smoking?" The doctor smiled weakly. "That's a rather odd habit to take up at your time of life, isn't it?"

Moira looked at her hands, at the cigarette between her fingers, and a torrent of words flooded her mind, happy afternoons with the babies, glimpses of transcendental moments in her life, and small deaths. Everyone she loved looked away as she died. She remembered Brian and catering and meals and lamb, recalled sunshine and sleep and midnight trips to the toilet for a drink of water, memories of screams on bridges and sudden jolting plastic smells.

Swamped, her head reeled back on her neck. They could have been kind to her. They could have asked how she was, what she was doing. *Hello, Mum, having an affair? Hello, dear, killed a lady today?*

She heard him speak through the fog of white noise in her head.

"Moira, Mrs. Appleton? Have you been feeling hot at all? Any unexplained sweating?"

She stood up, eyes fixed on the doctor, lifting the cigarette to her mouth and sucking hard. She wanted to look straight at the living-room door, look through the mottled glass at her sons and husband, but she couldn't turn her neck or make her eyes leave his yellow face. She was not invisible anymore, she took up space and left mess, she hid the remote and had killed a stranger.

Moira opened her mouth wide, tipping her head back to let the jagged, clinging words out of her throat, but when her voice came it was small and strangled.

"I am a ripple."

Purrz, Baby

Vicki Hendricks

When Mary Lou came to the door in a red velvet robe, exactly like mine—except for the size—I knew it was no coincidence. What I'd been suspecting for months was clear. How smart of Jack to save time on Christmas shopping by making one stop at the department store, a robe for his wife and one for his lover! I saw the competition in her eyes as she boldly sized me up, thinking she could snatch him away from me by sheer intelligence, never mind looks. She was only wondering how long it would take. I saw his eyes flick down the front of her robe, which was loosely tied, although there wasn't much to see in there. She must have worn the robe to taunt me, secretly, not figuring that I had one just like it. Of course, mine didn't have embroidered initials. That *ML* stuck in my mind. It was early morning, and we were dropping Purrzie off before we flew out to visit my mother. Jack had suggested that ML, as a cat lover whose elderly pet had just passed away, would take good care of our little sweetheart. After seeing the robe, I wouldn't have entrusted my beloved Purrzie to her, but we barely had time to get to the airport, and Purrz seemed comfortable sniffing around her living room, which was the most important consideration, after all.

I had to wonder what Jack's motivation could be in taking me to this lair. Did he want to get caught? More likely he thought I was too stupid to have a clue. His underestimating my intelligence had been an issue for years, mainly because I didn't read continuously like he did or appreciate the arts. I was proud of my down-to-earth personality, but he just got snootier as the years went by. He'd been spending a lot of time away from home lately, but I wouldn't have figured on a lover if I hadn't seen that robe and the calculating look on ML's face.

Maybe ML had suggested the idea of watching Purrzie so she could check me out. Of course, Jack wouldn't have thought she'd wear the robe. On the way to the airport I mentioned the identical style, and he shrugged as if he was barely listening. His acting was decent when he was desperate.

I forced myself to put all my feelings aside while we were at Mother's. After the trip when we picked Purrzie up, I looked around her place. She had her Ph.D. diploma on the wall and tons of books, Shakespeare plays and novels and poetry I was supposed to read in high school but never had time for because I had to work. She had a lot of female poetry writers that I never heard of—Marilyn Hacker, Elizabeth Bishop, Adrienne Rich, many more. I glanced into the kitchen. Only a toaster on the counter. She was no doubt a feminist who couldn't cook. Women's poetry was her specialty. While ML and Jack were discussing "school business," I scribbled down a few of the poets' names, thinking I might catch up.

Back at home, I'd kept my suspicions to myself for a couple of weeks, when I heard Jack having a quiet phone call. "Who was it, honey?" I asked him.

"Somebody from school about a meeting. Nothing."

I let it go, but my guard was up. I heard him again, with that same tone, two days later. Then one morning he was on the phone before I even got out to the kitchen. I punched *69 on the extension, and checked ML's number on information. I was no fool.

Jack was slathering cream cheese on a bagel when I confronted him.

"Why were you talking to Mary Lou so early?" I asked him.

"What?" He looked up from the newspaper like he was dazed.

"I just did star-sixty-nine on the phone."

"Huh?"

"Six-nine. It redials the last caller."

"Oh. Why'd you do that?"

"I wanted to know who called so early. So answer my question."

"Mary Lou is having trouble with her department head. I was just giving her advice."

"Oh, really?"

"Yes, Georgia. What's your problem?"

Of course, I shouldn't have tipped. He was too fast to get caught like that. However, he wasn't aware that I could hear the change in his voice, the soft tone like he used to use on me, and I kept that to myself.

By afternoon I started to feel bitter. I tried to concentrate on reading e-mail, but it was tough. I slopped a shot of Wild Turkey into my chamomile tea and took a long gulp. Son of a bitch. For fifteen years, I'd cooked, waited on him, and taken care of the home so he could keep his nose buried in print. Now he's sniffing up another woman. In the fall, when ML took the job teaching English literature, he'd mentioned that they had known each other in college. I should have been more alert. I remembered her name from years before. She was a fantasy that never came true. Now was his chance.

I heard Purrzie's toenails trickling down the wood hall floor and called his name. He always came when I called him, unlike Jack. He stopped at the doorway of the office and yawned. This cat was a beauty, streamlined and muscular, a lovable, perfectly marked tabby, and smart as all get out.

"Oh, did I wake my sweetie? Com'ere, sweetie."

He came to me and I petted his back and gave him smooches on the head. He was warm all over, probably just got up from his window ledge. "Oh, precious sweetheart. How's my sweetie?"

He took a leap and settled on my lap. He loved me more than anything else in the world, including food. You couldn't say that about any dog, or dog's best friend.

I started down the spam awaiting my attention, deleting the hundred or so about Viagra, penis enlargement, and the latest assortment of sleazy sexual promotions. *Masturbate to dilated teen rectum movies, Mature lesbians rubbing their vulvas, See me playing with my rectum.* Christ. Rectums? I couldn't really understand the attraction. Nobody would have believed this five years ago, or twenty years ago, when Jack had tried to woo ML.

It was bad luck that she'd turned up now, when adultery seemed minor compared to the popular sexual perversions. ML wasn't gorgeous, but different from me. Neither of us was a spring chicken at forty-five. I was stocky and muscular with a round face and dark hair, while she was a tall blonde, thin and sleepy-eyed, with narrow shoulders and dangling arms that seemed to lack solid bone or muscle, the feminine kind of woman Jack always looked at. ML had a slight edge that gave the impression she was only interested in what life could do for her, and the world could go fuck itself otherwise. I might've enjoyed her attitude if she hadn't been enjoying Jack.

I closed off the e-mail window and started typing up a list of Jack's new behaviors and the times and dates of the calls when he'd walk into another room to talk. I realized that lately, he'd mentioned going on a diet. Damn, that made sense. Bony ML wouldn't like sweaty flab interfering with her breathing, and Jack was smart enough to figure he'd better get rid of some before the newness of the sex wore off. Of course, he hadn't yet managed to cut his food intake. I could probably end their relationship if I just kept cooking his favorites, but it wasn't a sure bet, and could take a while.

Had he started getting haircuts more often? Tweezing the hairs from his nose and ears? I wasn't sure, but in general he was a little more attractive these days. It didn't look good for him.

I made a note to keep track of the crossword puzzles. It occurred to me that I hadn't seen Jack with his pencil poised over the newspaper in weeks—so romantic for the two of them, fact master and wordsmith, the perfect couple.

I had counted the condoms, the stash in his nightstand. I was sure he'd bought a full dozen in the month when I'd forgotten to take my pills, and his sex drive hadn't been that strong. Now there were only three left. He was thrifty enough to finish up the open box rather than buy a separate supply for ML. I hadn't had the sense to check the quantity before I confronted him about the phone calls. Since then the three hadn't been touched. I went back and continued to delete spam. It was comforting to know that if I ever needed sex, *of any kind,* I could find it easily. I'd put dinner in the oven earlier—lasagna, rich with cheese and tomato and béchamel sauce—and it began to send its aroma my way. I'd also gotten in a couple bottles of good Chianti. Italian food was Jack's favorite. I planned to start over that night, convincing him that my suspicions were gone so he'd be off guard. I wanted to catch him for pure shock value and to show him how smart I was, in spite of what he thought. Then maybe we could restart our marriage on more equal ground, him being in the hole he dug with his guilt.

I used to think Jack was cute and funny when he got into a rant, but now I realized that most of the joy he got from our marriage was by emphasizing my stupidity, and more than that, he enjoyed the company of somebody on his own level. I began to resent his intellectual monologues and use of words I didn't know. He was a professor of history, with his endless stories and details about wars and slavery. On a weekly basis, I listened to repeated critiques of Dee Brown's bad writing and poor research in *Creek Mary's Blood*. ML was, no doubt, impressed that Jack knew the facts better than the guys who wrote the books.

I hadn't attended college, but my life had never lacked for it, until now. I had my restaurant and made a much better living than Jack did teaching, but I knew deep down that he was only concerned with facts, how many he knew and how many I didn't. He'd always thrown me crumbs about how our differences made us so good together, but being smarter than me was what puffed him up, besides eating the great food I cooked. I think those were the reasons he was keeping me around, since he'd found ML again.

I tried to pay the phone bill online, but I was so upset I kept misspelling my password. I pictured ML and Jack together in the library at school, fondling each other under the table, her reciting poetry or him explaining how the Indians had eaten six pounds of meat a day in winter because they had no vegetables—Indians as thin as her, he'd say, and poke her in her flat stomach. It would be his dream to have a woman who enjoyed listening to all his factual crap. I poured the empty teacup full of Wild Turkey, chugged it. I wondered if they snickered together about all the things they figured I couldn't understand.

Purrzie stretched and jumped off my lap. I followed him into the kitchen to heat his rotisserie chicken. I shredded it into tiny bits so he wouldn't gobble big pieces and choke. He wasn't piggish by nature, but I wanted to make his life safer and more enjoyable in any way I could.

I looked into the oven. The lasagna was beautiful, but couldn't compete with ML. Besides being an intellectual who shared Jack's tedious book interests, she was the lost love of his life, and now he had a chance to regain his self-esteem. Years before she surfaced, he'd told me they'd once smoked dope and had sex. Now he probably didn't remember telling me, or more likely never realized I would put together the name with the information after so long.

I'd made the salad and was just sliding the bread into the oven when the keys rattled in the door. I reminded myself to keep a lid on conversation about ML.

Jack came in and gave me a big hug and kiss, and I sniffed his mustache and neck for any unfamiliar scents. I wasn't sure. He started to sniff, too, maybe at the Wild Turkey, another thing he was always on my case about.

"Lasagna, your favorite," I said. "Garlic bread on the way."

"Yum. I don't deserve you, Georgia."

"Why not?"

He kissed me quick and headed into the bathroom, his mind already elsewhere.

The Wild Turkey had a kick. I realized I'd better calm down. I wanted to ask him if Mary Lou could cook, although I knew it didn't matter to him anyway. It's one of those things you list when you're judging your pros and cons, but it doesn't weigh a feather against that hot rod of wild passion. I'd been riding the hot rod less and less.

I was pulling the pan of lasagna out of the oven when the phone rang. Jack was still in the bathroom. I shoved the pan on the counter and answered it.

"Is this Mrs. Brown?"

"There is no Mrs. Brown," I said. Telemarketers. Shit.

"Oh, sorry."

I'd been pretty harsh and I could hear apology in her tone. Maybe she thought Mrs. Brown was dead, or else that I wanted to be Mrs. Brown and couldn't get Jack to marry me. The truth was I'd never changed my name. Whatever she thought, she hung up fast—something to remember for future use.

Jack yelled from the bedroom. "Who was that, sweetie?"

"Telemarketing."

"What were they selling?"

"I don't know. They asked for Mrs. Brown and I said there wasn't one."

"Oh?"

"Yeah. She hung up."

"Good job." Jack came strolling out in his jeans and Ivy League shirt, looking his casual academic self, his face a little too happy for a weekday. It could have been because I was pouring the wine, and the lasagna was browned perfectly and bubbling in the center of the table, but I started to think. We'd had a telemarketing call a week earlier, and about an hour later he went to the gym and didn't come home until near midnight, after supposedly meeting friends and having a few beers. I'd fallen for it at the time, but now I realized the call could be a trick, in case I answered the phone, or a signal that ML was waiting for him.

I remembered something else, too. Jack had been keeping his cell phone turned off while we were together. That way he could get back to her at his leisure. Fucking asshole. He thought he had it made because I was such a dope.

I set the garlic bread on the table, sliced out a chunk of lasagna, and put it on Jack's plate. It was oozing cheese and red sauce and he licked his lips. He was so good at this. Getting ready to chow down and enjoy his dinner, then take off for some poetry and wild sex, leaving me with the mess.

He held out his wineglass and toasted me for the nice dinner. It started to gnaw at me, the way he was so cool. I used to admire that in a man, but now I saw the downside. They never flinch, no matter what you do. Teflon personalities. Nothing sticks—until the Teflon gets scratched.

I got involved in my plate as he started up a lecture about slaves. Topics were always swimming around in Jack's head. I nodded and chewed.

"I was reading the other day about cat-hauling."

"Cat-hauling?" The word *cat* caught my attention. "A service to take Purrzie to the vet?"

"No, the slave owners did it before the Civil War as a form of punishment, to make examples of the tough, hard-to-coerce slaves. It's in Charles Ball's slave narrative."

"Were the cats all right?"

"I guess. You might not want to hear about this during dinner."

"As long as the cats were fine."

"The idea was to tie a man down on his stomach, naked, with his arms and legs staked out, drop a big tomcat on his back, and pull it by its tail. The cat clawed and ripped into the skin and muscle, trying for a foothold to get away."

"I can imagine."

"They would do this until the slave was unconscious from the shock. Of course, there were no antibiotics, so the infection was often deadly."

"Holding the cat by the tail. Ooh." I cringed. "Brutal." I looked over at Purrzie on the windowsill, who was licking his paw peacefully. "God, that's horrible."

"Certainly was. Imagine getting ripped to shreds then left to get infected and die."

"The cats were probably scared to death." I took a big slug of my wine to get past the vision of an agonizing cat, screaming and being yanked, not having done anything wrong, not knowing why he was being punished. I shivered. "I didn't know cats were kept as pets back then."

"I don't think they cared for them like we do." He looked at Purrzie still licking himself and shook his head. "Not like His Majesty. Cats were kept to kill mice."

I ignored his cut at Purrzie, but it registered in my brain. He started up about some Civil War battle tactics, where the Union Army made tunnels like mice, but there was no further mention of cats, so I lost interest. When he stopped talking, I smiled. Now I was just waiting to see how long he'd hang around.

"There's ice cream for dessert."

"No thanks. I'm stuffed. I'm going to head over to the gym after I digest this great dinner."

It was an hour and a half between the time of the telemarketing call and the time he left the house. I figured he didn't want to jump up from the table immediately and risk trouble. I thought of telling him I was going along to the gym, but I hadn't worked out in two years and I knew he'd be suspicious. I didn't want to follow and risk getting caught. I was biding my time to figure out a better plan.

He came home late again that night and said the guys wanted to make racquetball and drinks a weekly thing. He had showered, so there wasn't any evidence to sniff. These were guys I hadn't met, so I couldn't call to check anything out. I didn't bother objecting. The jig would soon be up.

The next morning he made love to me, payback for the lasagna, no doubt, so he wouldn't feel guilty. I started to think maybe I was making too big a deal out of all this and I could win him back.

"I was thinking we could take a long weekend and go to Cancún or somewhere to get away from the cold," I said.

"I don't know. I have to keep up with my syllabus."

"Oh, take a day or two! The students will be happy. My treat." I knew ML, being a teacher, couldn't compete when it came to money.

"We practically just got back from Christmas. How can you take more time off from the restaurant?"

"I trust my new manager completely." I studied his face to see if the word *trust* made him flinch, but it didn't.

"I'll think about it. It's true we have Mary Lou to take care of Purrzie now. She still hasn't gotten another cat." He smiled. His whole demeanor brightened up at the thought of ML watching Purrzie. So why didn't the cunt get a new cat? I bet she couldn't wait to have Purrzie to herself again.

He was off to school early. Said he had papers to grade and had forgotten to bring them home. I bet they were meeting for coffee. My stomach started to burn as his car backed down the drive. So that was it. Purrzie was his ace in the hole—working better than what he had in the hole during his younger years. He knew I'd never let Purrz go, but ML didn't. ML knew a one-of-a-kind cat when she saw it, and Jack was a fringe benefit.

I couldn't take it any longer. I wasn't a wimp who could live like that, waiting and hoping. I took another day off at the restaurant so I had time to work out my scheme. I sat down at the computer and looked at my e-mail. All crap. Not a single note from a friend or relative. Nobody I could talk to.

I deleted more rectal spam as I formulated the details to catch Jack and ML. I closed my AOL and used Jack's password to open his account. Sure enough, there was e-mail from mljonson45. What luck! It had to be Mary Lou, and she was on AOL, too.

The mail wasn't anything interesting, just a fast note: *Don't worry. I have a great idea. Will talk to you at school.*

It didn't sound like good news for me. I deleted it. I'd heard about setting up false accounts where the address was one letter off from the real address. If I used a capital *I* instead of a small *l*, and pretended to write from Mary Lou, Jack would never know the difference, and I would receive his reply. I went back to my account and added a new screen name, mIjonson45. Only the computer could tell what letter that line stood for. I was damn smart.

I decided to keep the note to Jack plain and mysterious, since I didn't know their little love names, or what fancy expressions an English professor might use.

Come to my place at 8 pm tonight. I have a secret surprise for you.

I thought about the word *secret*. Was it too much? *Surprise* sounded too ordinary. I wanted him to build up anticipation so when I answered her door, his balls would shrivel into prunes.

I also wanted to be sure ML was home that night or I wouldn't have any way of getting inside. It was complicated. Jack's e-mail address was historybuff1860@aol, which I changed to historybutt1860@aol, and sent the message to ML: *Busy with grading today. I can come to your place tonight at 7:00. Let me know if it's okay.*

The address change was little risky, but it was too cute to resist. If ML thought it was a hoax, she might still be home anyway. At worst, I was wasting my time and would have to try something else.

I knew Jack would check his e-mail a few times from school. I sometimes left him messages there instead of calling. I was a little worried that he might say something to ML, but she was in a different building, and if they thought they had secret plans for later, they'd be unlikely to look for each other. Worst case, he would mention the e-mail and they would figure it was some kind of mistake. It might give them the creeps, but they couldn't trace it to me.

I took the gun from my panty drawer and tucked it into my big purse. My brother had given me the Glock when Jack and I moved to the big city. Jack didn't know I had it. He'd never have let me keep it. My gun in his face would show him I was serious, and teach him a good lesson. He would see how smart I was and never try anything again. I found a roll of duct tape to use on ML. I loved it. A dope like me teaching two professors a lesson.

ML's reply came back to historybutt within the hour: *Okay. I'll be home tonight. See you!* She was already excited, the tart. I checked the other screen name at noon and still nothing. I needed to know whether my plan had worked, so I could beat Jack to her place, surprise ML, and get her out of the way. Finally, at three o'clock Jack's reply was there. It was also brief: *Why so mysterious? See you there.*

I had defrosted homemade minestrone soup and bread from the restaurant for dinner. I wasn't in the mood to cook. Jack came home acting normal, as he was so skilled at doing, and we ate and he talked some facts about the Seminoles' turbans and jewelry. I couldn't really pay much attention. I thought I heard the name Mary Lou, and almost questioned him, but then I realized it was my imagination playing tricks. My mind kept racing over my plan and my feet were in a nervous jitter under the table.

Jack ate two full bowls of soup and I thought he'd never get done. When he finished, I said I had to help out at the restaurant for the evening. Actually, since I hadn't been there for two days, there was plenty I should have been doing. I slugged down some Wild Turkey in a corner of the kitchen and then put Purrz in his carrier. Jack knew Purrzie always sat on my lap while I did book work.

It was six forty-five when I left. I'd be a little late to ML's, but she wouldn't expect Jack exactly at seven. He seemed relieved to see me go, so I knew he was planning to keep his date at eight o'clock.

It was dark when I arrived. I walked to the porch, set the cat carrier down, pulled out the gun, and rang the bell. Footsteps started up immediately and ML opened the door. She gasped. Her face was priceless.

I had the gun pointed at her skimpy chest. "Keep quiet and move backward into the house."

She was good at taking orders. I kept the door open with my foot as I picked up Purrz and stepped inside. I set him on the couch and closed the door behind me.

"We're going to play a little trick on Jack," I said.

She started to disagree, but I poked at her small tit with the Glock and directed her to sit on a chair. She didn't put up a fuss, not that I gave her much chance. I pulled a piece of tape off the roll and slapped it over her mouth. She knew it was her own damn fault for starting up with Jack. I made her tape her own legs and one wrist to a wooden chair so I could continue to hold the gun. I put the gun down, wrapped the last wrist and tightened up the rest, then scooted her into the bedroom and moved Purrzie into the kitchen.

It wasn't long before I heard a car pull up. I got into position behind the door, expecting that Jack had a key, but he rang the bell—as formal as ever. I opened the door. He started sputtering something when he saw my face behind the Glock, but I barked my order, "Not a sound. Get in here or die," and he moved fast. I kept the gun on him and told him to march into the bedroom. He acted like he didn't know where to move, but I mentioned that the gun was loaded, and he backed up till he nearly fell over ML's chair. He looked at her all taped.

"Why are you doing this, Georgia?" he said in a controlled scream.

"You know damned well why!" I yelled back.

"No, I don't. What kind of stupidity is this? Put that gun down. You don't know how to use it."

He couldn't resist bringing up my "stupidity" and that set my head on fire. Any regard for him or my own good burned up with those hateful words. At this point I would have expected him to be begging my forgiveness so I would put the gun down. I couldn't believe he would continue to insult me and play out the lie this far. I was going to get a confession, one way or another.

I pointed the gun toward his chest. "Sit."

He sat on the bed and I tossed him the roll of tape I'd been wearing on my wrist. ML's bed was perfect for the job, kind of old-fashioned like I expected a poetry reader to have. "Lay down and tape your ankles to the bedposts," I said. I glanced back at ML, wondering if the word should have been *lie,* knowing she would catch that kind of error, but she just looked terrified. Jack gave me a look like he was humoring me, but he started unreeling the tape. It was a double bed, so his legs reached okay, but he was slow at taping and the result didn't look too secure. I wouldn't dare let go of the gun to help, so I pointed it at ML's head.

"Hurry up, and tape it right, or your girlfriend's gonna git it." I was starting to enjoy my role.

"Girlfriend? What?" He looked at ML, blank for a second. "She's gay!"

ML started to squeal behind the tape, like she wanted to tear him to pieces for calling her a lesbian.

I had to laugh. "Good try. Keep it up, asshole. What are you doing here, then?"

"I told you I was stopping by."

I could see him searching his head for another lie. His mouth moved, but despite his intelligence, nothing came out of it. Finally, he took a breath. "Look, we can clear this up. Put the gun down so we can talk. This is ridiculous."

"Oh, Mr. Information can't come up with a lie fast enough!" I pointed the gun back at him. "Tape your wrist to the top post."

He followed orders clumsily, and the time he took enraged me more. He was muttering that he didn't deserve any of this and that I was insane, but I ignored him as usual.

"This is nothing compared to what they do on the Internet," I told him. I had him tear off a long piece of tape so I could hold the gun and finish the last wrist. Finally, I set the gun down, slapped a piece of tape over his mouth, double-taped the wrists, and then went back over the ankles.

Now that he was taped up solid, I realized I had wanted him facedown, but there was no way I was about to start over. Faceup might even work better to get a confession. However, it was impossible to get his shirt off like that.

I went into the kitchen to look for scissors and also found a bottle of Cuervo Gold. Two quick shots and I felt adequate to the job. Jack went white as the bedspread when he saw scissors in my hand. The shirt was an ugly striped golf shirt, so I enjoyed cutting straight up the front, watching his chin quiver. I pushed both halves back over his arms to expose his chest. I opened his zipper and slid his pants partially down his thighs and took my time snipping off the Fruit of the Looms. Mostly I wanted to freak him out, not hurt him too much. He wouldn't have the nerve to press charges once his lies were exposed. I looked at ML to see how she liked the look of lover boy's balls right now, but she had her eyes closed tight. She might have thought I was about to cut those balls right off.

I heard yowling from the kitchen and went to get Purrzie. I felt terrible that I'd left him in that carrier so long. I took a second to pour myself another shot. When I stepped back into the bedroom with Purrzie, Jack's eyes popped. He knew what I had planned—we were going to do a little cat-hauling. "See, I remember everything you tell me," I said. "This form of torture comes from so-and-so's slave narrative."

I slugged from the bottle of tequila that I found I'd carried with me and lifted Purrzie from the carrier. Jack was squirming, a frown on his face, and I knew he was itching to name the slave I couldn't remember. No doubt he thought I was drunk, too, and I'd taped him wrong side up in my usual dumb-ass way. "We'll be working on your chest, so you can watch," I told him, to set the record straight.

As mad as I was, I couldn't imagine grabbing Purrzie by

his tail, so I held him under his armpits. "Now we'll see if you have something to confess." I pulled Purrz down Jack's chest noticing the evenly spaced stripes that immediately began to bleed. Jack moaned. Purrz was squirming and sure enough trying to get a grip with all four paws, just like the history book said. I held him a little lower to extend the rows of scratches and realized he'd gotten a foothold into one of Jack's balls. It was an accident. The son of a bitch moaned real loud. Purrzie was yowling even louder in my face, but even as I pulled the claws from Jack's right ball one by one, not a single word of confession came from those lips. I closed my eyes and gritted my teeth in frustration. "I'm listening—whenever you want to start!" I yelled.

Purrzie dug his left front paw into Jack's dick before I could lift him to threaten again, and it took some time to detach each hooked claw without further injury. I didn't want to ruin Jack for life. I had just pulled out the last claw when Purrz broke loose, scrambled up Jack's chest, and leapted to the floor. I watched him dash into the kitchen to hide.

Jack was still quiet, the damn fool. I looked back. "Shit!" The tape was covering Jack's mouth and he couldn't say a word.

He looked to be passed out, so I ripped off the tape and gave him a few slaps. His mouth fell open and some mine-strone fell out.

I gave him a few more slaps. "Wake up, Jack," I said. "Now it's time for your fucking confession." I decided to play it like I'd planned it this way, rather than have him think I'd been too stupid to take off the tape.

In a minute, I realized he wasn't going to wake up. I didn't figure he'd lost that much blood, but he must have choked on those words I wanted to hear. That minestrone had backed up and clogged his windpipe and nose. My cooking had killed him. I felt a black mood come over me.

ML was conscious. I ripped off her tape and stuck the gun in her face to think, but I knew I had to kill her to get away with this.

She started to cry. "Okay," she said. "I'm sorry. I confess everything. Please don't kill me!"

Her confession was meaningless by now. I was in big trouble, and my gun hand fell down by my side. The deed was done. The victory was shallow.

I left her taped there sobbing and coaxed Purrzie out from under the kitchen table. Cat-hauling was better in the telling than in the doing. The facts hadn't given a clear picture. I realized I would miss Jack when the shock wore off, even his stories. I put Purrzie in his carrier and drove home.

The food is lousy in prison and the restroom facilities are primitive, but I've had plenty of time to catch up on my reading. I even found some of ML's women poets in the prison library. Come to find out, they're all lesbians. Thinking back to the look ML gave me, I'm sure she was sizing me up in a different way from what I thought. It's possible I imagined all the evidence.

However, one thing is sure. ML came out on top. She wrote to me that she adopted Purrzie from the animal shelter—at least he has a good home. Despite my mistakes, I feel like the smartest person here at the prison. Being smart just isn't the daily thrill I expected.

The Next Nice Day

S. J. Rozan

Doris opened an eye, looked at the clock, and sighed. Nine-thirty. Bright sun filled the bedroom, the first nice day of spring. Doris was disappointed. She'd hoped not to wake at least until ten, maybe even ten-thirty. She tried going back to sleep, but it was no good. She threw back the blankets and began to dress. *Oh, well,* she told herself. *I can read the paper . . . that'll take an hour . . . and I'll hem the blue dress . . .* She looked bleakly at the sun lying on the lawn.

She made herself breakfast, noticing they were almost out of eggs. Good; she'd go to the supermarket, get something complicated to make for dinner. George would like that. "Honey," he'd say, "you shouldn't have worked so hard. You shouldn't have to spend your day cooking."

And she'd say, "I like to cook. Besides, what else have I got to do all day?"

George would grin and kiss her, flattered that she considered pleasing him more important than anything else she had to do.

But Doris didn't mean she had nothing more important to do. She meant she had nothing else to do at all. Period. Nothing.

Before she married George six months ago, Doris had worked in kitchenware at Wal-Mart, hating every minute. She'd been there eight years, three months, two weeks, and four days, and when she quit, the girls threw her a party and told her they'd miss her. She'd said she'd miss them, too, but she knew she wouldn't and she hadn't, not at all.

But somehow she'd thought marriage would be different from . . . well, from this, anyway. George, who'd first asked her out after she'd sold him a waffle iron, had lots of money and he loved her. And she loved him. But . . . but she had nothing to *do*. At least in the Wal-Mart days it had been a challenge, getting up in the morning and forcing herself back to kitchenware, going without lunch so she could afford to go to the movies, bringing home each measly paycheck like some great trophy marking a hard-won victory.

Now she got up in the morning and the challenge was in filling her days. Sometimes she watched soaps, but that disgusted her, sitting in front of the TV in the middle of the day getting fat on Almond Joys. (Not that George minded the added pounds. "More of you to love," he declared.) She'd have liked to go visiting, but the three other houses on the isolated (the realtor had said "secluded") curve of River Road all belonged to young families with children in school and two working parents. *Those women had something to do all day,* Doris thought resentfully. *They not only had jobs, they had ca-reers.* Maybe when she and George had kids it would be different, but George wanted to wait on that. "Just you and me for a few years, babe," he'd say, nuzzling her neck. It was sweet of him, but what it meant was this: Doris alone in a big empty house, where she ate too many candy bars and took too many naps.

She was drinking her morning coffee when the doorbell rang.

The man at the door grinned as soon as she opened it. His uniform shirt had *Appliance Sales and Service* embroidered above the pocket.

"Oh," Doris said, annoyed at this chunky man for . . . she wasn't sure what, maybe grinning at her. "You're here to fix the washer?"

"Yes, ma'am."

"Come in." Doris led him through the hall and silently pointed out the door to the basement. During the half hour he was down there, she washed the dishes—by hand, it took longer—and read the morning paper. The repairman came upstairs just as she finished the comics.

"I think it's fixed," he said, wiping his hands on a cloth from his pocket, "but if it gives you trouble, call me and I'll put in a new part."

"I thought that's why you were here."

"Nah. For now I just kinda adjusted the old one. I ain't sure it needs it and the company'll charge you a hundred fifty bucks for that part. That's how come I get repeat business around here. Hate for the customer to get screwed, know what I mean?"

He leered at her in a conspiratorial way. *Yes, and I hate for my washer not to work,* Doris thought. Still, she supposed he was trying to do her a favor.

"You got a place I could wash up?" he asked.

"The powder room's right there." He was the sort of man who should shave twice a day, and he hadn't shaved this morning, Doris observed; but he'd been nice about the washer, and he was a living, breathing human being. "Would you like some coffee?" she asked impulsively.

He looked at her and grinned again. "Sure," he said. "Coffee. Sure."

She took cups from the cabinet and poured a quart of milk into a heavy pitcher. He came out from the powder room and smiled as she put the pot from the Mr. Coffee on the table. He waited until she'd set it down and then grabbed her by the waist and kissed her hard on the mouth.

Doris broke away so violently she had to steady herself on the countertop to keep from falling. "What the hell was that?" she screamed. "What do you think you're doing? Get out of here! Get out!"

"Knock it off, lady," he answered. "You invited me to stay."

"What?" Doris couldn't believe it. "I asked you to have some coffee, not to wipe your filthy lips all over me—" She was so angry she couldn't go on.

"Oh, come off it," he said. "If you wanted a cup of coffee you'd go next door. A dame like you don't ask a guy like me to stay for coffee except to, ah, help fill up her morning in a fun sorta way, know what I mean?"

"I know just what you mean," Doris answered, picking

up the milk pitcher, "and if you come one step closer, I'll break this over your head."

"Screw you," he said. He stopped smiling and began to move toward her.

If he touches me I'll swing it at him, Doris thought, but when he reached her she almost didn't. She stood there frozen, watching him finger the buttons on her blouse, but then something snapped and she swung the pitcher fast and hard into his head. The kitchen exploded in fireworks of milk and blood and glass. Then the man was on the floor, and the table was covered with splotches of red and white and pink, and Doris had to run to the powder room and be sick.

Ten minutes later, after great quantities of cold water, Doris felt in control again. The repairman hadn't moved, so she felt his pulse. It was still.

I've killed him, she thought listlessly. *I'd better call someone . . . The police . . .*

She was dialing the number when a thought stopped her, sending a chill up her spine. What was she going to tell the police? That he'd tried to rape her? A fat, boring housewife attacked in her own kitchen in the middle of the day by a well-liked local repairman? And besides, he hadn't tried to rape her, really. He didn't have a weapon and he had all his clothes on and she *had* asked him to stay for coffee and Doris had read about cases like this, where the woman went to jail because the jury wouldn't believe it was really self-defense.

I'll call George, she thought. *He'll tell me what to do.*

But George, law-abiding George, would tell her to call the police. Or worse—what if George didn't believe her? What if George thought—what the repairman had thought?

No. No police, no George. *I,* thought Doris, *I am going to have to deal with this. I am going to have to make it look as though this never happened.* She sat motionless for a long time, stunned by the enormity of it. Then she roused herself suddenly. She looked at the clock. It was just noon. *Oh, God, I wonder if I have time to . . . to what?* Doris thought. *Bury the body—maybe in the yard—clean up the kitchen, take a bath—his van, get rid of his van, abandon it somewhere . . .* And a thought struck her. It struck her with such force that she drew a breath, held it, let it out slowly.

She was busy.

She had something important to do, something that had to be done, and only she could do it. And—and—after George came home, after she was through burying the body, after she got rid of the van and cleaned up the blood, she would still be busy. She would have to make up a story to tell George—an alibi, that's what she needed—and in case anyone knew the repairman had planned to come out here, she'd have to be ready to swear he hadn't. (Here she realized with satisfaction that her neighbors, because they had *careers* and were out all day, wouldn't have seen his van.) Oh, there were so many things to do!

When George came home that evening, with the sun lying in cheerful golden stripes on the lawn, she had beef Stroganoff on the stove and a scotch and soda ready for him. He kissed her. "Well, honey, what did you do all day? I see you've been digging in the garden."

She smiled. "Yes. I was planting zinnias. The weather report says it's going to rain, so I thought I'd get them in before it did."

He smiled, too. "I'm glad you're enjoying the garden. Just

don't work too hard." He sipped his drink. "By the way, honey, I got a call from the roofer. Obviously he can't come in the rain, but he says he'll be out to look at the chimney the next nice day."

"Will he?" Doris turned to him, her smile slowly spreading. "Good," she said. "Oh, good."

He Said . . . She Said

Marcia Muller

Cal Hartley heaved the last of the five-gallon water jugs into the back of his van and slammed the rear doors. Then he coiled the hose onto its holder on the spigot. As he got into the driver's seat he glanced across the parking lot at the White Iron Chamber of Commerce building; only two cars there, both belonging to employees, and no one had seen him filling up, or else they'd have come outside by now, wanting to know where their so-called voluntary donation was. Three bucks well saved.

At the stop sign at the main highway, Cal hesitated. East toward home? West toward town, where he'd earlier run some errands? West. He didn't feel like going home yet. Home was not where the heart was these days.

The Walleye Tavern was dark and cool on this bright, hot August afternoon. Abel Arneson, the owner and sole occupant, stood behind the bar under one of the large stuffed pike that adorned the pine walls, staring up at a Twins game on the TV mounted at the room's far end. When he saw Cal enter, he reached for a remote and turned the sound down.

"What brings you to town, Professor?" he asked. Professor because Cal was a former faculty member of the University of Minnesota, recently moved north from Minneapolis to the outskirts of this small town near the Boundary Waters National Canoe Area.

"Water run. Hardware store. Calls on the cell phone; it doesn't work outside of town." Cal slid onto a stool. In spite of him and Abel being native Minnesotans, their patterns of speech could not have been more different: Cal sounded pure, flat middle America, while Abel spoke with the rounded, vaguely Scandinavian accent of the Iron Range.

Abel, a big man with thinning white hair and thick horn-rimmed glasses, set a bottle of Leinenkugel in front of Cal. "Not so easy, living without running water, huh?"

"Not so bad. The lake makes a good bathtub, and we've got a chemical toilet; all we need the fresh water for is brushing our teeth, cooking, washing dishes."

"And from the hardware store?"

Cal smiled wryly. "Heavy-duty extension cords. I think I told you the power company allowed us to hook into the pole up on the road till we finish with our renovations. Seems like we need more cords every day."

Abel shook his head, looked at his watch, and poured himself a shot of vodka. "I don't envy you, trying to bring back that old, run-down lodge. Thirty-five years abandoned by old lady Mott, just sitting there rotting. Some folks around here say it's cursed."

"Yeah, I've heard that. But I don't believe in curses."

"No?"

"Definitely not. A place is only what you make it. You saw the main building when you came out; it's livable and will be a fine home eventually. We think we can save three of the cabins for when our kids and—someday—grandkids come to visit. The rest we're demolishing."

"By yourselves? Didn't any of those contractors I referred you to get back with estimates?"

"The roofer, and he's done already. The others we only need for the septic system, plumbing, and electrical. They'll be in touch."

"Your wife . . . Maggie, is it?"

"Right."

"She doesn't seem the type for hard labor. Wasn't she some kind of artist in the Twin Cities?"

"Interior designer."

"How does she feel being dragged off to the end of the road here?"

Cal felt his throat tighten up. He took a sip of beer before he said, "She feels just fine. It was her idea, in fact. She found the property."

"Good for her." Abel looked up at the TV, reached for the remote, and turned the volume up slightly.

Good for her. Yeah, right.

You won't say that when I tell you she's trying to kill me.

———

Maggie was painting the floor of the one-room cabin with red enamel when Howie, her black Lab, ran in and stepped on the wet surface.

"Howie!" she yelled, and the dog—perverse creature—began to wag his tail and knocked over the paint can. Maggie stood up, shooed him out the door, and wiped her damp brow with the back of her hand. It must have been ninety-five degrees, and the humidity was trying to match the temperature.

She regarded the mess on the floor, then turned away and went outside. The red paint had seemed a good idea two days ago—it would conceal the poor quality of the wood and the indelible stains from years of a leaking roof, plus lend a cheerful note to a cabin that was perpetually dark because of the overhanging white pines—but now she decided she didn't really like it. Better brown, or even gray, covered in colorful rag rugs from the White Iron Trading Post.

She stood in the shade of the trees and looked down the gradual slope to what had once been the main building of Sunrise Lodge. A long two-story log structure with many-paned windows and a sagging porch, it sat in a clearing halfway between this cabin and the shore of Lost Wolf Lake. Over the thirty-five years that the property had sat abandoned, pines and scrub vegetation had grown up, so only a sliver of blue water was visible from the porch's once-excellent vantage point. In time, the trees would be cleared, but first the lodge and three salvageable cabins must be made habitable. Each structure already had a new roof, but that was it. So much to be done before the long winter set in, both by Cal and herself and local skilled laborers, none of whom seemed prone to speedily working up estimates.

Maggie shook her head and trudged downhill, giving the evil eye to Howie, who was rooting around in a thicket of wild raspberries. She mounted the steps of the lodge, avoiding loose boards, and fetched a beer from the small refrigerator beneath a window in the front room, which she and Cal had claimed as their living quarters. Then she went back outside and followed a rutted track down to the lakeshore, stepping gingerly to avoid the poison ivy that grew in abundance there. A rotted wooden dock tilted over the water; she navigated it as she had the lodge steps and sat down at its end.

Lost Wolf Lake was placid today; on the far side a small motorboat moved slowly, and near the rocky beach to her left a family of mallards floated, undisturbed by human intrusion. Maggie shaded her eyes and scanned the water for the black-and-white loons she'd often spotted in late afternoon, but none were in evidence. The sun sparkled gold against the intense blue. Another day in paradise . . .

Paradise? Who am I kidding? And what the hell *am I doing here?*

Well, she'd found the property, hadn't she? Up on a visit last July to Sigrid Purvis, an old college friend who operated an outfitter's business in White Iron—canoe rentals, sportsmen's gear, guided trips to the Boundary Waters. The talk of the town that month had been about old Janice Mott dying and her estate finally putting Sunrise Lodge on the market. Friends of Sigrid's had pretended interest in buying it, just to get a look at a local legend, so she and Maggie decided to take a tour, too.

A tour that Maggie now regarded as her undoing.

At the time, the property had seemed the ideal solution. To Cal's failure to gain tenure and his growing boredom with his work at the University of Minnesota in Minneapolis, where he was a professor in the English department. To the empty-nest feeling of their spacious home in St. Paul. To the staleness that had fallen upon their marriage. To her having to deal with clients, mostly housewives, who were too uninventive or uninvolved to decorate their own homes.

Some solution. Now she was one of those housewives, who couldn't even decide on what color to paint a beat-up, water-stained floor in a cabin that one of their two boys— both now in graduate school on the West Coast—might use for a week or so every summer.

But she was not only a housewife, Maggie reminded herself. She was a brush clearer. A demolition expert. A stringer of extension cords. A patcher of chinks between logs. A glazier of broken windows. She could prop up sagging structures. Remove debris from clogged crawl spaces. Empty the chemical toilet. Cook on a propane stove and wash dishes in a cold trickle of water from a five-gallon container.

The house part she could deal with just fine. But the wife part . . . That was another story.

She didn't feel like a wife at all anymore. The deterioration of her relationship with Cal had been gradual since they'd arrived here at Lost Wolf Lake in April. At first he'd seemed excited about their new life. Then he'd become remote and moody. And then, after he'd taken a bad fall through the rotted floor of one of the cabins, he'd barely spoken to her. Barely made eye contact with her. Barely touched her.

And when he did . . .

Maggie drained her beer and looked out at the center of the lake, where one of the loons had surfaced and was flapping its wings. So free, so joyous. Resembling nothing in her life. Nothing at all.

Because when Cal speaks to me, or looks into my eyes, or accidentally touches me, there's a coldness.

A coldness that makes me feel as if he wishes I were dead.

The ball game ended—ten to three, Twins—and Abel shut off the TV.

Cal signaled for another Leinie, his third, and the bartender set it in front of him. It was warm in the tavern in spite of the air-conditioning. Cal brushed his thick shock of gray-brown hair off his forehead.

Abel frowned. "Nasty cut you've got there."

Cal fingered it; the spot was scabbed and still tender. "Roof beam fell on me while I was taking down one of the cabins."

"You have it looked at?"

"Not necessary. One of the staples at home is a first-aid kit."

"You must use it a lot." Abel motioned to a burn mark on Cal's right forearm. "Last week it was—what? Twisted ankle? And before that a big shoulder bruise."

"Accidents happen."

"You always been accident-prone?"

"No, but I've never done this much physical labor before. Stuff around the house in St. Paul, that's all."

"Told me you'd built a whole addition yourself."

"Well, yeah. But I was a lot younger and more fit then."

"What are you? Forty-five? Fifty, tops."

"Forty-six."

"And you still look fit. I'd say you're not keeping your mind on the job at hand. Everything okay out there?"

"What d'you mean?"

"Well, a man who's got problems—say, financial or marital—can let his concentration slip."

Cal studied Abel Arneson. The man wasn't a friend, not exactly, but he was the first resident of White Iron who'd welcomed Maggie and him, driving out to the lake with a cooler full of freshly caught walleye and two six-packs. He'd steered them to contractors—who had shown up, promised estimates, and someday might call. He'd arranged for the purchase of a used skiff and ten-horsepower Evinrude outboard motor, which were to be delivered this week; and he'd promised to go out with Cal and show him all the best fishing sites. He was the logical person for a worried man to confide in . . .

Cal said, "To tell the truth, if anything, my concentration's heightened." He paused, sipped beer broodingly. "You see, all these injuries I've had—I don't think they were accidental."

When the motorboat was about a hundred yards away, Maggie recognized it as Sigrid Purvis's. Sigrid waved, cut back on power, and the boat swung toward the dock—a little too fast, bumping its side and making the rotting timbers groan. As Maggie went to help Sigrid secure it, Howie ran down the rutted track from the lodge, barking until he recognized the visitor.

Sigrid stepped out of the boat, grinning up at Maggie from under the bill of her Purvis Outfitters baseball cap. She was a tall, thin woman with a wild mane of blond curls and a weathered face—one made for laughing.

Howie bounded up to her, and she leaned down to pat him, the cap coming loose and nearly falling in the water. Sigrid snatched it up, then reached into the boat and pulled out a plastic sack.

"Blueberries," she said. "My crop's so big I'm getting sick of them."

"Thanks! We could use some fruit; our raspberries're really tiny, and mainly the birds get them."

"Got a beer?"

"Sure. Come on up."

When they were seated on folding chairs on the lodge's sagging porch, Sigrid said, "Things better or worse with Cal?"

"Worse. The coldness and the silences are really getting to me. And I'm getting vibes off him. Bad ones. Almost as if . . ."

"As if?"

"Forget it."

"Mags, this is Sig you're talking to."

". . . As if he wants to kill me."

"Cal?" Sigrid looked shocked. "That's impossible."

"Is it?"

"Of course. Your imagination's in overdrive, is all. Look, you're living on a huge property miles from town. You're both under stress, spending your savings like crazy and trying to get the place in shape before winter sets in. Everything's overgrown, the ruined cabins are creepy, and most of this lodge, except for the front room, is uninhabitable. Cal was depressed at not making tenure to begin with, and now he probably feels this project is more than he can handle. No wonder he's acting weird. And no wonder you're reading all sorts of extreme things into his behavior."

"I wish I could believe that."

"Believe it. It's better than believing he wants to harm you. Or that the place is cursed."

"Cursed?"

"Oh, you know, the local legend. Janice Mott and her husband were having a hard time keeping the lodge going. Old customers dying off, newer ones finding the place too primitive. Then her husband died in a freak accident, and she abandoned the property and moved to that tiny house in town."

"Right. And she never returned here again—or allowed anyone else to set foot on the property. Who would, given that kind of tragedy?"

Sigrid was silent for a moment, squinting through the trees at the sliver of lake. "But why not sell it?" she asked. "Why put up an electrified fence and hire a private guard service to patrol it every day? Why, at fifty-five, retreat to that little house in town and never again have contact with anyone, except for random encounters at the grocery and drug stores?"

"The husband's death made her a little crazy?"

"A whole lot crazy, to live in near poverty, paying out all that money to a guard service, while holding on to a prime property like this. And to let it deteriorate the way she did . . ."

"Maybe I'm beginning to understand her brand of craziness."

Sigrid shook her head. "No, you're not. You've just hit one of those temporary bumps in the road of life. But Janice Mott . . . It makes you wonder if there's something on this property she didn't want anyone to find."

Abel shook his head. "Professor, if what you say is true, you're in big trouble. But why on earth would Maggie want to kill you?"

"Well, there's a substantial life-insurance policy. And our marriage has been pretty much dead for a long time."

"Still, murder . . . Besides, how would she know to rig those accidents?"

"She worked around contractors in the Twin Cities, knows more than the average person about construction. Easy for her to weaken a floor joist or roof beam, or to cause an electrical fire."

"I just don't buy it."

"I didn't want to believe it, either. But as I told you, each time I've found something that indicated the accident was rigged."

"Wouldn't she be able to hide the evidence?"

"Some things you can't hide."

"I don't know, Professor."

Time to go. Cal stood. "Whether you believe it or not, I want you to remember this conversation. If anything happens to me, repeat it to the police."

On his way out of town, Cal adhered to the speed limit. The local law was strict on speeding, stricter yet on drinking and driving. He didn't want to call attention to himself, not that way.

After Sigrid left to motor back across the lake, Maggie decided to begin clearing out one of the bedrooms. Cal had insisted they make outdoor work and the cabins their priority before it grew cold, and reserve interior work on the lodge for the long snowy winter. But under the circumstances, there was no way she could endure even part of those months living in the single front room; the more space she freed up now, the better she'd survive till springtime.

The bedroom she'd chosen was on the first floor, behind the dining room and kitchen—most likely the former owners' living space, as it connected to another room with a stone fireplace. Both spaces were crammed with heavy darkwood furniture, probably dating from the late 1940s. The curtains, the rugs, the upholstery, and the mattress had been ravaged by mice and mildew. In the closet, clothing hung in such tatters that it was unrecognizable. The walls were moldy and water stained, the floorboards buckled.

It's more than I can contend with.

Nonsense. Look what you've contended with already.

She began with the bedroom, heaving the mattress from the bed and dragging it through the kitchen—outdated appliances, restaurant-style crockery on sagging shelves, rusting pots and pans on a rack over the stove—and out a side door. The rag rugs and curtains and what remained of the clothing went next. She'd build a pile and hire a hauler who posted on the bulletin board in the supermarket to take it away.

Inside, she looked over the furniture. The bed frame and springs were good; add a new mattress, and it would be a huge step up from the futon in the front room. The bureau's attached mirror had lost much of its silvering; Maggie looked into it, saw herself reflected patchily. In an odd way, she liked the image; she looked the way she felt.

Other than the mirror, the bureau was a fine old piece, and she was sure mice hadn't been able to penetrate its drawers. She began exploring them. The top one on the right was stuck tight, and it took a few tugs to open it. Inside were a man's possessions: handkerchiefs, a pocket watch, a scattering of miscellaneous cuff links, a ring with a large blue stone, a wallet in its original box, obviously a gift that hadn't been used. The drawer on the left was empty.

The second drawer protruded an inch or so from the ones above and below it. Maggie tugged it open, found a man's clothing: T-shirts, underwear, pajamas. Something thudded at the rear, and she pulled the drawer all the way out and removed it.

A blue cloth-bound book. Ledger of some sort.

She flipped back the cover. Not a ledger, a diary, in a woman's back-slanting hand. Blue ink fading but still readable.

April 2, 1948

> Our first week here at Lost Wolf Lake! It is so beautiful. I can't believe that John and I had the good fortune to buy the lodge. The owners, who built it in 1913, are old and ill, and made us a very good price. There is a large clientele, and all of the rooms are reserved through the coming season. We've left the guest rooms and the cabins as they were—they have been very well kept up—but I've ordered all new furniture for our suite, and delivery has been guaranteed for

tomorrow. I've never kept a diary before now, but from here on out I will, to document our happiness.

Car door slamming below. Cal returning, hours late, with the water and extension cords.

Maggie hesitated only briefly before she shoved the diary back behind the drawer where she'd found it.

"You're limping, Professor. What's the story this time?"

"Bruised foot. I was bringing in some firewood and the pile collapsed on me."

"You been to the hospital?"

"For a bruised foot?"

"Well, I was thinking you ought to be documenting these things that're happening to you. If Maggie *is* responsible—"

"Look, Abel, forget what I told you."

"Thought you wanted me to remember, in case—"

"I shouldn't've said the things I did. Nothing's going on out at the lake, except that I'm clumsy. I was in a bad mood and I'd had a few Leinies before I came in here. I talked out of turn."

"But—"

"Speaking of Leinies, can I get one, please? And then we'll talk about more pleasant stuff, like the streak the Twins're on."

"Maggie, I think there's something you ought to know."

"Sig! I thought I heard your boat. Help me with this armchair, will you? The guy's coming to haul the junk away tomorrow."

"It can wait a minute. We have to talk."

"What's wrong? Cal . . . he's not—?"

"So far as I know Cal's fine—physically. But mentally . . . I was talking with Abel Arneson at the Walleye Tavern last night. Cal's been spending a lot of time in there on his runs to town."

"I suspected as much. But a few beers, so what?"

"Drinking beer isn't all be's been doing. He's been saying some nasty things to Abel. About you."

"What about me?"

"Cal told Abel . . . He told him you're trying to kill him."

"What?"

"He only talked about it once, over a week ago. Said all these injuries he's sustained lately were your doing. The next time he was in, he claimed he'd had too much to drink and 'talked out of turn.' But Abel doesn't believe him."

"My God! Cal's injured himself a lot, yes, but that's because he's clumsy. He's always been clumsy. Does Abel really believe what he said?"

"He doesn't know what to think."

"Do *you* believe it?"

"I believe I may have been wrong before. You should watch your back, Mags. You just may be living with a crazy man."

"I took your advice and went to the hospital this time, Abel. The cut required stitches, and now there's something on record."

"So you've changed your mind about talking."

"Yes . . . Last time I was in, I was feeling a misguided loyalty to Maggie. All those years, our two boys, et cetera. But this last 'accident'—that tore it."

"You've got to look out for yourself."

"From now on, I will."

Maggie took to watching Cal, covertly, through lowered lashes as they worked side by side or sat on the porch in the evenings in the light from the mosquito-repellent candles. His gaze was remote, his expression unreadable. But every now and then she'd catch him watching her with the same guarded look she employed.

After a few days, he began working alone on tearing down one of the uninhabitable cabins, encouraging her to complete her renovations of the owners' suite. Grateful for the respite from his oppressive presence, she replaced floorboards and primed walls and refinished the heavy old furnishings. Occasionally she thought of the diary she'd put back where she'd found it behind the second drawer of the bureau. She intended to read more of it, but the work was grueling and made the time go quickly. She told herself she'd save it for the winter months ahead.

Right before the Labor Day weekend, Sigrid reported that she'd seen Cal and Abel Arneson in intense conversation in the Walleye, and that Abel had later refused to tell her what they'd been discussing.

After that, when Cal went out to work alone on the cabins, Maggie covertly followed him. And just as covertly documented his activities.

———

The roof beam was thick, and even though the wood was brittle, it was taking Cal a long time to saw through it. He couldn't risk using power tools, though. Maggie wasn't to know about this particular project.

The wind blew off the lake and rustled the branches of the nearby pines. He heard the whine of an outboard motor and Howie's excited barking—probably at the flock of mallards that frequented the water off their dock. The dog had followed him down here to this cabin by what Cal had privately christened Poison Ivy Beach, then wandered off. The mallards were in no jeopardy, though; damn dog—Maggie's choice, not his—was a lousy swimmer.

Cal hummed tunelessly as he worked. Tomorrow the cabin would be ready.

Maggie crouched behind a thicket of wild raspberries watching as Cal sawed at the beam of the ramshackle cabin. Its front wall had fallen in, so she had a clear view of him. After a moment she activated the zoom lens of her digital camera and took a picture. Last week she'd photographed him deliberately inflicting an ax wound on his arm that had sent him to the emergency room for five stitches. Now it appeared he intended to fake another accident—that of a major support beam dropping on him.

Why is he doing these things to himself? Why is he blaming them on me, telling Abel Arneson I'm trying to kill him? Sigrid said he hasn't spoken to anyone else, or the police. What does he hope to gain from hurting himself?

Just before he'd sawed through the entire beam, Cal used a pair of long metal wedges to brace the beam in place. Each piece had a thin piece of rope tied to it. Then he climbed down the ladder, moved it to its opposite end, climbed back up, and began sawing again.

Maggie documented the activity.

"You look kind of ragged around the edges, Professor."

"I'm not feeling too well tonight. For days, actually."

"How so?"

"Just tired. Haven't been doing too much work out at the property. To tell you the truth, it just doesn't seem to matter anymore."

"Thinking of throwing in the towel?"

". . . Yes, I am. The Twin Cities are looking pretty good to me right now. I've just about decided to confront Maggie about what she's been doing, move back, and divorce her."

"But you haven't said anything to her yet?"

"No. God knows what she might do if I did. She'll find out from my lawyer. Besides, she's hardly ever around."

"Oh?"

"Every day she disappears into the woods, down by the beach, where the last few cabins are. Says she needs her space. Damned if I know what she's up to."

"If I were you, Professor, I'd follow her the next time. And do it quietly."

Maggie studied the images on the digital camera's screen, one after the other.

Cal sawing one end of the fallen-in cabin's beam; Cal sawing the other; Cal constructing his elaborate system of braces and ropes like trip wires. The braces and ropes themselves, in close-up.

God, I never knew he had such mechanical ability.

He's planning another accident—a big one this time. The kind that will send him to the hospital. And maybe send me to jail.

How did it come to this? He was depressed and acting out against me when he was denied tenure, but the therapy seemed to help.

Until we came here.

My fault, he'd say—

"Maggie!" His voice, coming from one of the cabins by the beach.

She got up, went to the porch railing, and called, "What is it?"

"I need your help down here."

"Be right with you."

She took the camera into the lodge and set it on the counter. Evidence of Cal's mental instability.

What am I going to do with it?

"Maggie!"

"Coming!"

Take the image card to a lawyer? The police? Destroy what's left of our marriage? Destroy Cal? I don't love him anymore, probably haven't for a long time, but those years together and the boys have to count for something, don't they?

"Maggie!" He wasn't distressed, just insistent.

As she descended the slope to the beach, she took deep breaths, told herself to remain calm.

Cal stood on the ladder inside the cabin, holding the end

of the beam that he'd first sawed through yesterday. He was smiling—falsely.

"Sorry to bother you," he said, "but I need you to get up here and hold this for me."

"What?"

"Just climb up and hold it for a minute. You can do that, can't you?"

She pictured the braces and trip wires. Pictured what would happen when everything came tumbling down.

And realized what Cal's plan was. What it had been all along.

The knowledge hit her so hard that her gut wrenched. She fought to control the nausea, said, "Cal, you know I don't like ladders."

"Just for a minute, I promise."

She made her decision and moved toward him.

"Just for a minute?" she asked.

"Not even that long."

"Okay, if you insist—oh my God, look over there!"

She flung her arm out wildly. Cal jerked around. His foot lost purchase on the ladder, and then his hand lost purchase on the beam. He clutched instinctively at one of the ropes.

The dilapidated structure came crashing down, taking the ladder and Cal with it.

Maggie's ears were filled with the roar of falling wood and Cal's one muffled cry. Then everything went silent.

Slowly Maggie approached the cabin. Through the rising dust she could see Cal's prone body. His head was under the beam, and blood leaked around the splintered wood.

Dead. As dead as he planned for me to be.

She fell to her knees on the rocky ground. Leaned forward and retched.

Howie's barking penetrated the silence. After a time Maggie got up shakily, put her hand on his collar, and restrained him from charging at the rubble. She remained where she was, face pressed into the dog's rough coat, until she had the strength to drive to town to notify the police that her husband had had a final, fatal accident.

Five days later, Maggie returned to the lodge for the first time since Cal's body had been taken away by the county coroner's van. Most of the time, until today's inquest, she'd stayed in Sigrid's guest room, unable to sleep, eat, or even communicate her feelings to her old friend. Now it was over.

The verdict had been one of accidental death while attempting to commit a felony. It was the only possible one, given the existence of a large life-insurance policy on Maggie's life, taken out at the time she was a partner in an interior-design firm, as well as the photographs of Cal self-inflicting wounds and rigging the cabin. In his testimony, Abel Arneson had said he had doubts about Cal's stories all along: "The professor was an unstable man. Anybody could see that."

So it was over, and she was alone. As alone as Janice Mott had been after her husband died tragically on the property. Janice had fled to town and lived the life of a recluse, but Maggie didn't see that as an option. She didn't even see returning to the Twin Cities as an option. In fact, she saw no options at all.

Howie was whining at the door. She let him out, sat down on the futon couch that folded out into a bed. Stared around the large room and wondered what to do with her life.

Don't think so cosmically. All you have to decide now is what to do tonight. A walk down to the dock? No, too close to where Cal died. Quiet contemplation on the porch? Not that. A book? Couldn't concentrate. Wait . . . there's Janice Mott's diary.

Maggie retrieved it from the bureau drawer where she'd left it.

Janice Mott had kept to her resolve of documenting John's and her happiness at Lost Wolf Lake to the very last day. But the happiness had not lasted. At first the entries had been full of delight and plans for the future. Then Janice's tone changed subtly, with the discovery that she and John were physically incapable of having the family they'd counted on. It grew downbeat as the lodge's clientele eroded, depressed when she realized he was having an affair with a waitress in town. Paranoid as she began to fear John wanted her out of the way so he could marry the woman. And lonely. Very lonely.

May 8, 1970
> *John is gone so much. When he's not in White Iron with her, he works on the cabins. Getting them ready, he says, for the season. But the guest list is short and most will never be occupied again. For years I've been so wrapped up in him and, in the season, the guests, that I've made no friends. No one to spend time with, no one to confide in.*

May 10, 1970

I heard some sawing at the cabin in the pine grove and went there, wondering what John was doing. He was working on the roof beam, and made it clear he didn't want me there. I don't understand. That roof has always been in fine shape. I wish he would stop this needless work and at least spend some time with me.

May 11, 1970

John spent the whole night in town again—with her, of course. He came back this morning and went out to work without an explanation. I think he is ready to leave me, and I don't know what I'll do then.

He's calling out to me now. He says he wants some help. He spends the night in town with her, and now he wants me to help him!

Under this last entry, there was a space, and then the words, scrawled large, *May God have mercy on his—and my—soul!*

Maggie set the journal down. Rested her head on the back of the futon sofa and closed her eyes.

Same acts, different cabins. History repeating itself? Accidental similarity of events? Or some form of intelligence reaching out from the past? Something in the land itself?

One thing she was sure of: if there ever was a curse, it was gone now.

Her future was now decided.

She was staying.

How to Murder Your Mother-in-Law

Suzann Ledbetter

Annie DeArmond thumbed the button on the garage door's remote control. Thirty, maybe forty-five seconds had elapsed since she'd peeked out a slit in her living room's drapes. The proverbial coast had been clear. *Two minutes,* she thought. *Please, gimme a couple more minutes.*

The opener's chain clacked in its loop; the motor droned like mechanical hiccups. Noxious fumes swirled out, as though displaced by sunlight creeping, then blasting into the jam-packed, one-car garage.

There'd been time—plenty of it—for an immaculate white Cadillac with a monster behind the wheel to materialize in the driveway. Annie didn't trust the reflection in the rearview mirror. Was Maple Heights really as deserted as a working-class neighborhood should be at nine-thirty on a Tuesday? Or was a mirage ever the absence of something you prayed Jesus not to see?

Daring to break the spell, if that's all it was, she shifted to reverse and pressed the remote again. The aging Beemer's front bumper would clear before the door rumbled shut.

Still no Caddy. No daily 8:17 A.M. phone call, either, which Annie couldn't ignore, lest by 8:41 her mother-in-law would bang on the front door, babbling about being afraid the unanswered phone meant something terrible had happened.

From the street, Annie finger-waved and blew a kiss at the red-brick bungalow next door. The front windows' homespun flax curtains hung as creased and droopy as a thrift-store linen suit. Bagworms festooned the evergreens and yellow jackets circled above them. Both thrived on the earth-friendly insecticide Barbara Amos spritzed on the boughs with a recycled glass-cleaner bottle.

About now she was preparing a snack for her three-year-old daughter, Isla, and Annie's son, Tyler. The towheaded epicure said Barb's wheat-germ cookies and soy milk tasted "icky-nassy." They probably did, but drizzle on enough honey and the kid would eat baked gravel.

Aside from their same-age children, Annie and Barb orbited different planets. But her neighbor wouldn't tell Buddha himself that Tyler was there, what time Annie left, where she went, or how long she'd be gone.

"If you ever want to knock off your mother-in-law," Barb said, when Annie had smuggled Tyler through her back door, "no jury in the world would convict you."

She was joking, of course, and it was an old saw, at that.

The woman was such a pacifist, she couldn't snap bagworms off her bushes and roast them in a coffee can, like the guy at the hardware store advised. Barb had just tossed off the remark, as people do to commiserate, coax a smile, or better yet, a chuckle.

Chances were, she assumed Annie's complaints about Thalia were exaggerated. Barb knew the Cadillac commandeered Annie's driveway two or three times a day and cruised past the house at all hours, but "Didn't you say Lars's dad died a few months before you got married? Well, my guess is, Thalia's lonely. Losing her husband, then sort-of her son . . ."

Annie's fingers tightened on the Beemer's steering wheel. "Yeah, and I'll bet Lars DeArmond Senior's first words to Saint Peter were, 'What the hell took you so long?' "

Lonely was your parents and younger brother dying in a freak interstate pileup when you're a freshman in college. Lonely was quitting a dream job rather than take maternity leave because your husband loathed day care and insisted his perfect mother was willing, able, and eager to babysit for free.

"Over my dead body," Annie told him then, and repeated now to the dashboard. "Want to know what lonely is? It's sneaking out of your own freakin' house and taking the truck route through town for a doctor's appointment so the monster-in-law won't spot your car and tail you."

Miracle of miracles, today's getaway had been clean. Except staying off the main drags fostered conspicuousness of a different stripe.

A population migration and subsequent business relocation to Haupberg's south side hadn't been kind to its historic commercial district. Every decade or two, an influx of federal grant money kindled a sort-of municipal CPR to resuscitate what the fifties urban-renewal projects hadn't demolished and paved over. Preservation was a lovely idea, residents agreed, but who had time to drive downtown to shop, when the mall was an exit-ramp away?

The plywood-clad storefronts and warehouses Annie passed seemed more ominous than desolate. So did the human derelicts staring from doorways and weedy lots strewn with garbage and God knew what else.

Zagging around potholes, jouncing over railroad tracks, she regretted the false economy of buying regular tires, not run-flats. Focused on a traffic signal several blocks ahead, she wished something heavy metal and anarchist—Led Zeppelin, or Slayer—would kick up on her mental jukebox to drown out *Sesame Street*'s singsongy, *One of these things is not like the others; one of these things doesn't belong.*

The roads less traveled and leaving early to compensate for a long-cut put her at the Medical Arts Center with lots of time to spare. She hurried across the parking lot, eager to speed-read waiting-room copies of *Metropolitan Home, Vanity Fair, Town & Country,* and *Time.* The "Sexiest Man Alive" issue of *People* she'd seen on the supermarket rack would be snuck into the exam room to distract her from the strip down to a paper gown and gynecological body-cavity search.

Magazine subscriptions were slashed from their postnuptial budget when the two-can-live-as-cheaply-as-one adage became the world's third biggest lie. Particularly for her and Lars, who'd literally bought into the Y generation's "live for today, pay the minimum balance due, tomorrow."

All she'd had to show for four years of busting her chops

at an ad agency were two closetsful of clothes, some excellent furniture, thousands of accrued airline miles, a brushed chrome Jura Capresso machine, the loan on the BMW, and nine platinum credit cards.

Lars's financial situation was similar, excluding the wardrobe, furniture, and cool kitchenware. And on his debit side was forty-some grand in student loans.

In a panic, Annie demanded they live on his salary and devote hers to digging out of the money pit. They'd rented the cheap, crappy house in Maple Heights, frozen one emergency credit card in a former orange juice carton, closed the others, and pared expenditures to bare essentials.

Within months of rededicating her income to saving for a house, the baby boy who would be Tyler John DeArmond, not Lars Prescott DeArmond the Third, became the oral contraceptive's tenth-of-one-percenter.

Now entering the medical center's windowless lobby, Annie was temporarily blinded by the eclipse from sunlight to the windowless gloom. A shiver slithered from nape to belt line. The interior's meat-locker chill had less to do with the thermostat setting as the blouse glued in the swale between her shoulder blades.

It brought to mind Tyler's cute little bubble butt wreathed in the toilet paper her mother-in-law slipcovered the seat with, whenever he needed to "do a number two."

Fine for public restrooms, Annie allowed, though studies showed doorknobs were germier than the commodes and catching an STD from a toilet seat was an old wives' tale. But Thalia didn't layer just public facilities with yards of commercial-grade-one ply before her grandson ascended the throne.

"She damn near gift wraps *our* toilet," Annie fumed at her husband. "But hers? Uh-uhhh. Tyler goes bare-ass commando at *her* house."

"He's her first grandchild," Lars said, in that be-reasonable tone Annie had come to despise. "You can't blame Mom for being overly cautious."

Men were from Mars. Women were from Venus. Lars sometimes acted like he was from Pluto. And levelheaded, fiercely independent orphan Annie McGruder fell for him before the cop called to the scene of their fender bender finished writing Lars a ticket for following too close.

Kismet, their friends called it, ignoring the fact that Lars was an insurance agent's nightmare: an entry-level engineer prone to build castles in the air and neglect to register the significance of mundane objects, such as stop signs and glowing taillights.

"Aw, give the guy a break," she muttered, twisting the doorknob to Dr. Blaine's office. There'd been strides. He hadn't caved anybody's bumper since Tyler was born. Most days, his socks matched his slacks and each other. He wasn't exceptionally ambitious, but worked hard and without complaint. Bit by scrounged bit, their savings account was growing again. If an alien abduction could be arranged for his mother, life would almost be lemonade.

In the meantime, she thought, get the Pap smear over with, otherwise known as the annual gynecological extortion paid for pharmaceutical birth control. Then splurge and take the only man you've ever loved to lunch.

Come to think of it, wasn't Tuesday buy-one-boiled-shrimp-basket-get-one-free day at the Crab Shack? If they ordered ice water instead of sodas, they could stuff themselves for under ten bucks.

Special-schmecial. Live a little. By default, the kitschy seafood joint was the only restaurant in town that had stayed exclusively and sentimentally theirs. One whiff of crab boil and Thalia broke out in hives and clutched at her throat, wheezing and gasping for air. Poor dear.

A definite cheerful lilt inflected Annie's voice as she gave her name to Wilma, Dr. Blaine's receptionist. A fat-barreled highlighter rambled well down the appointment schedule before it fluoresced *Ann DeArmond*.

Glancing at her desk clock, Wilma said, "You might oughta check your watch, hon. Seems it's running a mite fast." Disinclined to reveal her magazine addiction, Annie said, "I used to fly standby a lot." Wilma's blank expression prompted, "You know, get your name on the list for an earlier flight, then if a passenger is late . . ."

Business-class road warrior evidently wasn't part of Wilma's work history. Annie motioned *fuhgeddaboutit* and headed for the longer leg of the L-shaped room.

An unspoken physicians'- and dental-office-waiting-room protocol clustered most patients in chairs the farthest distance from the corridor leading to the treatment rooms. Nurses weren't fond of tracking down and flushing out their quarries, but the arrangement was a boon to Annie. Periodicals in what she dubbed the Ix-nay Zone were always current, undog-eared, and nobody'd ripped out an article's last page to pocket a coupon for a quarter off a tub of margarine or a roll of paper towels.

Rounding the corner, she halted, then rocked backward,

like a mime simulating a collision with a utility pole. On the vinyl-cushioned settee abutting a lamp table crouched Thalia DeArmond, perusing the eye-candy issue of *People* Annie had mental dibbies on.

Her mother-in-law wasn't one of Dr. Blaine's patients—the primary reason Annie was. Because Lars told Thalia everything, Annie hadn't mentioned her appointment, or noted it on the calendar magnetically attached to the refrigerator. The old witch couldn't have followed her and beat her to the waiting room, unless she'd traded her car for a way-back machine.

"What are you doing here? Better question—how'd you know I was going to be here?"

Thalia's lipless mouth bowed into a smile. "I told you yesterday, Wilma had called to remind you of your appointment while you were out in the yard with my grandson."

"No, you didn't—"

"Since you didn't ask me to babysit, I presumed you were bringing him with you." She crossed her arms at her chest. "Lars agreed, little boys have no business in an examination room with their mothers. I promised I'd come and keep Tyler company out here."

Leaning sideward to peer around Annie, she inquired, "He is with you, isn't he?"

Before Annie could respond, Thalia jolted upright and shrieked, "Oh my Lord, Annie. You didn't leave the baby locked in the car, did you?" implying "again," loud and clear enough to be heard at the Quick-Shop a half block away.

Trembling, pulse throbbing in her temples, Annie felt a reddish skim veiling her eyes—it was pale where the cone of light projected upward from the lampshade, but a deep, almost scarlet hue washed the mauve wallpaper, the magazine rack, and her mother-in-law's bottle-black hair and smug, triumphant leer.

No jury in the world would convict you. No jury in the world would convict you . . . The litany pounding in sync with Annie's heartbeat had a strange, hypnotic quality—calming, and gradually congealing into an icy, viscous hatred.

"Tyler is not in the car. Please, don't take my word for it. Go see for yourself, then get in yours and go home."

For the benefit of the gawkers watching from the room's far end, the angles and planes of Thalia's face melted into a whipped-puppy expression. "Why are you always so mean to me? I was only trying to help."

A blond lab tech whose name Annie couldn't have mustered had it been tattooed on her brow shouldered open the door to the office's inner sanctum. "Oh—hi, Mrs. DeArmond. Wilma told me you were early. Good thing. The doc wants a urine sample and some blood work done, before the exam."

Casting a glare at Thalia, Annie followed the tech, waiting for the pneumatic door to reclose, turning a corner into a narrower hallway before asking, "Is there a back way out of here?"

Rachel, Annie remembered belatedly, chuckled and said, "I'm a wiz at drawing blood. Scout's honor, you'll barely feel the needle."

"I meant for after I'm finished with Dr. Blaine. Is there another exit, so I don't have to walk through the waiting room?"

"Sure." Rachel pointed a purple envelope file at a door marked AUTHORIZED PERSONNEL ONLY. "It locks from the inside, though. Forget something, and you'll have to hoof it all the way around the complex to the main entrance."

Forget. Forgive and forget. Forgive us our trespasses, as we forgive those who trespass against us. Annie envisioned a laminated sign her younger brother had bought at a gift shop in Yellowstone National Park and taped to his bedroom door: NO TRESPASSERS. VIOLATORS WILL BE BEATEN, SHOT, STABBED, AND LEFT FOR BUZZARD BAIT.

Nice sentiment, Annie thought, *but one peck at Thalia, the ultimate trespasser, and the birds'd york all over themselves.*

An hour later, she was slumped over in her car, crying into a wad of Burger King napkins, feeling like her head would explode, like she was about to throw up, like she was being persecuted for an unpardonable sin she didn't remember committing.

"What are the odds of my birth control failing twice in three years?" she'd raged at Dr. Blaine. "Less than being struck by lightning is what you said after Tyler was born."

The gynecologist shook her head. "I think you misheard me, Mrs. DeArmond. Ninety-nine-point-nine percent effective isn't quite the same—"

"Ninety-nine, a hundred, ten *thousand* percent—the numbers don't matter. Not if my mother-in-law switched them with something else. And that's exactly what she did—no freakin' doubt about it. Why else would she be here, camped out in the waiting room?"

Pushing off from the exam table, Annie paced the room, her feet bare, the flimsy paper gown swishing around her knees. "For all I know, she did it three years ago. The old bitch was obsessed with having a grandchild. Except all the horror stories about day care she told Lars backfired, when I quit my job instead of letting her babysit Tyler like she'd planned."

Dr. Blaine said nothing, her gaze lowering to the file open on her lap.

"Hey, I don't expect you to believe me. I'm the crazy one, right? Totally bat shit, with a major Hansel and Gretel fixation. It's just coincidence that both times we started saving for a house, the money ends up paying the maternity deductible on our health insurance."

Reliving the scene she'd made set off a fresh wave of tears. Maybe she was crazy to accuse Thalia of tampering with her birth-control pills. Maybe, like Dr. Blaine suggested, the antibiotic the dentist had given her after a wisdom-tooth extraction had inhibited the oral contraceptive's plasma level—whatever the hell that meant.

During those three or four agonizing days, she might not have taken the Pill as usual at the consistent stroke of 8 A.M. Not with her jaw so swollen, she had to borrow Tyler's sippy cup to drink her morning coffee.

It would also have been the perfect opportunity for Thalia to pull a switcheroo. Grogged out on Vicodin, Annie wouldn't have noticed if the tablets in the dispenser had Scooby-Doo's face stamped on them.

She blew her nose into the now-soggy napkins, sighed, and let her head loll against the Beemer's leather rest. Dr. Blaine's verdict hadn't been a complete surprise. Insisting everything's fine. That you aren't a machine, or you are, thus minor malfunctions are givens, and that a deal made with God is a deal, not wishful thinking with religious overtones that don't always achieve the desired result.

Instead of the curse friends suffered every month, Annie's periods seldom escalated above a mild epithet. With the right attitude, spotting can be construed as the real thing, only less, probably because bikini season was on the horizon and she'd stepped up the exercise, the fresh vegetables and fruits, the water intake.

She was healthy, well-nourished, buff, and pregnant. And no way could they afford two kids on one paycheck. Before long, Mommy would be the frantic woman who raced out the door every morning and shuffled home exhausted around dinnertime. Tyler whining, "But Gammaw said I could" or "Gammaw does it this way, Mommy," would become a constant irritant, not just a frequent one.

Mommy. Annie's palm slid up from her thigh and caressed her belly. Still as flat as a jillion postpartum sit-ups could make it, yet something swelled inside, and she'd swear she smelled baby powder and lotion and that wondrous, indescribable scent of a newborn asleep in her arms.

Funny, in the manner her dad described as "hmm, not ha-ha." Who'd have guessed Ms. Hotshot ad exec would suddenly go marshmallowy at the thought of another baby to love and cuddle and sing lullabies to?

"Don't worry, kid," she whispered. "Your mom's a pretty smart chick, if she doesn't say so herself. I'll think of something."

She didn't take Lars to the Crab Shack for lunch. Not with her eyes buggy and bloodshot from crying. The dude at McDonald's drive-thru couldn't have cared less had she sprouted horns and fangs.

Besides, minutes after she got home, when Lars rushed through the front door in full wild-man furl, he already knew about the baby. Thalia had laid the groundwork for the announcement with her bogus concern about Tyler's potential front-row peek at a pelvic exam.

"She had to tell me," Lars said. "While she was waiting around at Blaine's office to apologize for the misunderstanding about Tyler, she overheard a couple of nurses talking about how upset you were. Mom asked the lady at the desk if she could go to the exam room—you know, for moral support. They told her you'd already stormed out the back door.

"Mom looked everywhere for you, then came to my office, thinking that's where you must have gone." Gathering Annie in his arms, he buried his face in her hair. "If you'd seen her—Christ, I was terrified the doctor said you had cancer or something. Mom didn't have any choice but to tell me about the baby. Then when you didn't answer the phone . . . I mean, she didn't come right out and say it, but from what she'd overheard, she was afraid you might—"

"Might what?" Annie pushed him away. "Haul ass to the nearest abortion clinic?" Her laugh melded bitter with manic. "Encores aren't usually her style."

"Oh, for—c'mon, Ann. Where do you come up with this stuff? If you were half as upset as those nurses said you were, you had as much business driving anywhere as my boss does after the company Christmas party."

Bullshit. His mother had mastered the art of verbal alchemy. From allegedly waiting to apologize to the soap opera at Lars's office, Thalia had stirred an ounce of truth into a cauldron of lies and pulled out a twenty-four-karat-gold halo for herself. Again.

"I'm warning you, missy," she'd said, when Annie found out she was pregnant with Tyler. "I read in the *Enquirer* about career women that get in the family way, then claim they had a miscarriage. If anything happens to my grandchild, I'll see to it that Lars divorces you so fast you won't know what hit you."

To his credit, when Annie told him, Lars went ballistic. He confronted his mother, who dissolved into tears. She never said any such thing. Couldn't imagine why Annie would tell such a bold-faced lie. The *Enquirer* article she'd referred to offered cost-conscious tips on transforming business attire into maternity wear, not abortion.

The poor guy is a human Ping-Pong ball, Annie thought, *and we're the paddles.* She felt sorry for him. Sorrier for him than herself, actually, when anger relented to reason. Lars didn't buy everything his mother sold, wholesale. But she was his mother and Annie was his wife and he was the demilitarized zone between North and South Korea.

Now cradling her face in his hands, he grinned, said he adored her, and began to sing hideously off-key that sappy Paul Anka song "You're Having My Baby."

Laughing, Annie stretched up on her toes and curled her arms around his neck. "And you, Mr. Tall, Dark, and Studly, are havin' a vasectomy before me and your baby come home from the hospital."

Spring passed into summer with little outward change, aside from Annie's circumference. Or so it seemed; her mother-in-law as yet unaware that the novice had exceeded the master's grasp of appearances' deceptive qualities.

That "something" Annie promised the baby she'd think

of never materialized. Her old boss at the ad agency sympathized, but said telecommuting smacked of the Three Musketeers: one for all and all for one equaled the entire office staff opting for bathrobes over business casual.

Myriad home-based income opportunities were researched on her semiantique laptop. The old-chestnut envelope-stuffing scams were still alive and well. Or she could DOUBLE HER INCOME peddling cosmetics, baskets, interior decorating, naughty lingerie, and toys for discerning adults. Which was true, as zero times two equals zero.

Mrs. Fields and Famous Amos had cornered the homemade cookie market eons ago; eBay auctions required inventory and inventory required seed money and square footage for storage. And her brain was hardwired to invent advertising slogans, not gadgets she could patent, then hawk for $19.95 (plus S&H) on infomercials.

Opportunity knocked by accident, not design. While she was scouring a borrowed Sunday newspaper's real-estate classifieds, her attention drifted from houses for rent to homes offered for sale.

The copy's slew of misspellings, typos, and bizarre phrasing included *walkin closets, a stunning vault with a loft room overlooking,* and a *quiet view of a pond*—as opposed to what? she wondered. One with an airport runway between the windows and the water?

On a lark, she crafted tongue-in-cheek e-mails to the respective listing agents to ask how, for example, a *scruplelessly manured lawn* was maintained and whether livestock was involved.

One respondent blamed the newspaper's "proofreeder."

Another threatened to lodge a spam complaint with Annie's ISP. Three inquired how much she'd charge to compose and copyedit their ads.

Before week's end, the stable of clients expanded to eleven agents, two mom-and-pop agencies, and she was writing the local board's bimonthly newsletter. Rich, she wasn't getting, but the beauty of freelance was in its multiplication factor.

All the work was done by e-mail, billing included. Payments for services were electronically deposited in an online account, leaving no paper trail for Thalia to sniff out.

And boy, was she sniffing. Sensing Annie was "up to something," but unable to figure out what, was driving Thalia nuts. Plying Tyler with ice cream, then interrogating him like Gammaw Good Cop/Bad Cop tipped her to the hours Annie spent at the computer.

Her drop-ins increased; Annie added locks to the doors to which only she had keys. Then Thalia logged when and for how long the phone line was busy and accused Annie of having a virtual extramarital affair.

Had Lars told his mother to get a life, another hobby, or psychiatric help, Annie would have told him the truth.

He didn't, so a half-truth sufficed. "For your information, I'm trying to find a bigger house we can freakin' afford that doesn't have freakin' burglar bars on all the freakin' windows."

Right on cue, Thalia poked in her beak, waving brochures about a new subdivision catering to first-time home buyers with Mason jars full of pocket change for a down payment.

"Been there, tried that, not interested," Annie said, abrim with newfound, albeit depressing real estate savvy. "They bundle the closing costs and down payment into a high-interest loan, wrapped in a lower-interest loan."

Thalia's eyes swept the rooms perfect for one, cozy for two, and claustrophobic for three. "Since you have the answers to everything, where is this baby going to sleep? In the bathtub?"

"Don't be ridiculous," Annie shot back. "It'll take months for the kid to outgrow the kitchen sink."

"Think you're funny, do you? Well, I wouldn't put it past you. You can't handle one child, much less two."

"My problem, not yours."

"No, it isn't just your problem. My son and grandchildren don't have to live like this and you don't, either. I've told you, I can loan—"

"And I've told you, I'll live in a cardboard box before I borrow a nickel from you. Get this straight, Thalia. Crummy as this house is, it's my turf. Every teensy inch of it. You can lie, connive, manipulate, interfere, criticize, whatever, till you're blue in the face, but if you think I'm stupid enough to let you own a square of the shingles over my head, you've got another think coming."

Whether by virtue of Annie's parting advice, or the speed by which Thalia took her leave, the door didn't bang the old bat in the ass on her way out. Nor did she darken it, surveil it, call Annie, or tail her anywhere.

Thalia's previous record for pouting represented the happiest seventeen days of Annie's life. Now, at the nineteen-day mark, the dread peculiar to Floridians monitoring a hurricane's progress had Annie edgy.

Hostilities would resume. Gammaw couldn't stand being away from Tyler much longer. Annie deliberated saying yes to his pleas to call her. Except giving in was the same as a declared truce and usually the losing side of battle's idea. "Let's let Gammaw call you, sweetheart. Okay?"

Lars remained oblivious to the feud, in part due to a bid proposal he was working overtime to complete. Salaried employees don't earn time-plus, but Annie scored a hundred-dollar coup when real-estate agent Roberta Pendergast sent an e-mailed SOS.

Roberta had photos of a new listing for Sunday's newspaper spread, but was showing properties to a "live one." Could Annie tour the house and submit the copy before deadline?

As she saw dollar signs for another service she could provide her customers, Annie's enthusiasm evaporated as hers and Tyler's footsteps echoed in the fifty-year-old, renovated four-bedroom rancher.

The original hardwoods had been restored throughout, their patina richer than new flooring could ever be. Two-and-three-quarter bathrooms. Gas-fired, wood-burning fireplaces in the living and family rooms. Granite kitchen counters, stainless-steel appliances, a utility room, and a bonus room off the kitchen that would make a fantastic home office.

"Lookit, Mommy." Tyler pointed through the family room's French doors at a cedar jungle gym surrounded by a humongous sandbox. Bouncing up and down, he beamed at her, as though Santa had come early this year. "That's mine, right?"

Incapable of telling him it was destined to be another little boy's, or girl's, Annie just shook her head and said, "Time to go home, son."

Composing the ad felt like doing color commentary on the Oscars from an alley blocks away. Annie copied the finished product to Roberta, along with the jokey aside about the house being one she'd kill to own, if she could get away with it, and if the owner reduced the price several zeroes, please let her know.

A simmering amalgamation of self-pity and envy short-ened Annie's temper and mocked her penny-ante entrepre-neurship. She tried, but couldn't shake it. Her mood swung from not giving a rat's ass when Tyler spilled milk all over the coffee table to obsessive housecleaning, until aches in her pelvis sharpened and branched downward to the backs of her knees.

In the twilight lull before sleep, she decorated and redeco-rated her dream house, painted accent walls, rearranged fur-niture, cooked tandoori chicken or tortellini with prosciutto, and watched Tyler from the window building real sand cas-tles to billet his army men . . . then jerked awake, hair plas-tered to her cheek, the nightmares of the house burning to the ground so vivid, she tasted ashes and wood smoke.

Roberta Pendergast's bonus was transferred from the on-line account to Annie's debit card. Every dollar was spent on Lotto tickets. The clerk at the convenience store smacked his lips and said, "Man, I ain't never seen nobody buy that many scratchers and not win back a buck 'r ten."

One day at breakfast, Lars said, "Been kind of down, lately, haven't you. Like with Tyler, the 'will this kid ever get here?' stage is setting in." He patted her arm. "I'll call Mom to sit with Tyler Wednesday night and take you out for a steak dinner and a movie."

His breaking the silence checkmated Thalia, but Annie sighed and gestured indifference. "Thanks, but let's wait till this weekend. Or maybe some night next week."

"Whoa, time out, sports fans. For once, in fact, for the

very first time ever, it's Mrs. DeArmond who's forgotten what day her wedding anniversary falls on."

And he insisted on celebrating it, even with a surly, stone-faced wife in a god-awful rayon maternity dress and swollen feet jammed into a pair of scuffed loafers.

"Take me home and I'll give bubbly and charming my best shot," she said, when Lars pulled over the car and took a silk scarf from the console. "I mean, really. Strangling your pregnant wife is so 2002."

"Humor me. I want your anniversary present to be a surprise."

Truth be told, riding blindfolded, listening for clues like a shrewd kidnap victim on *Without a Trace* was kind of neat, until the baby went ninja. Vicarious sensory deprivation, Annie presumed. She was about to push up the scarf, when the car veered right, *whumped* over something, and stopped.

Lars helped her out and wrapped a guiding arm around her. Scraping her shoes, she deduced that she was walking on concrete. Eat your heart out, Sherlock Holmes.

Step up. Scrape, scrape. Step up. Scrape. A clack, a fraction higher step, then . . . a slick surface, but not wet, or greasy. Smooth. And familiar orangey scent. Orange Glo? That's what she'd clean with for a baby shower disguised as a wedding-anniversary celebration.

Any second now, voices would chorus "Surprise" and the baby would go "Hee-*yah*" and karate-chop her bladder.

Lars fumbled with the knot in the scarf. He kissed her neck and murmured, "Happy anniversary, darlin'."

Eyelids fluttering, squinting against the light, a dizzy, sinking sensation staggered her, her heels skidding on the refinished hardwood floor.

Recessed halogen lights. Pristine white woodwork, trim and crown molding. Terrazzo marble fireplace surround. A giant, red satin bow stuck to the mantel. "You . . . *bastard,*" caromed off the pale sage walls. "Is this your idea of a *joke?*"

"No, no, listen to me." Lars caught her shoulders, turned her around. "It's ours. Or will be, in a couple of days." Grinning and nodding, as though transcending a language barrier, he went on: "I know, I know, you've been mooning about this place for days and I probably shouldn't have gotten cutesy with the blindfold, but I . . ."

His voice fading to white noise, Annie thought back to Roberta Pendergast's e-mail. To the drive over here that day, on guard, as usual, for a glimpse of Thalia's car. Telling her, *If you think I'm stupid enough to let you own a square of the shingles over my head, you've got another think coming.* Tyler's chubby fingertip squashed on the glass, pointing at the play yard. *That's mine, right?*

She raked back her hair, wadding fistfuls, her nails digging into her scalp. Thalia set her up. Laid a trap so devious, she'd not only fallen for it, she'd helped her spring it.

Roberta's agency represented that no-down-payment subdivision Thalia had been all excited about. After Annie smarted off, sent the old bitch packing, Thalia had hired Roberta to find a house Annie'd sell her soul to have. It was only natural for Roberta to mention Ann DeArmond, the freelance ad copywriter. When she did, Thalia must have thought she'd won the lottery.

One e-mail, a hundred bucks for bait, and wham. Annie was hooked and didn't even know it.

No jury in the world would convict you . . .

Her arms dropped to her sides. Tears rimming her eyes,

she looked at Lars, mystified why God had chosen to take her mother away and leave his to torture her.

"Thalia reeled you in first, though, didn't she. Like she always does."

"Honey, please, why are you crying? I thought you'd be thrilled. Thought you loved this house—"

"You knew all along that Thalia and I weren't speaking. That day you said you were taking Tyler to the park to play on the swings. You came here, didn't you, but Thalia couldn't, for fear Tyler would tell me he'd seen Gammaw. He didn't say anything about the house when he and I walked through. All he remembered was the jungle gym in the yard."

Lars clapped a hand behind his neck, pacing in a circle, cursing under his breath. "It was a secret, dammit. Like that one-woman ad agency you made Mom promise not to tell me about."

She did, of course, telling him how sorry she was about accusing Annie of online adultery and how proud she was of Annie's ingenuity. Her success was evident in their savings-account balance, which Annie realized had been enriched by Thalia's clandestine deposits. Not enough, though, for the down payment on the dream house Thalia later admitted she'd tricked Annie into touring.

Lars explained how Thalia had convinced him that a real-estate investment wasn't a loan, Thalia sold her patio home to another of Roberta's clients to provide the rest of the down payment. Freed of her own mortgage payment, Thalia would rent the room off the kitchen to offset their care for Tyler and the baby while Annie ran her Internet gold mine from a spare bedroom upstairs.

"Look, sweetheart, I know this is a lot to spring on you all at once, and maybe Mom butted in when she shouldn't have, but think how great it'll be for Tyler and the baby. And especially for *you*. As of nine o'clock Friday at the closing, you're gonna have it all. Everything you've always wanted. A beautiful house, a career, and you'll still be a stay-at-home mom."

All that night, while he and Tyler slept, Annie sat silhouetted in the glow of the computer terminal, desperately searching for a loophole to crawl through. File for divorce? Inform the mortgage company that her husband had forged her name on the sales contract? (Couldn't spoil the surprise.) Refuse to sign the paperwork at closing?

At this late date, if Annie did anything to kibosh the deal, the remodeling contractor/owner would sue them for breach of contract. Legally, the box Thalia had put her in was escape-proof.

After Lars left for work Friday morning, Annie took down a black maternity suit from the closet rod, eyed it, then returned it in favor of navy slacks, her favorite paisley top, and an off-white blazer.

In the bathroom, applying her makeup, she almost dispensed with the mascara. Without it, her lashes were invisible. What the hell. The brand she used was waterproof.

"Don't you look nice," Barb said, when Annie arrived with Tyler in tow.

"Thanks." Annie smiled the brave smile of a good soldier. "I shouldn't be gone over an hour, or so."

"Take your time. No problem." Barb winced, stepped out on the stoop, and hugged her. "It's a big house, Annie. If

Thalia stays at her end and you at the other—sure, that's a lot to hope for, but things have a way of working out better than we expected, sometimes."

"I know. Believe me, I'm trying my best to think positive. For Tyler's and the baby's sake."

"Atta girl."

Driving across town, not once did Annie look in the rearview or side mirrors. She entered the title company's office at eight forty-eight, precisely nine minutes after she waved back to Tyler, standing beside Barb in the doorway.

Lars strode into the conference room just after Annie had declined a foam cup of coffee and taken a seat at the table. Then came Roberta Pendergast and Brian Bowen, the dream house's owner.

Introductions were exchanged. The closing agent's name was either Nat or Pat. Small talk ensued as a tray with the coffee carafe, cups, and accoutrements went around. In answer to Nat or Pat's question, Annie said the baby was due in January. No, they didn't know its gender. Tyler wanted a boy to play with. She and Lars didn't care, as long as it was healthy.

Lars fidgeted, spun around in his chair, checked his watch against the wall clock. "I wonder what's keeping my mother. She's never late. Usually, she's way early."

"Maybe she forgot," Bowen said, obviously annoyed by the delay.

"I wouldn't miss it for the world," Thalia had chirped, at last night's bygones-be-bygones family dinner. "I can't tell you how happy I'll be to present that cashier's check for my share of our . . . investment."

Later, in the kitchen when Annie was rinsing the dishes,

she'd sneered. "Starting tomorrow, you're nothing but a squatter in *my* house, missy. And don't think for a minute I'll ever let you forget it."

Now the others seated around the conference table reached a consensus that traffic was to blame for Thalia's tardiness. Where do people learn to drive these days? From a correspondence course?

Annie nodded, gnawing her lip, unable to take her eyes off the door. Any second, Thalia could waltz in, gushing apologies and excuses.

Lars snagged Annie's hand, their skin equally cold and damp. Roberta reported that the machine had picked up her call to Thalia's house. Lars confirmed that no, his mother didn't have a cell phone.

The baby stretched and turned in utero somersaults. Annie flinched, sat up straighter, aware her escalating heart rate was the cause. Free hand splayed, the heel braced on the table edge, she studied the fingernails she'd clipped to their quicks yesterday afternoon. Not very attractive, all blunt and unpolished, but they'd grow back again in a few weeks.

Citric acid from the lemons she'd scrubbed her fingers with, then her hands, advancing up her arms to her elbows, like a surgeon prepping for a appendectomy, had inflamed the cuticles and left her skin paper dry.

Lars hadn't noticed. Neither did anyone else, that day.

Not the EMTs or the patrol officer responding to the 911 call Lars placed from Thalia's kitchen phone. Nor did the police detective who fingerprinted her and Lars. Routine procedure, he said. Just a formality.

The medical examiner's attention was riveted on the deceased sprawled on the breakfast nook's floor. By law, an autopsy would be performed, but the M.E. was all but certain Thalia DeArmond had died of anaphylactic shock. The medical history Lars provided, her distended throat, and the hives welting her skin were indicative of it.

The probable culprits were the dead yellow jackets found in a potted fern on a knickknack shelf and the Oriental-patterned area rug under the table. It appeared the wasps attacked while Thalia was reading the newspaper and drinking her morning coffee—lightened with her customary dollop of milk and three heaping spoonfuls of artificial sweetener.

"If your mother hadn't been on a beta blocker for her high blood pressure," the M.E. told Lars, "the allergic reaction to the wasp venom probably wouldn't have been as severe. The medicine suppresses the body's natural defense mechanism."

"Then it's my fault," Lars said. "She must've asked me a hundred times to mend that hole in the patio door's screen."

"Sorry for your loss, but there's no sense at all in blaming yourself. Accidents happen. That's all there is to it. From what I see here, that's all this was, Mr. DeArmond. Just a tragic accident."

The wasps duly sealed in an evidence bag, their cause of death assumed to be natural and recent. There was no reason to suspect they'd expired yesterday afternoon from a pesticide sprayed on Barb Amos's shrubbery. It was simplicity personified planting their stiff, harmless corpses here and there after dinner while Thalia, Lars, and Tyler were glued to a cartoon video on TV.

Given the circumstances, it wouldn't occur to the detectives to analyze the leftovers from the meal Thalia prepared herself last night, much less the sugar bowl on the breakfast table, half-full of artificial sweetener. Both were laced with oven-dried, pulverized bits of clam meat. Mixing the powder into the food had apparently diminished its effect. The amount stirred into her coffee was proportionately much higher.

Absent evidence of foul play, there was no probable cause to confiscate Annie's computer. A thorough examination of the hard drive might reveal electronic footprints from a Google search date-stamped in the wee hours of the morning after the younger DeArmonds' wedding anniversary.

Astonishing, how much information it yielded about beta-blockers, anaphylactic shock, anaphylaxis, and their causes, including an allergic reaction to shellfish and bee and yellow-jacket stings.

Soon, after the postponed closing was rescheduled, Annie would truly have it all and all to herself. The husband she'd loved from the moment they'd met, their little boy, his new baby brother, or sister, a beautiful house, and a home-based business headquartered in that tailor-made bonus room off the kitchen.

And no jury in the world would convict her.

Vanquishing the Infidel

Eileen Dreyer

I only heard the good parts secondhand. The parts that made my mother a legend in our neighborhood. I was part of the story, though. I was the catalyst. I'm the one who always gets to tell the story, especially on the anniversary of her death, when we're pulling out all her best stories like curled-up black-and-whites in a photo album.

I'm the one who measures with a yardstick of words and the memories of a six-year-old how deadly my mother was.

Deadly is such a relative word. Now that I'm in my sixteenth year as a trauma nurse, of course, I've seen the very worst that word can mean. Violence against man, woman, child, and beast. Self-destructive tendencies that can suck the light from a room like a psychic black hole. Idiocy and avarice and plain, bone-deep laziness that fail to prevent disaster.

And if I hadn't seen it in the halls, I sure see it on CNN. So I know what deadly is.

But you have to understand that back then my life was much smaller, much more intimate. My world was the size of my neighborhood, the great lessons taught in the voices of my parents, Sister Mary Alice, and, if I happened to be good and got to stay up late, Jack Buck on KMOX when the Cardinals played. So it makes perfect sense that deadly came in a five-foot-one-inch package on a soft spring morning, and that the story ended up becoming legend, not just in my family, but in the neighborhood, the city where I grew up, the parish.

It was just that kind of story.

My mother was just that kind of woman.

In fact, she was such a force in our lives that when we buried her a meager twenty-five years later, her funeral looked more like a movie premiere, with people spilling out of the doors and trying their best to hear the sermon from the street. Toasts were drunk on three continents, Khoury-league softball fields went dark for a day, and more than one bishop was heard to tell this story to whoever would listen.

To put everything into perspective, let me tell you a bit about our lives back then. We were nothing special. We were, in fact, small people. Not in size, although a good case can be made for that, too. We were simply not important in the greater scheme of things. No kingmakers or lawbreakers or trendsetters, not even anything more interesting than the odd horse thief lurking among the branches of the family

tree. Yes, we made a certain splash within our own neighborhood, even before the incident, but not really beyond its
bounds. There was simply nothing that set us apart from
any other family on the block.

We lived in a blue-collar neighborhood that was neatly
tucked into St. Louis County, where everybody seemed to
know everybody else, and everybody else's mother would
report back to your mother if you misbehaved anywhere
within the city perimeter. Where we actually did play kick
the can as dusk settled in the trees, and fireflies and black-
and-white TVs flickered in the sultry summer evenings.
Where arguments and laughter drifted out the open windows that let the tepid breezes in.

We were a block of working fathers and stay-at-home
moms, although nobody knew the term then. The women
were a sorority, more often than not found sitting on one of
the front porches sharing a beer as they waited for their kids
to finally give up on their games before bath time forced
everybody inside. They shared recipes and frustrations and
childen, until we all obeyed whichever voice barked out a
command and wandered into neighboring homes with im-
punity. Especially if that mother was a better cook than
ours . . . which, considering the fact that she was Irish, was
a good bet.

As for us, we were ten people living in a two-bedroom
house with no air-conditioning and one bathroom. Seven
kids, one grandfather, two parents, and a dog. It was *Leave It
to Beaver* meets EST.

God, how my father hates it when I say that.

"It sounds like we're white trash," he always complains.
"I had a good job."

"We still lived in a two-bedroom house," I have to remind him. "It was an oversize dollhouse. We were crammed inside like clowns in a Volkswagen."

That house was so small that I had to literally crawl under the yellow Formica kitchen table to get to my seat. Not that I minded. I sat in front of the window and got all the breezes.

But, in truth, he was right. He had a good job. In fact, he had the only college degree on the block. He was a CPA who could have played minor-league baseball or been a big-band singer. He chose responsibility instead, and gifted it to my mother along with her engagement ring after the war ended.

My mother lost her engagement ring that same night. She held on to the responsibility and her beloved husband until the day she died. He still holds her, deep, where we can only briefly glimpse the chasm that is his loss.

But in spite of his good job, we never had any money. We all attended the best Catholic schools in the city instead.

"You must do very well," people would say to him when they heard about his business.

"Not really," he'd answer very equably. "But the Jesuits are very happy."

So, really, were we. I know fifty-eight ways to extend hamburger, and as God is my witness, if I ever have to eat Jell-O again, I will commit violence, but we laughed a lot, and I don't remember any want gone unmet except for brand-new store-bought clothes. My mother sewed, and my aunt offered hand-me-downs, so that it wasn't until my junior year of high school before I got my first real new dress—a bright red and blue paisley suit with the shortest skirt I've ever worn. I have nothing but anecdotal proof, but I swear you can't look nearly as sexy in a hand-me-down as you do in a store-bought dress.

Oh, and just once, I wished I could have seen *The Wizard of Oz* on a color TV. I was thirty before I found out the Wicked Witch was green. Okay, I'd heard she was green, but good God, she was *green*.

Still, considering the need I've seen since I've stepped out into the real world, I think we did okay. Which is why it hit me so hard the day I first walked onto that ER hallway at nineteen. I had never met people like that. I had no concept of what it meant to know that someone could batter a helpless woman or try to slash their way into oblivion. I couldn't comprehend that those people who looked and acted so much like me could bear such a load of trauma and pain without it showing like jagged glass and barbed wire.

We, none of us, have anything hidden. To this day, no one is in rehab, no one on parole, no one in disgrace—well, except for my one brother who keeps forgetting that we always get together for the Labor Day barbecue so we can pick names for Christmas. But then, I think he forgets so the rest of us have something to talk about until the Christmas presents are exchanged and we can complain.

In fact, we're so unnatural that just a few years ago, long after we all reached adulthood, we earned a tag that we're trying to turn into a coat of arms.

There we were on vacation at the cottage my cousins have always let us use on the beach of Lake Michigan, all thirty-six of us ranging from forty to two, now crammed into two cabins with two bathrooms. Old habits just die hard, I guess. We're also less tolerant than the Volkswagen years. We last for exactly one week together before we reach critical mass and everybody has to go home before we kill one another. And then we talk about it the rest of the year (with time out for the aforementioned ranting about my forgetful brother).

Anyway, one morning there we were, every one of the thirty-six of us playing football down on the sand with all the requisite noise and mayhem, when this woman comes teetering toward us on heeled sandals, a Bloody Mary in her hands and her optimistically platinum-blond wig a bit askew.

"Hey!" she yelled, even slurring that, one magenta fingernail shaking in our general direction. "You . . . you be quiet! I . . . I'm sleeping!"

To which we politely responded, "Get off our beach."

Well, something to that effect.

Politely.

She blinked a couple of times, so that we couldn't miss the lovely garage-door blue of her eyelids, and then she did. Leave. Just turned around, teetering so precariously for such a long moment that at least eight of us started a pool on how soon the laws of gravity would win out, and then she quite simply minced back the way she'd come.

You'd think we would have talked about that for a while, but she got no more than a few shrugs before the football once again went aloft (never let it be said that we let problems prey on us). And to be frank, we thought no more of it until later that afternoon as we celebrated happy hour by mixing mostaccioli for dinner and drinks for the cooks, a sacred tradition in the family, especially in Michigan.

And suddenly there she was again, pounding on the

screen door and listing to the left. She had another Bloody Mary in her hand and a different wig—red this time. It still listed at the same angle as its owner. She didn't even wait for us to get the door open before she started up.

"I hope you don't . . . ah, mind," she managed, clutching that Bloody Mary like a microphone. "I need to a . . . a . . . apolo . . . gize."

"Oh, don't worry," my brother said, trying to quickly usher her back out. "We understand."

But she held her ground. "No. No, you don't. I was . . . I was *rude* to you all . . . today. But you . . . you see, I, uh, I just didn't know how to take you people. You see, I've never met a *functional* family before."

So we've dubbed ourselves the Last Functional Family in America.

And at the helm, that deadly mother of mine.

A tiny Irish nurse with a passion for baseball, a critical lack of patience for fools, and a passion for children. Of course, anybody who knew her would be hard-pressed to remember she was tiny. She had a big personality. Expansive and welcoming. Big ideas and a bigger heart.

Every relative ended up in our kitchen at one time or another. Every friend one of her kids had was welcome in her house at any time. Every pet they owned usually ended up in our washroom being mended. After all, my mom was the neighborhood nurse. And on our block that meant attending every living creature.

She almost treated a Clydesdale once. As in the Anheuser-Busch Clydesdales. Our neighbor was one of the first drivers. A massive man with hands like hams, he was even more gentle than his animals. Until they misbehaved, anyway.

One kicked him in the head as he was shoeing her. So he clocked her, just like in *Blazing Saddles*. He came to show my mother the hoofprint on his forehead. She almost left him right there to make sure the horse was all right. (She was. He assured us that at her size, his fist had been a negligible irritant.)

And when my mother ran out of kids and pets to spoil, she adopted priests. We had at least one over to dinner every week, usually the brand-new guys, who hadn't even broken in their collars yet. And if not them, relatives, friends, parishioners, and sundry workpeople. Mom lived by the rule that there was always room for one more.

There wasn't, really. At least not unless the priest wanted to crawl under the table to get to his seat. But somehow we all squeezed in. Because Mom said so.

She was notorious, but not in the way that should equate with a story connected with violent acts. In fact, the only times my mom heard from the police were when her dog— the legendary Gizmo—was caught on the wrong side of the fence after siring yet another litter of puppies (I think half the puppies within a twelve-block radius bore a startling resemblance to my dog) and on St. Patrick's Day.

Every St. Patrick's Day.

My mother wasn't just Irish. She was über-Irish. John Ford and Maureen O'Hara Irish. The kind of Irish who yearned to go home, and placed the blame for any and all indignities suffered by Ireland in the last millennium squarely where it belonged. On British shoulders.

My siblings and I were raised in St. Louis, a southern city with a large, active Jewish population. My parents were scrupulous about raising us without prejudice. Except for one. The words *British* or *English* were never said in our house without the adjectives *damn, goddamn,* or *stupid goddamn.* And lest you think this was because my mother actually remembered the auld sod, whence she came, don't get emotional. Our family's been here for at least a hundred fifty years. The only sod my mother has seen was on *The Quiet Man.*

My mother used up every Irish name in the States to christen her children. (And yes. The girls were named Mary. I hate that. The only people who still call me Mary are old nuns and the U.S. government.) She sang weepy Irish tunes in an off-key voice about going home. (She had a magnificently bad voice, but she always said, "God gave me this voice. He can just darn well listen to it." Which meant that she also delighted in throwing everybody else off key at mass every week.) She wept at "Kathleen Mavourneen" and considered John Kennedy a saint.

But St. Patrick's Day was the pinnacle of her Irishopathy. The High Holy Day, we call it, and still gather to raise a toast in her honor. On that day, as far back as I can remember, my mother and our cross-the-street neighbor Pa Quinn would hold a competition to see who could celebrate better.

It began with paper shamrocks in the trees. Then kelly-green bunting across the porches. Life-size cutouts of the patron saint himself on the front lawn, with rubber snakes at his feet. Green Christmas lights strung over every bush in the yard and cars decorated with carnations we crafted out of Kleenex and dyed green with Easter-egg dye.

And then came the pièce de résistance.

Sound systems.

Four-speaker, blow-your-hair-back, woofer-and-tweeter

specials the likes of which I swear could outdecibel an AC/DC concert.

Mom was the first to rent one, from the man who provided the music for the school picnic and Boy Scout jamborees. Pa got a bigger one from the VFW. Then the two of them would crank up the volume and blare John McCormick back and forth as if they were trying to drive Prince Philip screaming out into the street. There was just nothing like "McNamara's Band" at ear-bleed volume to get you out of bed for school in the morning.

The person who actually did come out into the street was Pa's son-in-law Roger, an unabashed German, who for the occasion dressed in all black with a black bowler (an orange band around it), who would march up and down the street holding a shotgun over his shoulder in silent and smiling protest.

The neighborhood reveled in the nonsense. Except for one person.

At the end of the block, we had a war bride, Millie Parsons. As you can imagine, she and my mom spent 364 days of the year in wary truce. After all, their children played together. They had to get by each other on the street and at church. But on the seventeenth of March, the gloves came off. The minute that sound system crackled on at seven-thirty in the morning (early enough so my mom's children could hear it on the way to school), Millie called the police and filed a complaint about noise abatement.

And so every year, at precisely 10 A.M., my mother called the Immigration Bureau and reported Millie Parsons as an illegal alien.

But other than that small aberration, my mom was pretty

much the pacifist. After all, she'd grown up in another Irish family populated by boys, in which fists were the favored method of problem solving. And, truth be told, the Irish have a weensy bit of a reputation for brawling. The donnybrook was named after an Irishman, after all.

But it was my mother's firm policy that she wouldn't put anyone on the list—and there is nothing more dreaded than an Irish list—until she'd given them three good and honest chances to piss her off. (Okay, she never said "piss her off." It didn't take a lot to translate, though.)

After all, maybe the mother of the bully in my brother's class had had a headache when she yelled at *my* mother for the turmoil her own son had caused. Maybe she had a miserable husband (she had). Maybe it was just one of those days.

Three good and honest chances. After that, if you continued to misbehave—if, say, you were rude to my grandfather, or refused to do the job you were being paid to do, or kept my mother in line too long with screaming children while you talked to your spouse/boyfriend/girlfriend/psychic on the phone, *then* you were on the list. And from that moment on, you were shunned like an unfaithful Amish farmer. And if you know anything about Irish lists, you know that once you're on the list, there isn't any getting off without a papal dispensation. In fact, the old joke goes, "Do you know what Irish Alzheimer's is? All you remember is the grudge."

That's pretty accurate.

So I always thought it was a rare thing that Mom was so very patient and understanding. That on the whole she tried to de-escalate situations rather than escalate them. She did, in fact, try her best to stretch those three tries out as long as she could.

There was only one exception to the rule. One reason to miss those last two chances altogether and head straight for jail, without passing Go.

If you hurt one of her children.

Which is how this story started in the first place.

My mother was tiny. She was bright and smiling and funny. But if you so much as made one of her children cry, then ducking wouldn't be low enough to hide. Three strikes were two strikes too many. You were damned faster than a heretic at an Opus Dei meeting.

You might be beginning to get the idea of how my mother was deadly.

So now that you know about her, I'll tell you my part in the infamous story. The Day Dodie Vanquished the Infidel.

It starts with school. We attended St. Mary Magdalen School about a mile from our house. Uphill all the way. In all weather. (It never hurts to remind my children of that.) We didn't have a second car until I was in high school, and our school couldn't afford buses. So we walked. Then we rode bikes.

It seems to me now that we were a bit too conscious of our travails in getting to school in those days. On the way, there was a fruit market, a shambling old wooden shack with two hanging scales and crates crammed with peaches and corn in the summer, pumpkins in the fall, and bags of salt in the winter.

It was the scales that interested us. I remember making it a point to weigh our book bags so we could later tell our children how abused we had been by being forced to carry such a load ALL THE WAY up to school and back every day. I can't remember now, for the life of me, what those book bags weighed. I just remember the sense of self-righteous in-dignation at the final tally as we tipped those bags into the tray.

The fruit market was about halfway to school, along one of two major thoroughfares in the area. It was a road we had to ride along every morning and afternoon. It wasn't safe by any means, but heck, that was just the way it was then. We didn't have to cross the street, after all.

We would leave our short, dead-end block at precisely seven-thirty every morning, and turn onto Lewis, a steep neighborhood street that emptied out onto Manchester. It was the street we rolled pumpkins down after Halloween to see them smash against passing cars.

Lewis dead-ended onto Manchester, where we would take a right and continue the other eight-tenths of a mile to school. Uphill. (My childhood memory demands I remind you. Again.) At the right-hand corner sat a service station. I think it was Shell. It was not well cared for. I remember that the asphalt was cratered and hilly and the windows were dirty.

Directly across Manchester sat Eberhardt's Tavern. It was a low-key kind of tavern, a family meeting place that held picnics in the back in the summer and passed beer out the back door to good customers on Sundays when the blue laws were in effect. They had the best lunch menu, which drew neighboring businessmen, and a TV for Friday-Night Fights, which drew the locals.

Fellow parishioners ran the place, a family with about a dozen kids who went to school with us. So we knew them well. Heck, we knew everybody in that school well. It was that kind of town.

But back to the service station and the busy road.

Because it was so dangerous to empty out from a fast hill onto a busy road, my mother told us to cut through the service station to gain the sidewalk up to school. This was especially important once we were allowed to ride bikes, which happened when I was in first grade.

I was quite the big girl. My bike was blue. I remember that, and the fact that I was jealous of the bar across my brother's bike. It was cooler than a girl's bike.

But I rode it to school every morning. Still at seven-thirty. There was never a question of being on time. We had mass at eight and doughnuts at eight-thirty. And no one. No. One. Was late to mass at that school. That was because our school was run by Dominican nuns.

Now, the important thing you have to know about the Dominican nuns is that the last fun thing they had to do was the Inquisition. So they gave them small children to teach. Needless to say, they were the only entity on earth that frightened me more than my mother. After all, my mother was merely a wiz with a pancake turner. It makes a hard, stinging slap on bare skin without leaving a mark. My mother went to that after she was going to smack my brother once in the butt with a hairbrush for mouthing off. My brother turned at the wrong moment. He got a black eye. My mother went to confession five times. Then she changed over to the pancake turner. Believe me. It was just as effective.

Yeah, my mom had a pancake turner. But Sister Mary Elizabeth had a spanking machine.

We never actually saw it, but the school was housed in an old, dark, cavernous brick building with high ceilings, peeling tile floors and a stage on the top floor that seemed to

yawn like a necromancer's cave, behind which was the re-
puted spanking machine.

Nobody misbehaved in Sister Mary Elizabeth's school.

So you can imagine that there was nothing short of nuclear attack that would keep us from getting to school on
time.

Such was the situation that spring morning. I know it was
spring, because we'd been cutting across that service-station
lot all school year. And all school year, the manager, a thin, fret-
ful man with lanky hair and greasy hands, would yell at us.

He hated it when we rode across his lot. He said it scared
away business. Personally, I thought it was the bumpy lot and
the dirty windows that did that. He said that we were trespassing. My brother asked where we should go, the street?

But we never really paid much attention to him. After all,
what was he going to do to three kids who were just riding
to school?

There were three of us around that time. Three of us in
school, anyway. There were at least two back at home. I can
be sure of that, because there was always a baby in that
house. So there was one then.

But it was time for school, and we weren't going to miss
it, even if the man at the station called us names I'd only
heard my dad call an umpire at a Cardinals game once. So
we coasted down the last half block of Lewis, focused on the
speed and the descent and the need to balance the book bag
on our handlebars when we swept right toward school.

My brother Larry was in the lead. That was because he
was oldest. Then Tom, who was actually younger than I
was, but would never keep his place. I also thought at the
time that that extra bar gave the boys some kind of unfair

advantage, like a retro rocket or something. I was just trying to keep up on my blue bike that was actually too big—like everything else I got as a child, it came with the promise "she'll grow into it."

I'd gotten around the corner, missing the rush-hour traffic on the street, and had just called to my brothers to wait, when suddenly that lank little man jumped out from behind one of the gas pumps screaming like an Indian.

Then he pushed me off my bike.

The bike went one way. I went another. I remember the shock of hitting that warming asphalt, the thunking noise of me hitting the ground. I scraped my knees and both of my palms. My books scattered everywhere.

"That'll teach you!" he shrieked, pointing his finger at me, much as that drunk woman would do years later. Except his nails were the color of grease. "I *told* you not to ride across my lot!" I think that for a long time I just lay there, sprawled like a frog on a driveway, my knees full of gravel and my sparrow chest heaving with the effort not to cry.

I failed. I cried. I sobbed. My brothers came back for me. They yelled at the man, who yelled back. They helped me lift my bike and get it going back in the right direction. They helped me get going.

To school, of course. If you're not certain why, when we were that close to home, we just didn't turn around, may I refer you back to the section on Dominican nuns. I was gasping for air and stinging like I'd taken the pancake turner, but I was *not* going to be late for mass.

I have to admit that Sister Mary Elizabeth surprised me. I always remember her as a tall nun, but, heck, at six, everything was tall. She had a white habit with a black veil that always seemed to be in motion. And she had great, clacking rosary beads hanging from her belt that warned you a block away retribution was coming.

That morning, she took one look at me and gathered me right into those nun arms.

She smelled much nicer than I thought she would. Starch and roses, I think. She patted me on the back and made cooing noises, and ushered me right up to her office to wash off my knees and be interrogated.

It's one of the reasons police don't really scare me. After getting hauled up three flights of dark stairs and behind that black, echoey stage and then grilled by that old nun, you'd have to pull out an iron maiden and thumbscrews to scare me.

She took me right back there, back behind the lurking shadows, the endless echoing of her hard-soled shoes against the hardwood floor. She sat me down, and then she sat in front of me.

"Mary Eileen?" (You expected her to call me something else?) "What happened?"

I was still a bit fuzzy on that. After all, what really happened made no sense. Why would a fully grown man push a six-year-old off her bike? What did he think I was going to do to his parking lot?

There was much sniffling and a hiccup or two, but the story came out, and I was distressed to see that certain frown gather on Sister's forehead.

Usually that frown meant that someone was going to serve detention. Someone was always serving detention, standing at parade rest along the wall by her office with their books in their arms. Even as I told her what happened, I was trying to figure out what I'd done to warrant such a fate.

"Is your mother home?" she asked.

Oh no. That was even worse. The only thing scarier than getting into trouble at school was having my mother find out. She'd double whatever the punishment was. I was going to be standing against walls till I drove.

"Um, yes, Sister."

Sister gave a brisk nod that sent that veil to shuddering again. "Good. Now, I want you to go down to Sister Maria Suzanne and let her clean off your knees. I'm going to talk to your mother."

I never did it intentionally (well, not often), but I'm told that at that age, when I leveled the injured innocent look on adults, they were prone to melt. I leveled it for all my worth. "Am I in trouble?" I asked, managing not much more than a whisper.

Sister seemed genuinely astonished. "In trouble?" she demanded, sounding outraged. "And what would you be in trouble for? It's that man who is in trouble, child."

Nobody told me nuns could be prophets, too.

Now, this is the part I could only get secondhand. After all, I was stuck in school. (Although I did get an extra glazed doughnut for being brave. I would have let them remove my appendix with a kitchen knife for a second doughnut.) But this is, to the best of my knowledge, what happened.

Sister Mary Elizabeth waited only long enough for me to leave before she started dialing. When my mother came on the line, Sister didn't even give her the chance to ask what her children had done this time.

"A very distressing incident," Sister told her. "Have you heard that your children had trouble with the manager of that Shell station on the corner by your house?"

"Yes, Sister. My husband and I talked to him about his behavior just last week. There's no excuse to be yelling at any of those kids who ride through his lot."

Sister sighed. "Well, it's gotten worse."

According to those who knew, my mother did not act right away upon getting the full story. She did, after all, have at least one baby at home (although I'm pretty sure it was at least two). She had no car, and my father was out of town. So she needed to wait long enough to get somebody to watch my younger siblings before she could venture forth from the house.

Not that she did much venturing. She marched like a legionnaire. She took those three blocks down to Manchester with murder on her mind.

It is said that at about that time, Englehardt's was packed with the usual lunchtime crowd. It was pretty much a normal day, as few had witnessed the earlier contretemps, the room noisy, smoky, and thick with men trying to grab a bite in a congenial atmosphere before heading back to hard work.

Suddenly one of the men did a double take. Blinking, he leaned closer to the front windows, which faced the service station across the busy street.

"Hey, you guys," he said. "Isn't that Dode Helm?"

Several other men gathered, one being the owner, who was co-coach with my mom of our softball team.

"What's that she's carrying?" he asked.

"It's an umbrella. What the hell's she doing with it?"

It was, in fact, one of those lethal black umbrellas with a metal spike on the end about a foot long. My mother was wielding it like Boadicea with a broadsword. Arm outstretched, the umbrella zeroed in on a certain skinny chest,

she was pacing the station manager back step-by-step, jab-
bing the umbrella into his chest with each step.

"Asshole knocked one of her kids off a bike today," somebody offered.

The owner whipped around. "You kiddin' me?"

"Should we help her, you think?"

There was silence as every man in the room heard a shrill
cry from the station manager. Then, to a person, they shook
their heads.

"Nah."

Not one of them had the courage to come between my
mother and her prey. Instead, they all piled out the front
door, beer and cigarettes in hand, to watch the show.

Not even the cross traffic could drown out the sound of
my mother's outrage.

"How . . . *dare* you!" she roared. "You brave, *big* man. Did
you feel *brave* shoving a little girl off her bike? Well, *did* you?"

She kept moving forward as he moved back, his eyes gog-
gled, his skin ashen, his hands up. Each step was punctuated
by a fiercer and fiercer jab, until shirt buttons flew.

"Well, how do you like it *now,* big man? How do you like
somebody else bullying *you* for a change?"

"Help!" he screamed like a girl, still trying to bat away
that umbrella.

"Should we tell him to run?" one of the men asked, taking a drag off his cigarette.

"She'll just follow him."

"Probably beat him to death with the thing."

My mother backed that man all the way into his own
work bay and up against the wall, the umbrella still striking
like a snake, her voice carrying just fine over traffic noise.

"You're a *dead* man, do you hear me? You won't have a pot to *piss* in after I finish with you. You're not going to hurt one more little girl *ever again*! Do you understand me?"

"She's crazy!" he shrilled to whoever might hear. "Get her off me! She's gonna kill me!"

Not a soul moved.

"Police should be here soon," the tavern owner mused.

There were nods all round.

"Just in time to pick up the pieces."

The police showed up five minutes later. By then she'd cracked one of the man's ribs and made him wet himself. By the end of the day, the police had run him out of the city, and my parents had convinced the oil company to yank his job. He was never heard from again.

Long after my mother stalked back up the street toward home, the umbrella resting on her shoulder like a spent rifle, the men at the tavern watched the empty street in awe.

"I could have told him what would have happened if he bothered her kids."

The owner shook his head. "I don't think he would have believed you." And then he grinned.

They all grinned. And then, that Sunday when they saw her at mass, they ribbed her unmercifully. But they did it with respect. Everybody had heard how my mother fought like a tiger for her children. Nobody had ever told them she also fought like a Cossack.

Deadly. That's what she was.

And sometimes, when you're a very small child who finds herself at the mercy of capricious adults, having a deadly mother can come in handy.

Still, even with the bits I didn't see, it's a good story.

Biographies

Nevada Barr was born an hour east of Reno, Nevada, and raised on a small mountain airport in the Sierras. Being a sufferer of the Seven Year Itch, she has changed careers many times from waitress to actress to ranger to writer. The marriage of the last two, ranger and writer, spawned her award-winning mystery series featuring Anna Pigeon. The most recent in the series is *Hard Truth,* set in Rocky Mountains National Park. Nevada now lives in New Orleans and is working on a stand-alone thriller that will be published in 2007. That done, she plans a glorious reunion with Anna in a park yet to be selected.

Barbara Collins is one of the most respected short-story writers in the mystery field, with appearances in over a dozen top anthologies, including *Murder Most Delicious, Women on the Edge,* and the bestselling *Cat Crimes* series. She was the coeditor (and a contributor) to the bestselling anthology *Lethal Ladies,* and her stories were selected for inclusion in the first three volumes of *The Year's 25 Finest Crime and Mystery Stories.*

Two acclaimed hardcover collections of her work have been published—*Too Many Tomcats* and (with her husband) *Murder—His and Hers.* Their first novel together, the Baby Boomer thriller *Regeneration,* was a bestseller and has been purchased by Hollywood; their second collaborative novel, *Bombshell,* was published to excellent reviews. They are now writing a new series for Kensington as "Barbara Allan," the first book titled *Antiques Roadkill* due out in 2006.

Barbara has been the production manager and/or line producer on *Mommy, Mommy's Day, Real Time: Siege at Lucas Street Market,* and other independent film projects emanating from the production company she and her husband jointly run. The Collinses' collaboration extends to a son, Nathan, a recent University of Iowa grad.

Once a daily-newspaper reporter in St. Paul, Minnesota, **Carole Nelson Douglas** moved to Fort Worth, Texas, in 1984 to write fiction full-time. Her fifty novels include mainstream women's fiction as well as science fiction and fantasy. Her Irene Adler Sherlock Holmesian suspense series began with a *New York Times* Notable Book of the Year citation for *Good Night, Mr. Holmes. Spider Dance* is the latest title. Midnight Louie, Las Vegas's cozy-noir feline PI, celebrates his eighteenth case in *Cat in a Quicksilver Caper. Cat in a Midnight Choir* received a starred review from *Publishers Weekly,* the first animal mystery so honored. Douglas's fiction and nonfiction work has won or been short-listed for more than fifty writing awards and she's had stories in eight *Year's Best* mystery anthologies. She and her husband are owned by several adopted cats and a dog. She has never been a housewife. (Web site: www.catolenelson douglas.com.)

Award-winning, bestselling author **Eileen Dreyer**, known as Kathleen Korbel to her Silhouette readers, has published twenty-two books for Silhouette since 1986 and, under her own name, eight suspense novels and seven short stories, including her most recent novel from St. Martin's Press, *Sinners and Saints,* in which St. Louis forensic nurse liaison Chastity Byrnes has to search New Orleans for her missing sister.

The proud holder of an Anthony Award nomination, Eileen is a rabid researcher, supplementing her twenty years' experience in the field of medicine—sixteen in trauma nursing—with training in forensic nursing and death investigation, and has graduated from the Tactical EMS School, which qualifies her to act as a medic on a SWAT team.

When not addictively traveling, she still lives in her native St. Louis with her husband and two children (and remains close to her extended family, of which she is now matriarch and current vanquisher of infidels). She has animals but refuses to subject them to the glare of the limelight.

Vicki Hendricks is the author of noir novels *Miami Purity, Iguana Love, Voluntary Madness,* and *Sky Blues.* Her short stories appear in collections and periodicals, including *Murder for Revenge, Best American Erotics 2000, Flesh and Blood, Tart Noir, Nerve.com,* and *Mississippi Review Online.* She lives in Hollywood, Florida, and teaches writing at Broward Community College. Her work reflects interests in adventure and sports, such as skydiving and scuba, and knowledge of south Florida environment. Her latest novel of murder and obsession, *Cruel Poetry* (2006), is set in South Beach, Miami.

For starters **Suzann Ledbetter** insists her mother-in-law is the world's best and a heck of a good sport.

Suzann's mother taught her tomboy daughter to read at the age of five, assuming the kid couldn't have her nose in a book and get in trouble simultaneously. It didn't work, but Suzann's insatiable curiosity, smarty-pants mouth, tendency to make up stuff, and love of mystery novels somehow became the basis of a writing career.

Suzann (www.suzannledbetter.com) is a popular speaker and an editor-at-large for *Family Circle*. Her latest books are the contemporary suspense caper, *Once a Thief* (Mira), and *Shady Ladies* (Tor/Forge), a collection of biographies of seventeen fascinating, but little-known, nineteenth-century females (both published in 2006).

Suzann and her husband, David Ellingsworth, live in the southwest Missouri Ozarks with three retired racing greyhounds, two cats, and about nine million books.

Elizabeth Massie is a two-time Bram Stoker Award–winning author of horror novels, novellas, and short stories, published by major houses including Simon & Schuster, Tor, Harper, Avon, NAL, and more. Her books include *Sineater, Welcome Back to the Night, Wire Mesh Mothers, Dark Shadows: Dreams of the Dark* (co-authored with Stephen Mark Rainey), *Shadow Dreams, The Fear Report, The Little Magenta Book of Mean Stories,* and others. Her most recent novel, *Twisted Branch: A Novel of the Abbadon Inn* (written as "Chris Blaine"), was published by Berkley in 2005. Elizabeth also writes historical novels for young adults. She lives in the Shenandoah Valley of Virginia with illustrator Cortney Skinner (designer/builder of the mutant and other props for the Sony-released feature film, *The Lost Skeleton of Cadavra*), and is mother to Erin, twenty-nine, Brian, twenty-six, and grandmother to Anya, not quite a year.

During her twenty-five years as a professional writer **Christine Matthews** has produced more than sixty short stories in the mystery, horror, dark fantasy, and western genres. Her Gil & Claire mystery trilogy began in 1999 and concluded with *Same Time, Same Murder* in 2005. Of the second novel, *The Masks of Auntie Laveau,* the *L.A. Times* said, "This is a blueprint for how to write a thriller." Her stories have appeared in three collections of *Year's Finest Stories* and her story "I'm a Dirty Girl" was optioned for a film. She has also published a collection of her short stories, *Gentle Insanities and Other States of Mind.* She was coeditor of *Lethal Ladies II* and a contributor to the book *Writing the P.I. Novel.* In addition she is a poet and a playwright. She is currently assembling a "reading theater" production of her work.

Denise Mina left school at sixteen and worked at a series of jobs before going to school to study law. After law school, she misused a Ph.D. grant to research and write *Garnethill,* in which a former psychiatric patient wakes up to find her married lover sitting in her living room with his throat slit. The book won the CWA John Creasy Memorial Dagger for the best first novel in 1998. *Exile* and *Resolution,* parts two and three of the Maureen O'Donnell trilogy, followed. Her first stand-alone book, *Deception,* is the discovered diary of a house husband whose wife has been convicted of murder. *Field of Blood* (2005) is the first of five books following Paddy Meehan through Britain in the eighties and nineties. She is now writing the follow-up *Dead Hour,* thirteen issues of *Hellblazer* for DC Comics, plus a short play "Lady-Mag." She lives in Glasgow, Scotland.

Marcia Muller has long been considered a pioneer in the mystery world because of her creation of Sharon McCone, a San

Francisco private investigator. The first McCone novel was published in 1977. The *Chicago Tribune* called her "one of the treasures of the genre." And the *Cleveland Plain Dealer* said, "Reading Muller is like watching a superb ballplayer at work." In July 2001, Muller published *Point Deception,* a departure from her longtime series set in the fictional Soledad County. Her latest novel, *Cape Perdido,* is also set in Soledad County and was published by Mysterious Press in 2005. She has received the Grandmaster Award from MWA, the PWA Lifetime Achievement Award, the Ridley Award, an American Mystery Award, and the Anthony Award. Muller has also written three novels with her husband, Bill Pronzini, and published four short-story collections and numerous nonfiction articles. She is currently at work on her twenty-fourth Sharon McCone novel.

Sara Paretsky was recently awarded the Private Eye Writers of America Life Achievement Award, the Eye, for her prodigious contribution to the PI genre. She has also been awarded the Diamond Dagger Award for Best Novel from the Crime Writers Association of Great Britain, but amazingly, the Eye is the first American award she has ever received. Her Chicago private eye V. I. Warshawski appeared on the scene in 1983 with *Indemnity Only. Fire Sale,* the twelfth Warshawski novel, was published in 2005. There is also a collection of Sara's short work, *Windy City Blues.*

Nancy Pickard is the author of the Jenny Cain and Marie Lightfoot mystery series. She is also the author of dozens of short stories and of three novels in the Eugenia Potter series created by Virginia Rich. She is the coauthor, with Lynn Lott, of the acclaimed nonfiction book about writing *Seven Steps on the Writer's Path*. She has won Agatha, Anthony, Macavity, and Shamus awards for her short stories and Agatha, Anthony, and Macavity awards for her novels. She is a three-time Edgar Award nominee. Her most recent novel is *The Virgin of Small Plans,* which is set in the Flint Hills of her home state of Kansas.

S. J. Rozan is the author of eight novels in the Edgar, Shamus, and Anthony award–winning Lydia Chin/Bill Smith PI series, including *Winter and Night,* which won the Edgar, Nero, and Macavity awards and was nominated for the Shamus and Anthony awards. Her most recent book is a post-9/11 novel, *Absent Friends,* published to rave reviews in 2004. Born and raised in the Bronx, she is an architect and lives in Greenwich Village.

Julie Smith is a former reporter for the *New Orleans Times-Picayune* and the *San Francisco Chronicle* who lives in the Faubourg Marigny neighborhood of New Orleans. Her first novel featuring New Orleans cop Skip Langdon, *New Orleans Mourning,* won the Edgar Allan Poe Award for best novel, and she has since published eight more highly acclaimed books in the series, including *Jazz Funeral, 82 Desire,* and *Mean Woman Blues.* Her most recent novel, *PI on a Hot Tin Roof,* is her fourth featuring African-American New Orleans private eye Talba Wallis, aka the Baroness Pontalba.

Critics have hailed Smith for having "a knack for reinventing herself with each new series while established characters are still going strong" and "her deft exploration of her characters' intimate relationships." For more information about Julie Smith, visit her Web site at www.casamysterioso.com.

Want More?

Turn the page to enter
Avon's Little Black Book —

the dish, the scoop and the
cherry on top from
the authors of
Deadly Housewives

Sweet Inspiration
Christine Matthews

I've had such a great time with this anthology, especially getting the chance to work with these thirteen talented, creative women. And I've wondered, as you probably have, just what makes them tick, where their inspiration comes from. Not the ideas for these wicked tales—ideas are everywhere—but the inspiration needed to make an idea grow into a full-blown story. And the wondering I've done has caused me to examine my own life, not just as a writer and editor but to the core of my being as a woman, mother, and housewife. All of this caused enough soul searching to make me appreciate two great influences in my life: my mother and my mother-in-law.

Coming from a traditional home, Mother was traditional in the beginning. But her artistic spirit took over somewhere after she joined the Waves during World War II. It was there she became a gunnery instructor. She was pretty and smart and ended up marrying a dashing navy pilot—my father.

I've often said that being raised by Mother was like living in an *I Love Lucy* episode. There was the time she tried drying Dad's wool socks in the oven. Getting involved in something else, she burned all of them. She was creative to the point of frustration. Our front hallway was forever metamorphosing. One time Chinese, complete with cherry blossoms painted on a black silhouette of a tree. Six months later, country. I never knew what I'd find coming home from school.

One year she decided to experiment and went to a hardware store, bought a dozen cans of gold spraypaint, and put us all to work on the Christmas tree. It was glorious. The real tree looked artificial when we were finished. So shiny and gold. The ornaments were gold; our shoes were tipped in gold. Like Mae West, Mother believed too much of a good thing was wonderful. The next Christmas she cut up her old fur jacket and made full-length coats for all my dolls. Mother was glamorous, fashionable, creative, and fun. I like to think I'm all those things, thanks to her.

The best piece of advice she ever gave me concerned my naive compulsion toward perfection. When my son was small, Mother came to visit. I was rushing around dusting, cleaning, doing the housewifely things I thought were expected. She watched for a few moments and then sat me down. "Relax. When Marc's all grown up," she told me, "what do you think he'll remember? That the house was immaculate? Or that you spent time with him?" Today my son is thirty-four. He's married, a talented writer, and constantly entertains his friends with stories about all the fun, weird times he had growing up. When I question him about dust on the furniture, he can't even remember the furniture, let alone what was on it.

And then there's Sophie, my mother-in-law. Literally starting her life over, she crossed the ocean on a boat crowded with hundreds of other refugees from Lithuania after World War II. She couldn't speak English, couldn't read the language, and had only a sixth-grade education. Tough, serious, and the only truly generous person I've known.

If I would complain about a hard day at work or how the neighbors were driving me crazy, Sophie would counter in her thick Lithuanian accent: "When I'm forced to leave my country, I have to run over bodies of dead soldiers. We have no food. No clothes. I see friends get shot right in front of me."

After I had a baby, I dared to tell her what a tough time I'd had. She told me, "I have my baby in a people's camp and passed out from the pain. We have no medicine. It was three days before Dennis (my husband, her son) was born. I scream for the doctor to let me die!"

Talk about putting things in perspective.

Sophie is now eighty-three, still fit, still sharp, still generous, even though I divorced her son twelve years ago. She is the toughest of the tough. When I was a teenager, she once told me, "I used to be nice like you, but I learned. I fought for my family. You have to fight, honey!" And I like to think, through osmosis, that somehow I've inherited her moxie. She's taught me to be unafraid, to suck it up and never try to upstage her struggle.

So there you have it. My two greatest sources of inspiration. The artistic, silly part passed through DNA and the tough, honest woman learned through example. I now run my household and conduct business inspired by these two great women. Housewife, mother, lover, friend, it all seems to come back to having known them.

Nevada Barr

I've been a wife a couple of times and, over the years, I've owned many houses, but the only time I was a housewife, in the classic and honorable tradition of housewifery, where I remained at home while the man went into the world to earn our bread, I was neither married nor did I own the house.

David, the man I'd been living with during the last year of college, and I had, upon graduation, moved to the town of Los Gatos, California. David was an electronic engineer and had landed a job in nearby Silicon Valley. I'd graduated with a B.A. in speech and drama and, at that tender age, still believed a degree bought you instant employment in your chosen field.

In a lovely old apple orchard we found a rental house. We could afford the rent because many of the ceilings were only six feet high. The owner explained that her grandmother had had it built for her gardener in the 1930s and "didn't want to waste the wood; the Chinese are such a little people. . . ."

David, ever practical, pointed out that he put in eight hours each day for "the common good" and I, as the unemployed "spouse," should put in a like amount. This was to include but not be limited to: cleaning, cooking, shopping, washing, ironing, making his lunch, the bed, etc.

Feeling I'd been somehow *had* but unable to refute his logic, I began my short career in housewifery. With no children and a tiny house, a strong young woman can get a good deal done in eight hours. For a time I tried to keep busy at it. A month or so passed, and as I was going about my assigned tasks, my sister, Molly, called.

When I answered she said: "What are you up to today?"

"I'm cleaning behind the stove," I replied.

And there came a long, dead silence. In my brain I began the actor's chant:

I am cleaning . . .

I *am* cleaning . . .

I am *cleaning* . . .

I am cleaning **behind** the stove. **Behind** it, for chrissake.

I packed. I left David a note:

Dear David—

Today I cleaned behind the stove. I'm moving back to San Luis.

Love, Nevada

Barbara Collins

My husband must love me for delights other than culinary.
Shortly after we married and settled in, I invited his
parents for a turkey dinner with all the trimmings—how
hard could that be? The day before I did the shopping,
cleaned the house, and set the table with our many recently
received wedding gifts of china, crystal, and silver. The
next morning I pulled the huge turkey from the freezer and
realized I should have thawed it. No problem. I drew a hot
bath in the tub—and from habit poured in some bubble
bath—then let the bird soak and bob in luxury for an hour.
Then I threw it into the oven. Later, the turkey, presented
on a sterling silver Reed and Barton platter, looked like a
thing of beauty straight out of *Ladies' Home Journal*. My
husband began to carve. Out of the cavity of the turkey he
pulled a plastic bag containing the neck and gizzard,
followed by a little white rope to tie its feet for cooking,
and finally the paper instructions. (I had no idea they could
stuff so much stuff in there!) At that moment the little
popup thermometer embedded in the bird's breast sprang
up. I rose to my feet and like in "A Christmas Story"
announced, "That's it. We're all going out for Chinese!"

Damn the Potatoes, Full Speed Ahead!: My Deadliest Desperate Housewife Moment
Carole Nelson Douglas

Despite having a mother who grew up cooking for farmhands from the age of thirteen, I've never been a cook. Still, in my early marriage years I felt duty-bound to give it the old college try, with such small success that my husband and I mutually agreed to feed ourselves, which means that these days we use the can opener, microwave, and the oven, period.

We were newlyweds living in a second-story duplex when I found myself preparing the Dinner from Hell. A sister reporter at the *St. Paul Pioneer Press-Dispatch* lived in an apartment building just a block away. Her husband was away on National Guard duty, so I invited her over for dinner even though she was a gourmet cook who tossed off things like rack of lamb. I'd stick to a simple menu: salad, main meat course, vegetable something. And it would be a good deed.

My real joy of cooking was presentation: the serving dishes and linens I found at estate sales paired with my wedding stainless-steel service (a knockoff of my favorite Royal Danish sterling pattern). Everything would look elegant and it would be fun. What could go wrong with just three people?

First, I came home from work, guest expected in half an hour, and found that I'd forgotten to take the meat out of the freezer. In those premicrowave days, I could only flood the sink with hot water and float the supermarket package in there until it drowned. Similarities to the *Titanic* should have warned me. Now, on to the evening's *pièce de résistance*. I'd always had a great eye for a tasty recipe, just no experience putting it all together. The layered sliced-potato-sour-cream-onion casserole sounded delish. First I had to boil the potatoes, pare them, and slice them. Only they didn't cook in the few minutes I'd expected. Isn't all that furiously boiling water supposed to actually *boil* things? Quickly?

Our guest had arrived. "Give her a cocktail," I whispered tensely to my husband in the kitchen, "and talk to her. It'll be a few minutes." The meat was now thawed but waterlogged. I minced onions and periodically forked the potatoes in their bubbling bath of death. Hard as rocks. Tines wouldn't pierce 'em. I did everything else, but the minutes were becoming an hour. Finally, firm but semicooked potatoes! I sliced and layered them with the other ingredients and then had to bake the mess for twenty or thirty minutes.

"Give her another drink and talk some more. It'll be only a few more minutes."

Remember, I barely knew the woman, and my husband had never met her. I sure hoped they had something to talk about out there while I was fussing and fretting in the kitchen. I finally announced dinner and could sit down and have a medicinal glass of wine myself. The meal was only ninety minutes late.

But it went so much better than I had feared. Our guest, we discovered, couldn't hold her liquor and normally stopped at one drink. Two cocktails kept her floating happily through the meal, taste buds numbed, and we walked her home. Upside? She never knew just how shaky that dinner was.

Carole's Slow, Sour Cream–Potato Casserole

½ cup finely chopped onion
2 tablespoons butter
2 eggs
1 cup sour cream
Salt and pepper to taste
5 large potatoes, boiled (or five cups cooked potatoes)
¼ cup dried bread crumbs
½ cup grated cheese

Saute onions in butter until soft. Beat together eggs, sour cream, and seasonings. Slice the cooked potatoes into a buttered or nonstick casserole dish, alternating layers with onions, bread crumbs, and ¼ cup grated cheese mixture and the eggs-and-sour-cream mixture. Save a last layer of eggs-and-sour-cream mixture and ¼ cup grated cheese to top the potatoes. Bake in a 350 degree oven until thoroughly heated through and the cheese is melted and golden.

Deadly Housewife Tip: *Allow plenty of time to cook five raw potatoes in boiling water!* A day ahead would be good.

Eileen Dreyer

Well, if you read my piece on my mother, you pretty much know what kind of cooks we are. A long line of Irish cooks who were left with no indigenous cuisine but potatoes and sour milk. And considering the fact that my own mother preferred to teach me the finer points of the infield fly rule and how to do point spreads on football than to cook (because she hated to do it so much herself), I'm left with not much more than the memory of a thousand ways to extend ground beef for ten people. But my mom kind of made it up as she went along, so none of us have ever been able to perfectly re-create her best efforts, like Mom's Goulash, which has no similarity whatsoever to the famous Hungarian original. Mom did make a great fried chicken, but the only time I tried to make that, my husband almost landed in the hospital with salmonella, so the less said about it the better. My siblings and I do remember one original concoction we all loved that our children don't seem quite so enamored of, however.

It's cheap, filling food at its finest, and I think it actually tastes great. But that may be because it's entwined with family memories. But if you're having a kind of "I don't know what else to do with the leftover food in my cupboard" kind of day, try it:

Dode's Hawaiian Sandwiches

English muffins
Deli sliced ham
A can of pineapple slices
Cheez Whiz

Warm up the Cheez Whiz. Fry up the ham. Toast the muffins.
Layer each English muffin with a couple slices of ham and a
pineapple slice. Pour on a nice coating of Cheez Whiz.
Enjoy! (Remember, I said she had an imagination.)

Vicki Hendricks

"Purrz, Baby" doesn't have as interesting a background as some of my stories do, but the explanation will, at least, serve to protect the innocent—namely, me. I'm in trouble on two points with my boyfriend, Brian, for the writing of this story. I'm always in trouble with somebody!

I was inspired to write "Purrz" by an old friend—possibly more than friend—of Brian's from nearly thirty years past. A few years ago, when we were staying at Brian's place in Chicago, his old girlfriend graciously agreed to watch my beloved cat, Snickers (aka Purrsnickety), while Brian and I headed to Colorado to visit my mother for Christmas. It was early morning when we dropped Snickers off, and coincidentally the old friend was wearing a red velvet robe exactly like the one Brian had just bought for me. Of course, my mind started working, since I was aware of their long-term relationship, and as a noir writer I'm always grubbing for dark ideas. But the facts end there. Brian is not a history professor—though he would have enjoyed that kind of work—and his friend is not an English professor and does not have the slender "boneless" look described in the story. The look came from a girl in my high-school class, Mary Lou something—which exemplifies how these details come from everywhere! I had no real plot against anybody. (Brian, my sweetie: I did not have suspicions or any feelings against her, and do not doubt your fidelity, ever. No one would think that. Besides, she lived way across town! I was grateful that she would watch the Snick, despite the fact that Snickers instantly scared "Kitty" into the basement and would not let her back up.)

Secondly, I am sincerely sorry that I borrowed, without asking, the historical information about cat-hauling from Brian, along with his comments on Dee Brown's writing. (Sweetie, nobody will connect that historical nutcase in the story with you! Most people who read "Purrz" have never met you and have no idea that you meander around the house spouting historical facts—at length. And there's no reason why you still can't put cat-hauling into your historical novel. True, you did the research. I accidentally soaked it up.)

I hope, sincerely, that this explanation serves to clear up any misconceptions that might arise. Brian and I are very happy together, he treats me wonderfully, and he never overindulges in my minestrone soup. This apology has received his approval. (Sweetie, yes, I'm perfectly clear on the fact that you did not buy her that red bathrobe.)

Mother Ledbetter's Lunchbox Laws
Suzann Ledbetter

Younger Son, aka Mr. Picky, who refused to eat anything green, or foods that touched one another on the plate, inspired this. Faced at 2 A.M. with the 189th consecutive lunchbox of that school year to pack, this essay pretty much wrote itself on the only paper on hand—approximately 45 inch-square Post-it Notes.

1. Those cute, reusable plastic containers perfect for pudding and applesauce have only a 50/50 chance of ever being brought home again. Their lids stand absolutely no chance at all.

2. Food editors of parenting magazines who divine ideas such as cutting sandwiches into cartoon-character shapes and poking whole cloves into peach halves to make smiley faces are overdue for a reality check.

3. It's impossible to convince a child that potato chips purchased in large bags for dividing into sandwich bag–size portions taste exactly the same as those manufactured in pricey, primarily air-filled baglets.

4. Jell-O becomes a beverage by approximately 10:15 A.M.

5. Limiting a child's choice of sandwich fillings to either "smooth" or "crunchy" is a tad unimaginative.

6. It's entirely possible that Robert Oppenheimer got the idea for the atom bomb the day his mom filled his thermos with a carbonated soft drink.

7. If on New Year's Eve you realize your child's lunchbox has been in her backpack since the beginning of winter vacation, classify it as toxic waste and call the EPA hotline immediately.

8. On the same day your child puts his school picture packet in his lunchbox for safekeeping, his guaranteed leakproof thermos will rupture.

Luckily, many school lunchrooms now provide standard cafeteria fare as well as branded burgers, pizza parlors, taco stands, salad bars, and a gamut of vending machines. Rather than rack your brain for two thousand, five hundred, and twenty mobile meals your child might actually eat, just think of his or her lunchbox as a portable ATM and pack it accordingly.

If This Is December, Those Must Be Coconut Cranberry Cookies
Elizabeth Massie

All right, I'll admit it, and I'm not bragging. I'm a good cook. I may not be able to do much with a sewing machine other than hem curtains. I may not be able to knit much other than a really long scarf. I may only know how to remove a cracked toilet float without properly installing a new one, but I can cook. Not fancy cuisine that consists of tossing hummus, escargot, and mandarin orange slices in balsamic vinegar and then embedding them in tofu puffs, but yummy, simpler stuff that, thus far, my household has enjoyed. Homemade chicken potpie. Homemade spaghetti sauce with fresh peppers, mushrooms, tomatoes. Homemade veggie chili and homemade olive and bacon pizza.

Back when I was a young mother, I decided baked goods were the way to go for Christmas gifts. Times were tight, and I had years' accumulation of tins crammed in my lower kitchen cabinet, left over from Figi's fudges, butter cream candies, and those Danish cookies from the dollar store. I found a recipe for coconut cookies that promised to be "excellent for gift giving." Since I couldn't leave well enough alone, and was just coming into my own as a cook, I played with the recipe and adapted it. I used fresh, sliced cranberries then, but these days I substitute the dried, raisinlike cranberries that work just as well. Now, coconut cranberry cookies have become a staple during the holidays. Give it a try. And I'll let you know if I ever figure out how to make a hummus/escargot/mandarin orange/tofu combination palatable.

Coconut Cranberry Cookies

1 cup sugar
⅔ cup packed brown sugar
½ cup shortening (I use nonhydrogenated shortening)
1 tsp salt
1 tsp baking soda
2 eggs
1 tsp vanilla
2 cups flour
1 cup flaked or shredded coconut, sweetened
½ cup dried cranberries
1 tsp water

Preheat the oven to 375 degrees. Mix sugars, shortening, salt, soda, eggs, and vanilla and stir until smooth. Add remaining ingredients, mixing well. Drop by rounded teaspoons onto lightly greased cookie sheet. Bake 7 to 8 minutes or until cookies are golden brown. Cool. Can be stored in an airtight container for up to three weeks. Makes several dozen, depending on the size of your "teaspoons."

Tablet
Denise Mina

In the words of Mike Myers's character in *So I Married an Axe Murderer*, most Scottish cuisine is based on a bet. This is a sweet recipe that is so delicious, and contains so much sugar, that regardless of personal fitness it's possible to kick your own height for forty minutes after ingestion, sometimes inadvertently.

For the moderate: Take a small square with coffee after dinner.

For the immoderate: Nibble a little bit and then another bit and then have just a wee bit more, just a taste. Stand up while eating because that doesn't count. Gradually, in a workmanlike manner, work your way through the whole tray. Sit still and berate yourself. Drink water to stop the dizziness. Promise never to do that to yourself again. Make another tray the next day.

110g (¼ lb) butter
250ml (½ pint) water
900g (2 lbs) castor sugar
225g (½ lb) sweetened condensed milk

Melt the butter and water together over a low heat. Add the sugar and keep stirring until it boils. Add the condensed milk, boil, then simmer for 20 minutes, stirring every so often. Take it off the heat and beat vigorously for five minutes to get air through it. Pour it into a greaseproof tray and, when partly cooled, score it into bars.

When it's set and cold, wrap the bars in greaseproof paper and store in an airtight tin.

E.J.'s Chicken Casserole
Marcia Muller

Sometimes characters from my novels contribute recipes that become old standards in my household. The following is an excerpt from *The Cavalier in White* (1986) in which heroine Joanna Stark's son, E.J., offers to make dinner.

"Ah, you're cooking. What are we having?"

"A new recipe I thought up while I was waiting to hitch a ride outside Willits. You take some boned chicken breasts, saute them in the marinade from those Italian artichoke hearts, then add mushrooms, black olives, Parmesan, lots of garlic—you'll love it."

"How do you know what it'll taste like if you've never made it before?"

"I've been imagining it for eight hours. It took a long time to get a ride."

Over the years readers have written to me about this recipe. Some suggested the introduction of sundried tomatoes; others thought it called for white pepper or onions or white wine. I've tried all versions, but I always come back to E.J.'s—although I brown the garlic and mushrooms and lightly flour the chicken, then bake the casserole in the oven at 350 degrees for half an hour. E.J.'s freestyle method of cooking leaves something to be desired!

Memories of a Mad Housewife
Sara Paretsky

I've been married for almost thirty years, and I'm happy to say that I've pretty much avoided housewifery all this time. But even someone who avoids domesticity has her moments. I married into a family of dog lovers. I myself didn't like dogs, but on my wedding day I gave in to the pleadings of my husband and three stepsons and agreed to look after some friends' golden retriever while they were in England for a year. (That year turned me into a lifelong slave of the golden retriever, but that's another story.)

Capo was five when she came into our lives, and we were her fifth family. Somewhere along the way she had been trained so well that we never needed to have her on a leash outside. She was smart, sweet, and responsive; she never ate garbage or tried to go after food on the countertops, but she had her doggie limits, as I discovered one raw November day.

My husband's parents were English and that day I thought it would be fun—as only an energetic and ignorant bride can think—to make a real English tea, ignoring the fact that my husband hates tea, both as a drink and as an afternoon meal. I baked currant scones, which came out of the oven with the specific weight of lead. My kind and infinitely obliging husband managed to eat one, as I pot-valiantly did myself, and we were then so ill we had to lie down for the afternoon. The other five bricks I left on the coffee table.

When we finally went back downstairs, Capo was lying in the hall. She thumped her tail feebly to let us know she knew we were there, but she couldn't stand. When we finally forced her to her feet for her evening walk, her belly was touching the floor. The poor thing had helped herself to the five scones I'd left in the living room, and they gave her several days of misery. I've never much cared for afternoon tea myself since then.

Why Housekeeping and Writers Don't Mix
Nancy Pickard

Here's what my house looks like now, when I'm deep into finishing a novel: Books and papers piled everywhere. Old food crusting on plates. Coffee cups with milky sludge floating on top. I think I mopped up the entire spot on the kitchen floor where the cat killed the mouse three nights ago, but what's my brassiere doing over there, draped across the table? I must have taken it off on my way to the shower one night and never noticed it again until this moment. And now that I'm looking at it, I see there's a pizza box underneath it, a box with, whew, only one old piece of pizza in it. I'll get to that later. To throw it away, I mean, not to eat it, although if I don't get to a grocery store soon . . . I've killed only one houseplant this time, but even the cactus is looking dry.

There are wet clothes in the washer—yes, I actually washed a few things—that I keep forgetting to put in the dryer, which means I will have to wash them again to get the mildew out. I lost one of my portable phones somewhere in this mess two weeks ago and haven't found it yet. Apparently the "phone locator" beep isn't loud enough to penetrate piles of stuff that high and thick. By the time I find it, the battery will be dead, but then so will every plugged-in appliance, too, if I can't find my last electric bill and pay it. My garbage disposal broke a month ago. One of the bathroom showers is leaking into the garage. I have enough dust bunnies to gather up and mold into a life-size sculpture of Winston Churchill . . . but the book is coming along nicely, thank you.

And people wonder why I have never remarried!

S. J. Rozan

For the past fifteen years I've shared a rented summer house—actually, a variety of houses—with the same group of friends. The domestic chores are divided thusly: they menu-plan and cook, I do the dishes; we all shop, I garden; and we hire a cleaning service. All this is to say that I only have three domestic talents: gardening, dishwashing, and ironing, which doesn't come into summer weekends. So I don't have much to say in terms of best, or worst, domestic moments. What I will do, though, is share a recipe.

I had a roommate in college, and for a couple of years after, named Kathy Craig. I spent a few Christmases with her family, and came home with care packages. Included among the cookies and the carrot cake were fudge candies made by her mother and loved by mine. As opposed to me, my mother was a fine cook; but she never minded a good shortcut. I don't remember what the Craigs called them, but my mother renamed them and they're now:

Kathy's Mother's Balls

6 to 8 ounces unsweetened chocolate
1 can sweetened condensed milk

Heat together until chocolate melts. Cool and roll into balls.

The Booze, Nuts, and Glitter Option

Add a teaspoon of rum or bourbon. If you do, use the larger amount of chocolate. When the balls are made, roll in nuts, sprinkles, sugar. . . .

Julie Smith

Several years ago a friend told me the only real-life amateur-detective story I've ever heard. Here's the gist:

Attractive divorcée Joy meets equally attractive Mel, a new guy in town, at a Jewish community center singles function. They date, things get serious, and finally, after dropping hints about their future together, he invites her to meet him for lunch at the best restaurant in town. He also sends her a gift certificate for pampering spa treatments the morning of the date.

Joy arrives manicured, pedicured, massaged, and expecting a proposal, but Mel's late. Half an hour later she calls him. Detained at the office, he says, "but go ahead and order—I'll be there when I can."

She has lunch alone, thinking, "Poor Mel, he works so hard," and arrives home to find an empty house. Really empty—of all her furniture and valuables.

Yep, she'd given him a key.

Detective Jones is sympathetic but comes up with nothing, so Joy takes matters into her own hands. The jerk's done it before, she reasons, and probably he'll do it again. So she gets on the phone to JCC singles clubs all over the country, finding that the outraged ladies are only too glad to help. They put the word out and pretty soon Joy gets a call—a man answering Mel's description has just started dating Natalie in Sioux City.

She consults with Natalie first, then Jones, who agrees to fly with her to Sioux City to make the ID. Natalie arranges a tennis date with her new beau, so Joy and Jones can get a good gander. Sure enough, it's Mel—and here's the icing on the cake: Natalie's wearing a necklace Joy could swear used to belong to her. Turns out Mel gave it to her.

Case closed.